SPIRIT OF THE LAW

LOUISE GORDAY

Joyce —

No more masks!!

Louise Gorday
2021

Book Cover Design by ebooklaunch.com
Formatting by Polgarus Studio

Printed in the United States of America

To Charlie

You've read every one and haven't asked me to stop yet.

I think that puts you in the super brother league.

Also by Louise Gorday

The Pickle Boat House

Bayside Blues

The Clockwise Carousel

The Church at Parkers Wharf

Contents

Chapter One
Dispatched

The sun was bright and the air balmy—a good thing, since the rust-belt town of McKeesport, Pennsylvania, offered little else. Hamelin Russell stood alone before a house in the typical style of these old mill towns: wide porch, two stories, its color forgotten beneath a layer of fine soot. He looked at the line of once-proud homes marching up the hill toward Grandview Avenue at the summit. Their battleship-gray and dark-green porches were faded, the lattice trim sagging. The vacant lot behind him had reverted to an urban prairie of tall grass, scrub, and unidentifiable weeds, and a pit bull bounced and growled behind the chain-link fence of the yard next door. The neighborhood housed older residents hanging onto properties long since paid for, and struggling young on Section 8 assistance. He looked for foot traffic on Grandview. Up there somewhere was a hole-in-the-wall grill selling killer kielbasa-and-onion hoagies.

A red minivan turned from Grandview onto Grover Avenue and continued down behind him, humming softly on the uneven brick pavers as it negotiated the steep descent. Time to get cracking. Hamelin pulled from his pocket one of his most precious possessions, a small black notebook, and consulted the list printed in the front. He ran down through the names starting with "Nathan Sturgess, 2850 Walnut

Street, McKeesport, Pa.," at the top.

He looked off into the middle distance and said, "Andrew, I don't even see *Malcolm Derby, thirty-three-oh-nine Grover Avenue, McKeesport.* I have Sturgess next. You positive Derby's for today?"

"Why do you ask me that every time I give you an add-on?" Andrew grumped, his quiet voice floating through Hamelin's mind. "Yes, I see he's not on your schedule, and of course I'm sure. Now, get in there and take care of business. I may have some additional names later."

Hamelin put his notebook away. "Yeah, well, you should give those to someone else. I have another appointment close by." He tuned the newbie dispatcher out and verified the house number. Satisfied it was 3309 Grover, he tossed his empty latte cup into the black trash bin at the curb and entered the residence through the front door. He passed quickly through the living room and made an immediate left into a short hallway that led him to the bedroom in the rear of the house. Slipping into the room without comment, he went to the head of the bed and opposite the crying woman holding vigil in a chair on the other side. The bedridden elderly man's pain-racked eyes shifted his way, and he smiled weakly at Hamelin.

The woman frowned. "What are you looking at?" she asked, staring blankly in Hamelin's direction.

"Water," the man whispered to the woman, his eyes never leaving Hamelin's face. "Water, please."

She nodded. "I'll be right back. Promise me you won't go anywhere while I'm gone."

"Promise," he whispered.

She let go of his old, bony hand and left the room.

"You're late," the old man said to Hamelin, but in a tone without admonishment. "I've had a rough time of it this morning. I thought for sure you would get here earlier."

Hamelin sat down on the edge of the bed. "Everything in its time," he said. "Would you like to wait until she comes back, Malcolm?"

Malcolm's gaze shifted to the bedroom door. From beyond came the click of a cupboard door and the hum of the water dispenser on the refrigerator. He shook his head. "Now, please, if you don't mind. I think it will be better."

Hamelin smiled warmly. "And so it shall be. Close your eyes and think of all the wonderful things in store for you."

"Thank you," Malcolm said, and he closed his eyes.

"My pleasure." Hamelin took up the frail hand. In an instant, the old man stopped breathing. Every crease in his face smoothed out, and his expression changed from one of pain to serenity.

Hamelin watched him a moment before reverently draping Malcolm's lifeless hand across his chest. Then he exited from the room, passing Malcolm's wife as she returned with the water. He was already out the front door when the wailing began.

"Mayday, Mayday! Abort, abort! Do you hear me? Stand down!"

Hamelin froze halfway down the steps. "Andrew?"

Andrew was yelling now. "Cease and desist! It's the wrong person. Thirty-three-oh-nine Grover *Street.* I repeat, *Street,* not *Avenue.* Tell me you haven't been inside yet."

"For God's sake," Hamelin muttered. His hands went to his hips as he searched his surroundings. At the bottom of the hill and up the other side was a two-story stone building with two red bay doors. "Engine Company Three on Grover Avenue. Get 911 and fix it. I have to be elsewhere."

Hamelin didn't wait for a response. He crossed the street and cut down the alley that would eventually angle up toward Grandview. Clearly, it was not going to be a good day. He was already late for lunch.

Chapter Two
Letter of the Law

Hamelin Russell would be the first to admit he was an immortal who enjoyed flying by the seat of his razor-creased khakis. Well, maybe "flying" wasn't quite the word. It gave the wrong connotation, of wings, angels. He wasn't that sort, but he did have a heavenly affiliation. He was a transporter of souls—a portal to the afterlife, one could say—to the lovely and celestial, or the ugly and hellish. He didn't make the allocation, just did the fetching and delivering to a predetermined final home. The work was rote and boring, with an instruction book that could choke the great thoroughbred Secretariat. Sometimes, he improvised. He was flawed, but he prayed on it a lot. Winging it didn't play well with management, and trouble followed him wherever he went, nipping at his heels like a crazed chihuahua. He had been chastised, reassigned, and demoted more times than anyone else in his unit—probably than any in the history of the afterlife. But he had never before been called before an ad hoc review panel of elders.

As he sat in the stillness of the conference room, he reflected on the white pickled furniture, bright white carpet, and bleached curtains. Everything screamed uniformity and conservatism. Maybe he had finally taken individualism too far. His gaze drifted to the three bowed heads across from him as they prayed for wisdom and guidance. So far, their stoic demeanor gave nothing away. Surely, if it were going to be really bad, Saint Peter would be here.

Stephen, the central figure of the three, stirred, bringing the group's silent prayer to an end. He stroked his silver beard several times as if reaffirming some decision, then reached for the pale-blue business envelope that had lain untouched in the center of the table. He studied the contents and passed it to the others.

When the letter returned to him, Stephen cleared his throat. In the countless years Hamelin had known the kind elder, he had never heard a catch of indecision in his sonorous voice.

"So, Hamelin, the problem we have before us today concerns dereliction of duty—"

"Was it the kielbasa thing?" Hamelin asked, trying to cut to the chase. "Because it didn't live up to the hype. Rest assured, I shan't be doing *that* again."

Stephen blinked at him a couple of times. "I'm sure Mr. Derby wouldn't refer to it as '*the kielbasa thing.*' The gross injustice of robbing a mortal of ..." He sighed in frustration. "Mistakes are unacceptable, Mr. Russell, and if one is ever made, you do everything possible to see that it is fixed immediately. Popping off to enjoy a kielbasa sandwich is not an acceptable option."

Hamelin hung his head and nodded. Two bad days in a row. He was on a roll.

"But let's not get sidetracked," Stephen continued. "While your lunch yesterday is a contributing factor, the main impetus for this meeting is your habitual tardiness in retrieving souls at the moment of death and transporting them in a timely manner to the afterlife." He picked up a clipboard from the table and turned it so Hamelin could see the color-coded line graph fastened there.

Hamelin skimmed it. The horizontal axis of the graph was labeled in months, the vertical in minutes. It was attachment A at every performance review his supervisor had ever conducted with him. He looked at Stephen and again nodded.

Stephen put his finger on the blue straight line running horizontally across the graph. "This is the target metric of two minutes plotted over the past twelve months." He moved his finger to another horizontal line, this one red. It meandered above and below the blue one, but never by more than a minute or so. "Here is the unit average. And finally," he said, tapping a third line, which was green, "this is *your* average over the past year."

Hamelin studied the peaks and valleys of the sinuous green wave. It looked like a skier's path on a slalom course.

Stephen's penetrating gaze shifted from the clipboard to Hamelin. "Your averages were so far afield from the target metric that we had to recalibrate the upper part of the vertical scale to *days* instead of minutes. And now we have yesterday's mishap."

"Were they able to revive Mr.—"

Stephen gave him a withering look.

"Oh. Most unfortunate. He was very appreciative when I was there." Hamelin glanced at the other two elders. Both were scowling, and each's hands were drawn into tight, prayerful steeples. He was in deep dirt. He focused on the graphs and took a moment to craft his next response. He would be the first to admit that the graphs looked a bit strange, but this observation probably wasn't what Stephen was looking for. "What happens when you average out the highs and lows over the twelve months?" he asked, running his finger along the green line.

Stephen set down the clipboard. "You don't."

"My bad," Hamelin said. He withdrew his hand and assumed the steeple pose. "I'd be the first to admit there are months where things weren't quite up-to-snuff, but look at the months where I've got collection down to a minute or less. Doesn't that count for something?" He shot a tentative look at Barnaby, the panel member to Stephen's right. His gaze was met with a reproving shake of the old man's bald head.

"Maybe," Stephen said, "if this were the first time you were being counseled. Unfortunately …"

"No, no, that's okay," Hamelin said, raising his hands in deference. "I'm glad you've brought it to my attention. I had no idea my performance has been that, um, *erratic.* And I can guarantee you that we will not be having *this* conversation *next* year."

Hamelin looked at each panelist. Stephen was absorbed in the graph, Barnaby's gaze was boring a hole through him, and the third, Patrick, appeared to be absorbed in transcribing the proceeding. The panel's silence was deafening and defining. This was not a mere admonishment to do better, and a simple promise to improve was not going to get him off the hook. Hamelin mustered all the contrite feelings he could find, stuffed them into a pleasant tone, and said, "Are there any other areas noted for improvement?"

"When performance on a critical element is deemed unacceptable, all else becomes irrelevant," Stephen said. He consulted the letter he had passed around earlier. "I'm sure you understand the severity of this. As a soul runner, you have but one function: go get the deceased and escort them home. We simply can't have souls arriving at heaven or hell in a helter-skelter fashion. And we *certainly* can't be engaging individuals who are not scheduled for departure." His gnarled hand swept across the lines on the graph. "It's clear that you can meet the metrics. You do it time and time again. But then, there are these …

lapses. No one else in your unit seems to have a problem. What, exactly, are you doing out there?"

Hamelin grimaced. "It's attention deficit, sir—a lingering mortal affliction. I battled it all my life, and I can't seem to shake free of it. Pray for me. I'm failing miserably, but I don't want to."

The elder looked at him sternly. "We will continue to pray for all your *afflictions,* brother. And we want you to do your own praying and soul-searching. You have enormous potential, and helping you—and all your coworkers—realize success is one of our greatest priorities. Rest assured that no one wants to quench your, um, unique spirit, and … er, zest for life, but this poor performance has to stop. *Today,*" he added, tapping the table with his index finger. "So, it pains me to inform you that, effective immediately, you have been placed on probation for the next thirty days. If, during this period, you are able to meet the requirements of your position, your provisional status will be returned to a permanent one and you'll have nothing to worry about. But if you can't straighten this out," he said, pointing to the wavy green line, "we shall be forced to terminate your services, and final judgment will be passed upon you."

Hamelin blanched. "You're sending me to hell?"

Stephen's expression softened. "No one here has the authority to decide—or even speculate—on that. But I've known you a long time, Hamelin, and I know that you can accomplish whatever you set your mind to. Don't dwell on the consequences. Concentrate on the satisfaction in doing God's work. There are untold riches to be found in that."

"I understand," Hamelin said, forcing a smile. He was capable of meeting any metric that management threw at him. What no one would understand was how boring he found all this. He had been floating between heaven and hell for eons, and for all his good works, he was no closer to setting foot in heaven than when he arrived. Now that they might punch his ticket out of this place—perhaps on less-than-stellar performance—was he ready to accept the consequences for *all* his works?

"Let's meet again a month from now," Stephen said, drawing him out of his brooding.

Suddenly, Patrick's pilot light seemed to ignite. He stirred from his writing pad for the first time in the meeting. "A moment please, Stephen?" he said, waving his pen at them. "Before adjourning, a question was asked that still needs addressing." He ran his pen up through his notes until he came to something he had circled. *"Hamelin Russell: Are there any other areas noted for improvement?"* With a satisfied glance at Stephen, he put his head down and began scribbling again.

Stephen nodded. "My apologies, Hamelin. It's an insightful question, which I failed to address properly. Nothing else in your record is cause for concern. But I would be remiss if I didn't ask you a similar question. Is there anything else in your performance that should concern us? If there is, we should discuss it now. Because it would be most unfortunate if something else were to come out later."

Hamelin got up and moved to the windows. The view from this set was always eternal night—not a dark, forbidding expanse or cosmic latte, but a wondrous cosmos of twinkling diamond dust, sweeping red elliptical galaxies, and spirals of blue—a firmament sparkling with incalculable, untold marvels. Oh, how he loved the nebulae—especially the Engraved Hourglass, which often appeared here. When he failed to find it, he put his hands on the sill and gave his recent activities an earnest review. He wasn't perfect, but then, who was? He could see only one other major deficiency in his soul running. He might be sorry for it all he wanted, but he would never confess it. Stephen was wrong about ignoring consequences and basking in the glory of the work. Hamelin's proclivity for ignoring Handbook Section 383 would get him bounced for sure. No, the only consideration for him now was how easily it could be found out. Management had all kinds of metrics, but he wasn't sure they could even measure for this transgression. His mind made up, he returned to the table, sat down, and looked into Stephen's deep sea-blue eyes. "Nothing, sir. I am extremely proud of my service and take very seriously the responsibilities that have been entrusted to me." Hamelin watched the almost imperceptible drop of Stephen's shoulders as he seemed to relax.

"Good to hear," Stephen said, smiling. "Now, go out there and turn yourself around. It's all in your hands."

Hamelin left them there. He could put his left foot in and his left foot out, but even the hokeypokey couldn't turn around the potential catastrophe hanging over his immortal life. First, he would pray hard that management never learned of what he really did in the mortal world. Beyond the gambling, loafing, and moonlighting at blues bars lay a secret that would get him never-ending torment and damnation. It wasn't something he was sorry for doing, but realistically, if he burned for eternity because of it, there might be some regrets.

The second thing on his agenda was to use the intellect the good Lord had given him and fix this dilemma. Common sense told him to refrain from any more Section 383 violations. He could live with that. There was also a lot of harping in his head about fixing all his current violations. He wasn't so inclined. It would hurt a lot of people. Some were old acquaintances, and it was probably time to cut the cord with them anyway. But others, like the bar owner in Nevis, were recent relationships, and he had taken quite a shine to them. He would regret terminating those. No, coasting along with what was in place would probably be okay. After all, he'd gone all this time without being discovered. What could possibly go wrong?

Chapter Three
Soul Runners

Hamelin moved from the senior staff's serene sea of white—known in the vernacular as the White Corridor—to the frenetic, kaleidoscopic world of the worker bees. He checked the signage on the conference room door and entered a large chamber that looked like a high school cafeteria set up for a PTA meeting—rows of folding metal chairs set up in neat rows, with a wide aisle dividing the room into two parts. The room was packed, and a speaker was already at the podium, gesturing at a PowerPoint presentation on a large pulldown screen. Hamelin signed in at the registrar's table, took a yellow orientation packet, and scanned the crowd. His colleagues appeared to be listening with rapt attention, every eye glued to the speaker. When managed correctly, they were a powerful force in carrying out the directives of the Godhead. But they had not yet shaken all the foibles of mortal life, and left to their own devices, they were also capable of cutting a swath of destruction across the universe. Senior-level management were there to ensure that it never happened.

He headed to the back row of seats and sat down in an empty chair in the middle. "Luke," he said, acknowledging the shag-cut fellow on his right. "Miss much?"

"Have you ever been anywhere on time?" Luke shoved his spiral notebook at him and pointed halfway down the page. "This is the final presenter. They're about ready to cut us loose. Afternoon sessions strictly for managers, same all day tomorrow, and then the managers will be out for a week. Where've you been?"

Hamelin ignored the question, refusing to be drawn into a discussion about his existential crisis. "Official business. Who'd they leave in charge?"

"Oh, you'll never guess," Luke said.

"Martin, huh?"

Luke nodded. "Of course. But there's a bright side. They're temporarily promoting him to full supervisor. He'll be out of our hair. The newest and lowliest member of the managerial staff will disappear in a fog of obscurity. No doubt you'll be designated a team leader and get an opportunity to shine. Scuttlebutt is, you were in the running to the very end. What'd you do, tick someone off?"

Hamelin shrugged. His image certainly needed polishing, but there was little chance of that happening. Petty rivalries permeated this layer of soul runners. There was no esprit de corps, despite management's rah-rah sessions assuring them they were the *team supreme.* Martin had snagged the promotion everyone coveted—an advancement that would put him that much closer to leaving this plane of existence and being elevated into the full rewards of the afterlife. Spoken of or not, such an elevation was, or would become, the goal of every newbie in the room.

"I've already redeemed myself with that tricky two-fer in Maryland last summer," Hamelin whispered. "At the moment, all I want to do is get out of here so I can hit a fiddlers' convention in Guthrie, Oklahoma."

"Picking up someone famous?"

Hamelin shook his head. "No, Byron Berline's playing. Best of the best in any musical style he chooses." His gaze wandered the group until he found Martin, sitting in the next row. He looked deliriously happy as he chatted with coworkers.

Martin Westwood Cobb was happy only when he was in charge—a taskmaster who carried out projects flawlessly with short, nonnegotiable deadlines and spirit-crushing micromanagement. He rarely contributed anything of substance. Others executed; he took credit—classic senior management material. Bosses adored him, and his coworkers hated him. From his lensless tortoiseshell poser glasses down to his trendy Yeezy footwear, Hamelin detested him. The feeling, though unspoken, was mutual.

Hamelin skimmed the notebook. When he handed it back, Luke was staring at him, a slight frown creasing his forehead.

"You took that better than I thought," Luke said. "Since you're in such a good mood, I'll confide something else. But you have to promise you'll carefully consider what I'm going to tell you and not go off half-cocked."

"Yeah, sure." Hamelin felt pretty certain there was nothing earthshaking Luke could tell him. He just wasn't that well connected.

"You know, don't you, that Martin was the reason they took you off runs to heaven and gave you the miserable ones to hell?"

"I suspect so."

"No, listen to me," Luke said, pulling on his sleeve. "He *is* the reason. It's in black and white. Down in the archives—in the dank, dark, recesses that only librarians would enjoy. I stumbled across the testimony. It started out as a single alarming confidential tip about how you played your way through a couple of pickups. When it succeeded in ruffling feathers, the tipster came forward and provided an official statement. Signed by none other than *M. W. Cobb.*"

"Son of a saint," Hamelin said, giving his rival in the next row the stink-eye. So *Martin* was the source of the initial complaint about his lackadaisical approach to collecting souls. He hadn't thought it possible to dislike the guy more than he already did. It had taken him years to work his way back up to heavenly runs. "You show me. Then I'll make him wish he hadn't."

Luke shook his head. "Uh-uh. Just promise me you'll behave, or I won't tell you anything else. No need to even any scores. You've worked past it. I'm only telling you so that in the future, you'll watch your back."

Hamelin didn't share that he hadn't worked past it at all. Quite the contrary, in fact—it had snowballed into something current and alarming.

"How did you get permission to access the archives?" he asked.

"Father Richard asked me to help him catalogue mortality data from the past two hundred Atlantic Ocean hurricane seasons. Evidently, someone thinks there might be outside meddling—or, God forbid, some sort of collusion between dark and light forces."

"In that case, I guess they wouldn't be *light* anymore, would they?"

"No," Luke said, chuckling, "but doesn't it seem reasonable to assume that there would be some sort of mixing of good and evil along a continuum? Anyway, they're gung-ho to stamp it out if they can find solid evidence."

"Could you get me a copy of the testimony?"

Luke flipped to the next free page in his notebook. "Dream on," he said as he wrote a heading across the top. "I like my job. If you weren't a friend, you wouldn't even have gotten a heads-up."

Hamelin looked at Martin again, half expecting to see him reading their lips. But the new golden boy was otherwise occupied. The air around him softly shimmered as he chatted up an infatuated, curvaceous newbie.

"So full of himself," Hamelin murmured. "How can they promote someone so selfish? There's a darkness about that man. He's the first place I'd search for collusion."

The final speaker walked off the podium to enthusiastic applause, and audience members began to drift out the door in small chattering groups. Hamelin finished the soda he had brought along, shoved the empty bottle under his chair, and waited.

Martin tapped the shoulder of David, the blond-haired man in front of him. David, and those near him, pivoted their chairs around. Several moments of shifting coffee cups and rustling orientation packets followed.

When all was settled, Martin glanced around the group and then broke into a beatific smile. "Looks like everybody's here, so let's get right to it," he said. "We're here to plan an end-of-year celebratory bash. We want to go big and we want everyone's suggestions." He flipped a page on his scratch pad. "So, folks, what'll it be: a spate of UFO sightings and Martian visitations, or just general carousing and mayhem? You brainstorm; I'll write. Then we vote. David," he said, pointing at the blond guy, "you made a list of past events? Just for reference?"

"All up here," David said, tapping his temple. "I think we should try for something a little more organized this time. And we should stick together. It's more interesting that way."

"Epic floods?" someone called out from the right.

David shook his head. "I'm not averse to repeating ourselves, but we did that two years ago. Whatever we choose, the activity should appear random to an impartial observer."

"You mean management."

"Well, yes, of course," Martin said.

"Plate tectonics are always fun," offered someone from the left."

"Tectonics a no-no," Martin said. "San Francisco got a little out of hand. Took 'em decades to build that place back up. We need to keep collateral damage at a minimum—ideally, zero."

Hamelin stretched out his long legs and pulled the brim of his Baltimore Orioles baseball cap down low over his eyes. Worker bees all turned loose at the same time, and management ignorant of their whereabouts? Destruction was inevitable. This "democratic" exercise was all for show; he'd seen it all so many times before. The suggestions were half-baked, thrown out by the youngest immortals, the idealistic ones still motivated by, and perhaps infatuated with, their positions in the afterlife. Martin would soon stamp that out of them.

Hamelin had once been like them, bursting with energy and itching to change the world. No more. He would let this little exercise in apparent free will run its course before things got serious and he offered his two cents. Hamelin couldn't control their actions. Martin would seduce them into doing what he wanted. But Hamelin could influence *how* it was done, throw a wrench in the process. It was the least he could do for dear old Martin.

Martin tapped his list. "I'm hearing all kinds of good suggestions," he said. "I'll add one to the mix. Yes, it's been done before, but not for a while. It'll be a hoot. And with minimal guidance, we can avoid inflicting much collateral damage. It's the perfect team-building experience for those not afraid to cut loose. *One ginormous bender.* It's been a while, right, David?"

David nodded. "Quite a while."

A sudden chorus of "*Yeah!*'s" turned the head of the registrar as she packed up near the door. Martin offered her a thumbs-up. She laughed and continued tidying up her space.

"Wait, wait," Martin said, holding his hands up to calm his rowdy group. "Even better, we can run the Tippy, a best-in-bar competition that never fails to entertain. Everyone gets to nominate their favorite bartender. It's spectacular fun watching mortals knock themselves out trying to win it."

A flabby-armed strawberry blonde shot up a hand as if she'd just won bingo. "Excuse me. The Manual says we can't drink."

"Section three-twenty, part five," mumbled Curtis, the crew-cut, fingernail-chewing newbie sitting next to Martin.

"Yes, Charlotte, you're speaking of Section three-twenty, part five," Martin said. "But the inference is clear: *while on duty.* Am I right?"

Hamelin watched her bristle. Her upset was understandable. Just like drinking and driving, inebriation and novice soul runners did not mix. There was no degree of control that Martin alone could exercise to harness the destructiveness of dozens of out-of-control immortals cutting loose in various earthly bars. While they couldn't end a life without authorization, they could leave the physical world in shambles.

The rest of the group ignored, or failed to grasp, any negative implications and roared their approval. Charlotte closed her mouth. And just as Hamelin had anticipated—and as Martin had planned—the group's activity was chosen.

"Then drinking it is," Martin said. He turned to David. "I'll bet you spent longer researching the history of our outings than it took this crowd to agree on that." Beaming, he turned back to the group. "As you may or may not have heard, I'll be hobnobbing with the big boys for a while. A temporary promotion. Even though I'll be off at the managers' retreat, I'll still be with you in spirit, and I'll most assuredly have your collective back."

Hamelin pushed up in his chair. It didn't make sense. The outing would be a free-for-all, and as its orchestrator, Martin would be responsible for any damage inflicted. Why would open himself up for that?

"Same rules as last time?" he asked, drawing Martin's attention for the first time in the meeting. The smile Martin flashed his way was a bit unsettling. A drunken rampage, no doubt, was the just the beginning of Martin's machinations. Was it possible he knew about the performance review?

"Yes, thanks, Hamelin. No change to the way it has run before. I'll set down a few guidelines, but basically, for those unfamiliar, we send out contest invitations, visit every bar in the running, then cast a vote for the best. Simple enough. And a word of caution: you may not offer a heads-up or assistance of any kind to any competitor. Evidence of cheating will result in disqualification of the barkeeper you've nominated."

Okay," Hamelin said, "but how are you going to keep this all running smoothly if you're off with the managers?"

Martin's smile widened. "Good question. And we'll get to that in the second half of the meeting."

He motioned for Hamelin's baseball cap. "Keep in mind, the invitation goes to the bartender, not the bar, so make sure you've got your bartenders in the right bars. Write down the name of the bartender and his location on a slip of paper, and throw it in this hat. Don't be shy. It's all confidential. First prize means bragging rights, so choose wisely, children." Martin passed the hat to the middle-aged woman on his right.

"Oh, and one more thing," he added, watching the hat as it traveled through the group. "This should go without saying, but just so everyone is clear, we work hard; we play hard. This is a serious team-building experience. There will be no communication with management. Once the game begins, all assignments you receive are to be stayed until three days hence. No exceptions. If you can't hack it, you might want to find a more compatible work group. In other words, get the heaven and hell out."

Gasps, then silence.

"No d-d-deliveries?" Charlotte bit her lip.

Martin shook his head. "None. Once the contest commences, and for the three days following, there will be neither ascents into heaven nor descents into hell."

"That's going to create quite a backlog on day four," Charlotte said, chuckling. "If I didn't know better, I'd think you were serious." Her gaze swept the faces around her. "My God, you *are* serious. Nobody else thinks this is crazy?" She took a nervous sip from her coffee mug.

"It's only a problem if we make it one," Martin said. "If you can't stand the heat, how are you newbies ever going to make it to hell and back? Hmm? It's not as if the *soul* is going anywhere." He gazed around the crowd, driving home his point. "Besides, what's three days? We can make it symbolic if it makes you feel better."

Charlotte choked on her drink. "That's blasphemous! Saint Peter will never tolerate anything of the sort."

"And that's exactly why we don't report out on group activities," David said.

Charlotte looked from Martin to Luke, to Hamelin and then back to Martin. "Disgraceful! I'm out of here." She pushed her way out of the cluster of chairs and headed for the exit.

Martin remained focused on the hat's journey. "No problem unless you go flapping your gums. Anybody else want to cut and run? Now's the time. One stroke of the pen, and I can have you out of the group and on your merry way."

Hamelin watched Charlotte huff out. It was refreshing to find someone with enough confidence and integrity to stand up to Martin. Better still, her seething dislike of Martin might prove useful someday. "Charlotte, wait. Hold up," he said, scrambling after her. He caught her at the door. "From one friend to another, keep your mouth shut. You haven't had your first performance review yet. Being on probation, a bad one would limit your career opportunities. Nobody likes getting stuck making deliveries to hell. I'd hate to see that happen to such a promising newbie. Keep a low profile and sit this one out." He gave her a wink, patted her on the arm, and returned to his seat amid a sea of wide-eyed stares.

"You had me worried there, Hamelin," Martin murmured. "For a moment, I thought you were going to walk, too. Let Charlotte be. She'd never make it in this group anyway." He took the hat back and shook the slips of paper inside. "We're done here. I'll get these tallied up and we'll regroup." He checked the clock on the far wall. "I have another meeting I have to pop off to. Why doesn't everybody take a break? Be back here at eleven twenty-five." He looked at Hamelin. "When I get back, will you count these with me? I'll call, you write 'em down?"

"Sure," Hamelin said. "I have something to attend to, but I'll be back by eleven."

He walked out into the corridor, toward the first exit door past the auditorium. Martin was an operator—always in the right place, at right time, with the right answer. Hamelin would never beat him in a head-to-head contest for a promotion, but the Tippy, now, *that* was a different story. Martin couldn't sway or intimidate a group this large into voting for his bartender. It was a level playing field for once, and

Hamelin could best him. If there was one thing he knew, it was the bar beat. He breathed the blues and had jammed in enough dives across the cosmos. After soul running, it was his second calling.

He pushed through the exit door and, a moment later, was walking down quaint tree-lined streets. Nevis, Maryland, was one of his favorite small towns on the East Coast. To his right, the sparkling waters of the Chesapeake Bay stretched from the boardwalk and public dock to the Maryland Eastern Shore on the horizon. And to his left, the town green ran like thick carpeting toward century-old oaks. Both were lovely and deserved attention, but today he followed his nose toward the town center. Without a doubt, the best bartender on earth would be found there. Short in stature but big of heart, Bennie Bertollini ran an outstanding bar with great ambience, excellent brew, and a manner that could lift the spirits of even the most downhearted. The Phoenix pub was the epitome of what a Tippy bar should be. Once Hamelin verified that Bennie continued to ply his skills here, he would nominate him, and the winner of this year's contest would be a shoo-in.

Then it was back to the meeting. Luke was right. If Martin wasn't participating in the contest, he would surely appoint intermediaries to run it for him. The delegating game was second nature and the perfect vehicle for placing blame on others. He fully expected Martin to make him the fall guy. And since he was already on probation, it was a risk Hamelin couldn't afford. So, he would have to ensure that fallout from the retreat was as wide and ugly as possible and that Martin would be culpable from the start—censured so severely that he would never be promoted again. Hamelin relished the thought of his nemesis remaining stranded between heaven and hell in perpetuity. At the first sign of trouble, Hamelin would go above his head—secretly, of course. Two could play the anonymous-tip game.

Chapter Four
The Mulligan

The sky over Nevis was bright blue and cloudless, yet darkness hovered over Ryan Thomas like a black cloud threatening rain. He looked at the photograph of the Whaler, taken as it sped away from the pier, then peered out from under the red beach umbrella to scan the same dock again. Every third boat was a Boston Whaler, but from what he could tell, none had a St. Paul port of registry, or the drop-dead gorgeous first mate he remembered. If only he had photographed *her.* It was the biggest mistake he had ever made, and his life had been littered with them. He would never find his wife, Livia, this way. He closed his eyes and pictured his last memory of her—a fleeting one: hot brunette sitting cross-legged on the bow of the boat. So different from when he'd had a relationship with her. Back then, she was a striking blonde with girl-next-door looks. It seemed a lifetime ago when he watched, helpless, as her life ebbed away on a Nevis sidewalk.

He couldn't blame Hamelin Russell, the immortal soul runner who had held her hand as she lay dying, for taking her. He understood that Hamelin had no control over whose soul he was sent to collect. And Ryan certainly couldn't complain about Hamelin's decision to spare her a trip into the afterlife by allowing her soul, momentarily free of the corporal plane, to migrate into the body of the woman Ryan had seen in the Whaler. No, his only beef with the rogue immortal was that he hadn't bothered to tell him the love of his life was still walking the earth. It was only by chance—or fate—that he had caught sight of her down on the docks that day. Despite the change in appearance, he knew her instantly. He would have known his soulmate anywhere. And he need only find her again, and everything would be perfect.

He checked the dock again, refusing to believe that this picture recorded her sole trip to Nevis. "Brunette, leggy bombshell," he muttered. And how many beautiful women could fit *that* description? He had no doubt that Hamelin Russell could find the exact number. But the immortal had left Ryan on a Nevis sidewalk with a dying wife, no celestial phone number, and no heavenly forwarding address. He just needed five minutes of Hamelin's time, or maybe even a peek at the black instruction manual he followed so religiously.

A new Whaler approached shore. Ryan fanned himself with the boat photograph as if he were melting. The picture and his memory of the Whaler had all but consumed him these past nine months, and he had traveled hundreds of miles based on a feeling. It was the feeling that no matter what this girl now looked like, or what new life she had assumed, they could resume their life together.

He shooed a yellow butterfly off his kneecap. It fluttered away and settled on the back of the empty canvas beach chair beside him, its antennae seeming to vibrate to the beat of the doo-wop band playing in the concert shell on the boardwalk. All life should be so simple and happy. And Ryan was surrounded by happy: diving and whooping volleyball players, sunbathers on colorful striped beach towels, boogying music lovers. He studied the strawberry daiquiri and the untouched piña colada sitting on the cooler next to him. Liquor wasn't about to do it for him. He took a swig of the piña colada anyway and set it back down hard.

A slender hand with shiny fire-engine-red nail polish brushed his hand to claim the other drink. "This mine?"

Ryan scrambled up and wrapped the woman in a tight hug. "Vanessa! I was beginning to wonder …" He pulled back and looked her over. She was all smiles and looking tanned and fit.

"Ryan *Doubting* Thomas. I told you I'd be here. I'm late but here."

Ryan's face fell. "Oh, no. Richard—did he …"

"Relax. The ex is fine. In fact, better than fine. Remission."

Ryan brightened. "Beaten the big C? That's great!"

"You should go see him," she said.

Ryan let the remark slide. It wasn't that he wished anything bad on his estranged father, but it was complicated, as was his relationship with Vanessa, his mother. Only Hamelin would understand the complexities. Unfortunately, he would coldly see it all as just an unfortunate byproduct of doing business.

"I'm late," she continued, "because I didn't realize there was going to be a party down here. I had to park way over by Roland's grocery. She shooed the butterfly from the chair and sat down. It fluttered off in Ryan's direction again."

Ryan uttered a profanity and waved it out of his face. "Oh, no, you don't."

She eyed him closely. "Shouldn't you and the butterflies be big buddies by now? They tell me that you spend a lot of time down here on the beach."

"Who's *they*?"

Vanessa chuckled. "My supersecret sources, whose names I will not reveal even under threat of torture. They also said you're clocking a lot of miles out of town."

He took off his sunglasses and rubbed his eyes. "If I ever find out who at the Phoenix has been talking out of school, I'll can them."

"I don't believe I said they worked for you."

"You don't need to. They keep tabs on me like I'm going to *off* myself as soon as I'm out of sight." He put his glasses back on and resumed his horizon watch. "So, who do you think is crazier: a grieving widower, or people who won't even let me go to the bathroom by myself? I just don't know," he said with a sigh.

"Heard about your new job. Investigative work going well?"

"Still sending out feelers, but a good response so far. The meet-and-deal will come later. Did you hear Maggie Sullivan's on board? Once we start accepting retainers, I'll probably bring her down and set up a real office. For now, we'll err on the side of caution and stay virtual, with her working out of New York. I'd feel terrible if I uprooted her and things didn't pan out. Thought I had a nice space right down the street from the Phoenix, but I didn't jump at it fast enough and somebody else scooped it up."

Vanessa poked her straw at the blobs of whipped cream in her drink. "Maggie, huh?"

"Listen, she's the best damn researcher I've ever worked with. If you're worried that old beau Hector Young might pay her a visit here someday and come after me again, forget it. He's too busy soaking up the good life in the Caymans, spending his ill-gotten gains. There's bigger fish…"

She put down her drink. "No. None of that. I just don't want any reminders of awful people. Loss is tough, and it takes time to heal. You do what you need to do, and you do it on your own time. I'm sorry I couldn't be here for you these past months, but I'm back, and with Richard on the mend, you now have my full attention again. Let me go get you a scotch. If that Zodiac's cover band can't soothe you …"

Ryan studied the bottom of his empty glass. "Just to bring you up to speed, I've probably had just a few too many of these lately. All I have to do is this," he said, crooking his index finger at her. He batted yet another yellow butterfly out of his face.

"If you think the butterflies are annoying down here, you should see what's going on up at the bar. It's positively *raining* yellow butterflies."

Raining yellow butterflies? Hope broke over Ryan like an ocean wave tumbling an unsuspecting child at the beach. Was it possible? "Don't go anywhere," he said. "I'll be right back." He beelined for the yellow-and-white striped tent near the boardwalk.

"What'll it be, boss?" asked a smiling, tanned Adonis manning a cluster of beer taps.

Ryan ignored him. He walked toward the swarm of yellow butterflies hovering around the only other person at the bar—a man of impeccable posture, lost in his thoughts as he polished off his drink and snacked from a plate of cantaloupe and pineapple. The air around him seemed to shimmer in soft light.

Ryan stopped a few feet short of him and said, "Should have known as soon as I saw the first set of antennae. Whose soul are you here for, Hamelin?"

Hamelin turned and fixed deep emerald eyes on him. "Fine, thank you," he said. "And you?"

Ryan sat down, leaving the stool in between them empty. "I've seen better. Where's Livia Williams?"

Hamelin frowned. "Williams? Name's not ringing any bells, Ryan James."

"You can drop the 'James.' I haven't seen my parasitic evil twin since you dragged his soul off to hell. Please tell me he hasn't escaped eternal damnation and is coming to get me."

"Oh, not to my knowledge. You're looking good," Hamelin said, nodding agreeably." He held up his glass, signaling the barkeep for a refill.

"On the house," Ryan said, "but cut him off after this one."

The bartender frowned. "Okay, but are we charging everyone else for water?"

Ryan turned back to Hamelin and blinked. "Why are you not drinking?"

"I never drink," Hamelin said.

"*Pfft.* You left empty beer bottles all over my Carrera when you stole it."

"Correction. Those were Dr. Pepper bottles. Furthermore, I was offered a ride and it was your cohabiting, 'parasitic evil twin,' Ryan Llewellyn Thomas, who had the car and was polishing off the brew. Not me. Uh-uh. This body is a temple. Besides, you wouldn't like me drunk."

"Who said I like you sober? Now, back to my original question. Where's my wife, Livia? Or whatever her name is now. I know what you did. I've *seen* her down at the docks."

"Where's Bennie?" Hamelin countered, eyes like slits as he studied Ryan over the rim of his glass. "Not at the Phoenix. I asked."

"You're here for *Bennie*?" Ryan fumbled off the stool, thoughts racing as he tried to think of a place to hide his bartender until Hamelin found another soul to occupy his time. Then his thoughts skidded to a halt. "You should know where he is … unless … unless you don't really have business with him. That is, if you were being honest when you told me that you know only what you *need* to know." He crossed his arms over his chest. "I don't know where he is."

Hamelin chuckled and popped a pineapple chunk into his mouth.

"I never lie," he said, chewing thoughtfully, "and I have no *official* business with the bartender. General, unofficial business, yes. Did you have a falling-out and fire him?"

"Of course not.

"Now who's not being honest?"

Ryan looked to the heavens in search of moral support. "Okay, it was a falling-out. And if you must know, he's back in New York. He has the soul of a New Yorker, so he's probably better off there. But you just leave his soul there."

"Oh, that won't do. That won't do at all." Hamelin dabbed his lips with his napkin and pulled a black leather notebook from somewhere. "Another bar, I presume. Name?"

Ryan shook his head. "I don't trust you."

"God have mercy. I held your life in my hands, and you lived to walk away from the experience. You can't trust *me*?" Hamelin put his hand over his heart. "You wound me, sir. I probably could have gotten the information out of the address book in your middle desk drawer, but I was respecting your privacy."

"Why were you snooping in my desk?" Ryan asked, looking askance at him.

Hamelin lowered the book. "Because the lady on the phone was asking about some beer delivery."

"You were taking my *phone calls*?" Ryan ran his hand through his closely cropped hair and paced a few steps away before returning. "Jeez, oh, Pete. You haven't changed. You haven't changed a single bit."

"Why would you expect an immortal to change?" Hamelin slipped two bills underneath his glass and got up. "Let me give you a piece of advice, Ryan Thomas. The afterlife doesn't change anybody. That's what *life* is for. Didn't you learn anything from our last encounter? Not to suggest that the workings in the afterlife are not trying. The politics might surprise you."

"Frankly, I just want you to leave everyone I know alone, and find a better place to roost than Nevis—or New York. Surely, there's a dead person somewhere in this vast world who needs your assistance in finding the pearly gates. Tell me where Livia is, and then run along and do your job. Everybody will be the happier for it."

"Very well. You leave me no choice." Hamelin reached in a different pocket and pulled another book—this one yellow striped—and started paging through it. "'B' for 'Bennie,' or 'B' for 'Bertollini'?"

Ryan took a swipe at the book. "Son of a saint. Give me back my address book."

Hamelin leaned away and kept flipping. "Ah, *Wandering Joe's.* Excellent. And I have no intention of roosting; I'm off. Please extend a warm hello to Vanessa and tell her I'd be most happy to swing by the Phoenix for an open-mike night. It would be great to have the whole gang together again: Vanessa, Bennie, Jean, Marla … and you, of course. Take care, Ryan James."

"Marla, as in Jean's daughter? What, you're not fully plugged in up there in the afterlife? She's dead."

"Really? They found her body?"

"No, just Meekae Skalski's. They pulled him out of Galveston Bay. He was headless and wearing a pair of cinder blocks for shoes. Never found Marla."

Hamelin stared a moment. "Hmm. Well, got to go."

Ryan slid in front of him to block his path but avoided touching him. "I know what you did. I saw Livia here, on a Whaler—different person, same soul. I looked into that woman's eyes and I *saw* her. You made her a mulligan just like me. A second-chancer. I'm not going anywhere, and neither are you until you tell me where my wife is."

"Or what?" Hamelin's eyes crinkled around the edges as if he were amused. He pushed the address book into Ryan's chest and then sidestepped him. "Sit down right here and don't fret. I'll be back and we'll see about catching up on old times." He pointed in the direction of the porta-potty. "I need a moment."

Ryan sat. "I'm trusting you, Hamelin," he yelled after him. Hamelin could set his life right. Finally, he felt sunshine peeking through the gloom.

***

Hamelin passed up the porta-potty, ditched the beach, and headed for Soho in New York. Wandering Joe's sounded intriguing, but he needed to make sure the place was worthy to compete. And then he had to split. Even though time moved more slowly in the afterlife, Martin would soon be wondering where he had gone.

Chapter Five
Section 383

Hamelin entered the same heavenly portal he had exited through several minutes earlier, and squeezed past little groups of young newbies congregating outside the conference room door. Martin was just as he had left him, alone and writing feverishly in a tablet. If it had been anyone else, Hamelin would have felt empathy for his lack of companionship.

Martin looked up and gazed past Hamelin toward the door. "Last-minute assignment?"

No, just a quick trip to make sure you're on the losing end.

Hamelin turned and followed Martin's gaze across the rows of empty seats to several group members engaged in a heated conversation with Charlotte. "Just following instructions. A quick trip to make sure my favorite bartender is where I thought he was."

Martin turned his focus to Hamelin. "Following instructions? Doesn't sound like the Hamelin I know."

Hamelin refused to be baited. He settled into a chair across from Martin and beckoned for the tablet. "You were a little hard on Charlotte, don't you think? Pissing someone off is the quickest way to have them run to management and squawk."

Martin flipped back a few pages and handed the pad and pen over.

"Don't worry. I'll put the fear of failure in her. She still won't participate, but she won't be tempted to cross us, either."

"By *us,* you mean *you,* of course. It'd be nice if you'd chill a little. This is a bonding experience and all about blowing off a little steam, remember? Group activity. If you want to hold the reins a bit tight, make sure there's no collateral damage in the group this time. The drinking in this contest should be limited to *tasting.* Nobody should be drinking heavily."

Martin locked eyes with Hamelin and frowned. "No need to be so restrictive. The whole purpose of this exercise is to get all these diverse personalities working together for the common good. We'll police our own. Fear not. We'll take care of everybody. And yes, I remember everything."

Hamelin clicked out the pen point. "Fire away."

Martin emptied the contents of the ball cap into his lap. "Harry Acardi's Bar in Venice," he read from the first slip, and tossed it in the empty hat. He unfolded another. "Summerbee's Royal Oak in Cheltenham, England. Oh, I like that one. Too bad there won't be enough time to hit the racecourse, too."

"Never been lucky with horses. Baseball? That's another story. They don't—

"Mickey Keen's Steakhouse, New York," Martin said, missing or ignoring a rare chance to bond. "Good one. Smoking pipes all over the ceiling. Ever been there?"

Hamelin grunted and kept writing.

"Kelly Wong's Gallery, Hong Kong. Mmm, bring your own booze. Where's the fun in that?"

And so it went as they worked through all the votes, including the blank slips submitted by the meek or undecided.

"How many, Hamelin?"

Hamelin held up a hand. "Twenty, but hold on, I still haven't voted." He tore a strip of paper from the pad and scribbled on it.

Martin took the slip. *"'Bennie Bertollini. Wandering Joe's. SoHo, New York.'"* He looked at Hamelin and hesitated.

From the studied look Martin was giving him, Hamelin had the strange feeling he was missing something. Martin was devious, and one of the few people Hamelin had ever met who could go eye to eye with someone and lie at the same time. "Problem with Wandering Joe's?"

"No. Add it," Martin said, pointing at the pad. "Twenty-one, you said? Circle every third bartender. We'll go with those 7." Then he took the pad back and drew a diagonal line cross the empty space at the bottom of the list. "Looks like you just squeaked through with Wandering Joe's. Good, although I am surprised you didn't nominate the Phoenix in Maryland. You were there quite a bit last year."

"That was last year, when Mr. Bertollini bartended there. This year, he's at Wandering Joe's. I am touched, though, that you thought enough to keep up."

"I keep up with all my friends."

So you can make anonymous complaints about their failings? Hamelin nodded in seeming agreement, took his cap back, and returned to his original seat.

Martin beckoned to one of the red-shirted conference coordinators still hovering nearby and handed the list over. "If you would input these, Samuel, we can all be on our way." And then, as if the official handoff of the list were a bell signaling vesper prayers, newbies began trickling back to their seats. Charlotte was not among them.

When it seemed all were accounted for, Martin began again. "Two more pieces of business, and then your day is yours. Administratively, the group's too big to handle out in the field, so we're going to divide you up." He pointed at the redhead in the middle of the group and said, "Colin, you and everybody to the right of you goes with Hamelin. Luke is team lead for everyone to the left."

There it was. With one seemingly innocent decision, Martin had ensured that the retreat's snafus would fall squarely on Hamelin's and Luke's shoulders. As soon as the meeting was over, Hamelin vowed to write a memo for the record, documenting how he had advised Martin to prohibit drinking.

A hand shot up in Hamelin's group.

"Put your hand down, Thaddeus," Martin said, staring him down. "This is not a negotiation. Anything else you need to know will come from your leader. Learn to follow. It's a virtue."

He returned his attention to the group. "Lastly, before you're up and out of here, I'm required to discuss some serious business. Section three-eight-three."

Hamelin pushed the bill of his cap up. *Section 383?*

"Everybody familiar with that section?" Martin asked. "Concerns mulligans? I see a few blank expressions, so let's review. Every time you get the name of an newly or soon-to-be deceased individual, it's your responsibility to go get them and lead them home. Be that to heaven or to hell, you do your job and take care of it in a timely fashion. Now, a mulligan results when one of you fails to live up to your obligation and leaves a soul dangling out there somewhere." He made a vague hand gesture. "So, you were just going to be a few nanoseconds late in picking up the package. You were blowing your nose, enjoying a particularly lovely celestial view, yada, yada, yada. *Not* acceptable, people. The soul in question goes into freefall. Things go haywire. And the worst that can happen? Creation of a mulligan. The soul of the deceased transfers into another recently vacated body, and it acquires a virtual second chance in the world. It's one of the most flagrant violations of the manual. Right, Hamelin?"

Hamelin gave him a thumbs-up as a feeling like electricity shot through his body and set his fingers and toes tingling with a burning fire. He *had* missed a couple of deadlines and left some souls dangling—well, maybe more than just a few. He also had a few mulligans floating around. Management's obsession with time was perplexing considering they operated in an eternal existence. Moreover, the passage of time in the afterlife was never at the same rate as on earth. Experienced immortals often extended and compressed time—within reason, of course—to suit their own needs. As long as he eventually transported the soul to where it belonged, what was the problem? He'd never uttered a word to anyone about it. It would be career suicide, not to mention the termination of the mulligan. What could Martin possibly know? And could he use it to torpedo a thirty-day probation period? Suddenly, winning a bar contest seemed inconsequential.

Chapter Six
Just Looking for a Home

Bennie Bertollini gave the patron a wink and slid the five-spot into his apron pocket. Wandering Joe's regulars swore that a few choice words from the portly bartender could solve all problems and were cheaper than therapy. It was nice to be appreciated, but Bennie's connection to New York was not as strong as it had been. Working at the Phoenix bar in Nevis, Maryland, had created stronger ties.

His short stay in Nevis was the only time he had ever ventured from the Big Apple. He was not given to gadding about, even if the ninety or so shot glasses lined up behind him suggested otherwise. Benjamin Franklin's admirers left pennies on his Philadelphia grave, Edgar Allen Poe's toaster offered cognac and roses, and Bennie's admirers brought shot glasses from everywhere—gifts from regs who lovingly hoped to pique his curiosity and nudge him out into the exciting world beyond the Hudson River. Bennie appreciated all of them but noted, with regret, that he had never gotten a glass for Nevis.

"Son of a biscuit." Bennie yanked the foam-filled glass back from the Bud tap and dumped it down the drain. He tried a second time and drew the same result. He put the glass down, and his hands went to his hips.

"Bennie?" It was the nearest bar patron, Jean, a buxom woman with bobbed red hair. She was packed into a white Baltimore Orioles T-shirt and black spandex jeggings so tight they forced her not altogether svelte figure to jiggle and even flirt with indecency. She put down her shooter and waved him over.

Bennie shook his head and let out a long, deep sigh. Then he turned to his dark-haired assistant. "Rick, didn't we change this out last night?"

"My bad." Rick disappeared through the double doors into the kitchen area.

"Benjamin!" Jean said, rapping her knuckles on the bar top to get his attention. "It's not the beer. What's up with you?"

"Bar burnout," said the guy at the end of the bar. He combed his fingertips through a tangle of sideburns and took another swig. "Seen it plenty."

Bennie leveled a fierce gaze at the moderately successful bookie whose territory reputedly stretched from New York to northern Virginia. Nicky Fincher could quote odds on anything Bennie wanted to throw out there, including what time his grandmother would leave the house tomorrow for her morning constitutional. He had a creep factor, following Bennie around the city as he changed jobs—even to the Phoenix bar in Maryland. Not that Bennie ever felt physically threatened by him. And it was okay when he came in for a quick drink and left. But most often, he nursed his bourbon and held court with an assortment of addicted bettors much like today's companions—a couple of derelicts who looked like holdovers from an old Bowery flophouse. Bennie preferred that Nicky Fincher peddle his betting odds and information somewhere else besides Wandering Joe's.

"Nicky, consider this your only warning," Bennie said. "I told you that you could sit there quietly and have a drink, but if you said anything, I would throw you out. Next time I hear you …"

Nicky threw his hands up. "Sorry, man, trying to be good here. But it's hard to sit by and watch a friend's opportunities go down the drain."

Bennie jerked a thumb toward the front door. "Out."

Nicky never pushed back. He was like the swallows of Capistrano. Bennie knew he'd return when he deemed the time was right. Today, he merely nodded, pulled an Alexander Hamilton from his pocket, and laid it on the bar. "I'll be on my way. Guess you don't want to know. I'll share the good news with Ed's Bar and Grill over on Fifth."

Bennie's lips moved without sound. He'd heard it all before. Nicky had his approach down to a science: toss out bait and wait for nibbles. Bennie wasn't going to bite today. He jabbed a finger at the exit again.

Fincher cast his line out one last time. "Here I thought the best-in-bar award was a big deal. Apparently, I was wrong."

Bennie's head jerked around. "Best of Bars? You know about the Tippy?"

"Possibly. Interested?" Nicky sat again, grinning as he began to twitch the bait.

"You have my full and undivided attention." Bennie put down the glass he had been holding, and joined Fincher at the other end of the bar. "Spill."

Fincher shook his head. "Uh-uh. Introduce me to your friend Hamilton and we can talk."

"Get out," Bennie said with disgust.

"Sure thing." Fincher hopped off the stool and headed out with nary a backward glance.

He had to be lying. A mere bookie would know nothing of the mysterious bar contest. Bennie watched him make a left out the door, heading in the direction of Ed's, the joint down a block and with better foot traffic. "Dag nab it all," he muttered. He hurried outside and called after Nicky Fincher, and when he had his attention, he waved the tip money at him.

Nicky returned with a smile and some more shtick. His eyes darted left and then right as he leaned in over the bar top and whispered in a voice so low, Bennie had to crane forward to catch it all. "Word on the street says to get ready *now*—It's coming. Others are saying it's already too late."

"Too late?" Bennie repeated, straightening up. "Not possible. I would have caught wind of it." He grew quiet, studying Nicky's eyes as he gauged the veracity of his words. Then his eyes narrowed. "How do you know all this?"

"I'm good at putting two and two together. Hit every big bar on my circuit between here and Virginia. The hush-hush is all the same—elusive award, bragging rights—but the devil's in the details, and nobody's agreeing on those. Same person that was feeding me good info on the Phoenix a few years back gave me a heads-up on this one. Naturally, you popped into my head right away."

"How come you're so tuned in to my life? It's like you've got my fairy godmother on the take."

"Maybe it *is* your fairy godmother. I'll ask her next time we share a beer. But that does raise the question: why you are so out of the loop?" He looked around the joint. "I hear only the cream of the crop compete for this one."

Bennie shook his head and walked back over to the Budweiser tap. "Cream of the crop," he muttered. "I'm never out of the loop. If that's all you've got, take your fairy godmothers somewhere else. Come back when you have something I can use."

Nicky offered a coy smile, slipped the tenner into his shirt pocket and left.

"Good riddance," Jean said, watching him go. "Nothing on the up-and-up about that guy." She turned back to Bennie. "What's a tippy?"

"*The* Tippy?" Bennie walked over to her and leaned his forearms on the bar. "I have a confession to make, my love. There is only one thing in my life that I've ever coveted. Besides you, of course," he added with a loving smile. "I've been tending bar for over thirty years, and for the last twenty all I've dreamed about is winning the Tippy—the bar award to end all bar awards." He sighed and looked around him, shaking his head. "But not here. Nice place, but in NYC, places like this are as common as a busboy with a screenplay. No, the Tippy is about a special little bar with good food, a cozy atmosphere, and an undefinable *it* factor. There's nothing you can do to create it. It's just there. Like at the Phoenix. Ryan Thomas would say it's the difference between a bar and a pub. His distinction, but he has the concept right."

He wiped along the bar top with his white terry towel and sent a white legal-size envelope skittering across the counter. He picked it up. "*Benjamin Bertollini,*" it read across the front in elegant cursive. Inside, the blue vellum card had a fine watermark in the upper right corner. He read aloud from the equally beautiful script:

The pleasure of your company is requested
The Tippy
Best of Bars Competition
Year of Our Lord
Two thousand and nineteen

Bennie and Jean exchanged looks. There was no one else within twenty feet of them. Where did … How did …? Didn't matter. Bennie slid the envelope and card into his breast pocket and pulled out his cell phone.

"Benjamin," Jean said, coming up off her stool. "I've seen that glimmer in your eyes before, and I hate it. Give me the phone and let's talk." She lunged for the phone, but Bennie took a step back and continued punching buttons. "Who are you calling? Please tell me it's not that son of a … Bennie!" she pleaded. "We've been happy here the last six months …"

Bennie gave her a preoccupied look and turned way.

"Hello, Ryan," he said into the phone. "Yeah, pretty good. You know that job you keep offering me? If it's still available, I'm in. The only hitch is that I need to come immediately … Perfect … No, verbal commitment is all I need. If you can handle everything on your end, I'm all yours. We'll work out the rest of the details later. Thanks, man. It'll be good to be back at the Phoenix."

He slid the phone back in his pocket and turned to Jean. "You know how much I love you, and you know I will always put you before all else, but this may be my last crack at something as magical as a unicorn, as untouchable as a rainbow, and as elusive as the fountain of youth. If you want to stay with me, you've got two hours to pack. I'm going back to work with Ryan Thomas in Nevis."

"You can't just run out on Wandering Joe's. What the crap just happened?" Jean asked, both palms smacking the bar top.

"Hockey has its Stanley Cup, American football its Lombardi Trophy, and thoroughbred racing the Triple Crown," he said, warming to his subject despite her baleful stare. "And what does bartending have? The Tippy. This invitation backs up what Fincher said. The best of bars competition is on. And if I know one bar that can win, it's the Phoenix. Joe's got half a dozen résumés begging to take my place. Go find your suitcase, my love. We're leaving."

***

Ryan slipped the phone back in his pocket. Hamelin might have ditched him on the beach, but good old Bennie would never desert him. Some things were looking up. He looked around his bar with renewed energy.

The Phoenix was running in the black, but it had seen better business—like half a year ago. That was before Bennie had decided to take a job in New York. At least, that was the fiction Ryan had spun so he could live with himself. Bennie had not left of his own accord. Ryan had fired the saintly man in a heated moment when he should have been counting his blessings for having such a good friend—one willing to risk his friendship and job to protect Ryan. Ryan Thomas, the two-legged jackass.

Ryan retrieved the Powder Monkey ale he had been drinking, and pulled up a stool across from his current bartender. "Delaney," he said to the lanky Irishman whom Bennie had recommended as his replacement, "a little more kick, please—from Kentucky, maybe."

He watched as Delaney poured two fingers of Old Rip Van Winkle. "Delaney, do you like this job?"

"Job's a job," Delaney said, sliding the liquor toward him.

Ryan nodded. "That's what I thought. Listen, you're an outstanding bartender, but this Irish-pub thing isn't catching on too well here in Nevis. I've decided, uh, to take the bar in a different direction—Italian, maybe. I know this may seem sudden, but I'm giving you immediate notice. I'll give you two weeks' pay to compensate you for the lack of advance notice, and I'm going to tack on another six weeks of severance pay—one week for each month you've been working here. That sound fair?"

Delaney dried the last of the glasses and put it in the rack. "Bennie's coming back?"

"Probably."

Delaney sighed. "Can't say I didn't expect it. But still, no notice—that's kinda rough, don't you think?"

Ryan winced. "Sorry."

"Come with me," Delaney said, waving him off his stool. "I want to show you something." He walked out the front door and pointed down the brick-paved street toward the town green. "The vacant building at the end of the street?"

Ryan walked behind him to the edge of the sidewalk and looked past the mix of ornate Victorian and sleek modern storefronts. "The one they just finished renovating?"

"Yep. New bar opening," Delaney said. "Their bartender bailed on them. They're desperate for someone else, and just last night I got a call asking if I'd like to jump your ship and come work there. Owner said *Delaney's* had nice ring to it."

"You were going to give *me* notice?"

"Nope. Decided to tell him I wasn't interested. I felt I owed you for bringing me in here to a pretty good thing. But, you see, loyalty is a two-way street."

Delaney untied his white apron and handed it to Ryan. "May the best man win." He skirted the side of the Phoenix and headed down the alley.

"Thank you, Jesus," Ryan murmured as relief swept over him. He looked at the apron and then walked it to the trash can just inside the door. "A round of drinks on the house," Ryan called to Mickey, the young assistant bartender.

"What're we celebrating?"

"Where do I begin?" Ryan said, sliding back onto his bar stool. "First, you're promoted to bartender until Bennie comes back. We'll toast both of those. You know how to make a Bennie Plenty?"

"Yes sir," Mickey said, and in no time, he had one in Ryan's hand and six more lined up on a hostess tray.

Bennie Plenties could make you forget who you came with, but Ryan downed the first one and claimed a second. For the first time in six long months, he felt light and free. Was he being disloyal to Delaney? Well, maybe a little, but he had been struggling with Delaney at the Phoenix, and Delaney had not been particularly happy, either. In the past few weeks of his tenure, he wore a sour temper on his humorless face like a badge of honor. If Delaney thought he could compete with the Phoenix, he was delusional. Nobody could beat Bennie Bertollini head to head. If he wanted a bar showdown, it was on! He looked at Mickey and raised a glass. "To life and the better days ahead!"

Chapter Seven
Best-Laid Plans

As Martin nattered on, Hamelin studied his archrival. His stoic expression gave away nothing, but Hamelin knew him well enough to understand that the poker face itself was the tell. Martin was playing hard at something.

Hamelin's mind raced through the memories of his morning meeting with the elders. No, there had been no discussion of mulligans. He had carefully worked his way around the subject. Yes, he was guilty of violating Section 383, but no one could possibly know that.

As Hamelin analyzed Martin's every twitch, a small measure of relief began to soothe the burning pins and needles in his hands and feet. Happily, there would be no inquisitive soul runners nosing around Ryan Thomas, his mulligan in Nevis. Bennie's move to New York had seen to that. It would be Wandering Joe's, and not the Phoenix, in the competition. Given all his damnable violations, it was small comfort, but Hamelin would take it. He took a deep, centering breath. Everything would be fine if he didn't panic and do something stupid.

His attention shifted to Samuel, who reemerged from the curtained area behind the speaker's podium. He came straightaway to Martin, whispered something, and handed him a note.

Martin read the note to himself and chuckled. "The list isn't five minutes old, and already we're making corrections." His keen blue eyes focused on Hamelin. "You'll get a kick out of this, Hamelin. Bennie Bertollini has switched bars. New York's loss is Maryland's gain—Wandering Joe's in the Bowery out, the Phoenix in Nevis *in.*" He tucked the note in his shirt pocket. "So, we're all set."

Suddenly, in the afterlife, where most human attachments and concerns had been forever left behind, Hamelin felt something. *Something.* He closed his eyes and let it wash over him like baptismal holy water. The Phoenix was Ryan Thomas's bar, and he was actually fond of Thomas. Then the holy water became a drenching sweat. Had he just signed off on his favorite mulligan's death sentence for the sake of a *game*? He couldn't afford to have Martin or these people within a hundred miles of Nevis. Was this finally the end of his existence as a soul runner? For a moment, he was surprised by the order of precedence in those two questions.

"Anyway, where was I?" Martin said, reading down through his notes. "Right, section three-eight-three: mulligans, transportation. Tallies for souls aren't adding up; deliveries are not equaling orders for delivery. The number crunchers in the main office have been having a cow, and management is taking action. The powers that be are theorizing that the discrepancies may be due to an increased incidence of mulligans. Jerome's software people have been tasked with developing a better system to track and report on discrepancies, and a new task force has been established to identify and collect any mulligans identified." Martin looked up, a smug look on his face. "I'm honored and humbled to report that my new temporary assignment will be to direct this group."

Everyone but Hamelin applauded. *Humble Martin—an oxymoron if ever I heard one.*

Martin acknowledged the adulation with a nod and then shushed them again. "What's the takeaway here?" he asked. "Simple: get to your appointments on time. In fact, my advice is, don't even let your book accidently fall open to section three-eight-three. It will only invite temptation."

Thaddeus raised his hand again but lowered it when Martin gave him another nasty look.

"If you've already made the mistake of applying three-eight-three," Martin said, keeping his eyes glued on Thaddeus, "you'll fess up now before I catch you. And if you know of any violations, please report them. Okay? Simple enough." He looked around and smiled, seemingly pleased with himself. "But let's not end the session on a down note. We're the team supreme, and good times are ahead. You've got some time to take care of whatever you need to do, and then, crew, we're off to pick a winner!"

Hamelin elbowed Luke and stood up. "Point of order. Three days for a global bar crawl? That isn't long enough to do it all justice. Perhaps we should limit the geographic area to the west coast of the United States."

"Or just English pubs," Luke offered. "Or better yet, the Burgundy region of France. Quite doable in the time frame you've suggested."

"How about we stick to global and everybody gets a shot at greatness," Martin said. He pushed his chair back—a little too forcefully, Hamelin thought—and stood up. "Now let's have a great retreat, blow off some steam, and then come back energized for heavenly service."

As the others trickled out, Hamelin approached Martin. "You're right. Even with a bunch of newbies, we'll have plenty of time. But I think we should change one of the bars on the list. It would be a mistake to include Nevis. The place is a mind-numbing bore, another

Chesapeake jerkwater town. Let's go with La Mer in Nice, instead."

Martin frowned. "Well, if the purpose of the exercise is to ensure a good time for all, we certainly don't want a dud in there, do we?" He thought a moment, rubbing his finger along his chin for a moment. "No, all votes count. Besides," he said with a chuckle, "I'm looking forward to knocking back a few at the Phoenix."

Hamelin arched an eyebrow. "You're coming with us? I thought you were heading out with management. And then there's the task force." He immediately regretted throwing that last one in, but Martin at arm's length was better than Martin all up close in his business.

"Actually," Martin said, gathering up his belongings, "I'll be splitting my time between senior-level duties and the task force. If things go well, my detail might be made permanent, but until the mulligan study is completed, I'll be doing double duty and pulling long hours. I seriously doubt anyone will care if I take the occasional break to unwind. Nevis could be just the ticket. I'm dying to find out what the appeal is."

Hamelin felt as if someone had wrapped forty yards of barbed wire around his chest and yanked it tight. Without a doubt, Martin was already investigating him.

"Don't you think you need to stay tuned in with the managers?" Hamelin asked his boss. "This might be your big chance to move out of the rank and file. Besides, somebody needs to stay connected and cover for us."

"Trust me, Hamelin, I provide cover all the time." Martin glanced toward the few stragglers at the door. Apparently convinced they were out of earshot, he said, "I'm breaking protocol here, but friends take care of each other, right? Your assignment to retrieve the soul of Ryan Llewellyn Thomas last summer in Nevis, Maryland ... The report is rough, man. There's no way to fully reconstruct what happened, and you know how Saint Peter hates reports like that. Maybe it's as simple as a missing page." He massaged the back of his neck as if it pained him to bring it up. "The operation was according to protocol? No veering off the reservation to have a little roguish fun in Nevis?"

Hamelin dismissed the suggestion with a sweep of his hand. "Standard procedure."

"Then fix your report before you take off. It would be a pity to come back from a nice outing and find yourself being called on the carpet for a narrative that isn't clear. You can handle that, right?"

Hamelin nodded. "I'll find the missing text."

Martin clapped him on the back. "Great. I'd sure hate to see you fall from grace. No one wants to see that happen again. And a poor showing by one gives us all a bad rep." He looked around the empty room. "Let's get out of here before they lock us in."

At the door, they headed in opposite directions: Martin toward the elevators, and Hamelin seeking the nearest exit.

Luke fell in step with Hamelin almost immediately. "What a disgusting charade; it was Martin's way or the highway."

"Can't talk right now, Luke," Hamelin said, outpacing him.

Luke grabbed him by the arm. "Slow down, man. Where's the fire?"

"Obviously, elsewhere," Hamelin said, giving him an exasperated look. "I need to bolt away on something urgent."

"Cool it, dude. Maybe there isn't one. It's not the change-of-bar thing, is it? Because what's it matter whether your bar is in New York or Maryland? It's the bartender you're nominating. The Tippy is just a game. And there will be a new one before you know it. What am I not seeing here?"

"Who."

"Who what?"

"It's a who and not a what."

Luke cocked an eyebrow and waited.

Hamelin lowered his voice and whispered, "I might have left a mulligan somewhere thereabouts."

Luke stepped back and bumped into the wall. "God save me! Section three-eight-three? You broke code and left a—"

"Shh!" Hamelin placed a hand over his mouth and pushed him into a side hallway.

Luke yanked his hand away. "You violated three-eight-three? Are you out of your ever-loving mind? You always walk a fine line, but God save us, you're looking at expulsion with this—a one-way ticket to Hades. How do you get yourself into these messes?"

Hamelin sighed. "It's complicated."

"Yeah, well, the Merriam-Webster dictionary has a picture of you under that word. I thought you were turning things around. Who else knows?"

"No one."

Luke slumped against the wall, slack jawed. "You're sly, but oh so cooked. I can't believe Martin doesn't know." He stared a moment. "Wait … He knows?"

Hamelin shook his head. "When have you ever known Martin to be honest and forthright? He's up to no good—probably making a play for a permanent move up into management, and I'm in his crosshairs. Something's up with him."

"So, you keep quiet and hope they don't catch you?"

"Certainly not. I can't have Martin in Nevis, or anywhere east of the Alleghenies, if possible. If he gets within smelling distance, he'll know there are mullig—"

"Dear God! More than one?" Luke began massaging his temples as if his brain were in danger of exploding.

"Yeah, but I didn't breach the Section three-eight-three protocol in all of them. Some are still open cases. I used part B in Section eight-nine-five and created a sort of pending file. Those are somewhat better protected. They won't ever show up on an active transport list."

"Heaven help you, Hamelin Russell, because I certainly can't. The only thing you've got going for you is that Martin will be with the managers. You lucked out there. Can't smell what you're not near."

Hamelin peeked out into the main hallway. Martin had his back to them, staring at the elevator buttons for the north tower. Charlotte was nearby but hanging back in a small group of whispering sympathizers. Hamelin turned back to Luke. "Yeah, well, he's suddenly taken an inordinate interest in small Maryland towns, and he's talking about joining us. Even if he doesn't, there will be a constant stream of soul runners venturing into the state. I'm not sure any of the newbies can spot a mulligan, but a few of the more experienced runners might. It wouldn't even surprise me if he throws in a ringer just to rat me out."

Luke leaned past Hamelin to get his own look. "Where you are concerned, I wouldn't put anything past him."

"Not if past inclinations are any indication." Hamelin silently cursed the north tower's slow elevators. The hallway was emptying, and he wondered whether he should risk Martin seeing him hit one of the portal doors, or wait him out. He turned to Luke and said, "You know why I was late this morning? Because somebody's been bad-mouthing me. That complaint by Martin? Not over by a long shot. This is the worst possible time to risk exposure. They've put me on probation, and I need to implement some damage control."

Luke's eyes widened in disbelief, and maybe even a little admiration.

"You never cease to amaze me. And I'll never understand why you're constantly sabotaging yourself. But you've never done me wrong. So what can I do? Within legal limits, of course."

"You really want to help? Poke around in that archive of yours and see what makes Martin tick. And if you need help, try Charlotte. She would probably like to get in on a little bloodletting." He elbowed Luke aside. "I gotta go."

Luke grabbed his arm. "Whoa! Let me check first." He looked around the corner again. "I'll see what I can find, but you're going to have to work your way out of this hole by yourself, man. It's clear now. Scram."

Hamelin darted for the nearest exit. He had no explanation for the things he did. If it satisfied, he went with it, and somehow it always worked out. Until now. But he had a plan. A mulligan here or there? Okay. But a *pattern* of abuse? Some of the mulligans he had created needed to go. It was cold and calculating, and he didn't relish the thought, but sometimes that was how survival worked.

***

At the north tower elevators, Martin scoped out the stout youth in wire-rim glasses and the Purple People Eater T-shirt. Blindly ambitious Curtis was his favorite in the current newbie class. A closer relationship could be mutually beneficial. He waved him over. "Curtis, what do you think of the contest?"

"Looking forward to it, sir."

"You're in Hamelin's group?"

"Yes sir. And I consider it an honor to be serving with the likes of him. He's, ah, sort of, I don't know ..." Curtis adjusted his glasses as he searched for the right word. "*Larger than life,* sir."

Martin bobbed his head. "You might say that. Listen, Curtis, I've noticed your participation in our group meetings. You're quick on your feet and motivated—just the sort management is always on the lookout for."

Curtis grinned broadly.

"I need someone to do something for me," Martin continued. He pulled the newbie close and lowered his voice. "It's confidential and requires a deft touch. Interested?"

Curtis's smile grew. "Absolutely. You name it, sir."

"Excellent. Meet me on the south terrace after vespers."

Chapter Eight
The Gray

The South Terrace was a portico with smooth white columns that held up a dome of stained glass in shades of yellow and blue. At one end, steps led down to a grape arbor, with a path for reflection on the other side. Scattered about the compound were many terraces where one could revisit a favorite moment of life or create a new one. When he first arrived, Martin had delighted in them—moving from roaring waterfalls crested with double rainbows, to dense primeval forests where the only sound was the rustling of leaves in a quiet breeze. He reveled in it all. But eventually, he had grown jaded, ever searching for something that could not be satisfied by even the most fantastical images he could conjure. Now he obsessed over finding a way to move on from this place to the one of permanent peace and happiness—the place where you didn't have to imagine anything. And so he gave up on the terraces and concentrated on people—those in positions of power who could be flattered into boosting him up and out of here, and the pawns who could be manipulated and, if need be, sacrificed.

He sat down on the wide ledge of a fountain beside the arbor and watched water spray from an enormous water lily in the center. He didn't think Curtis weak or easily led. To the contrary, he was a smart, independent thinker, and Martin was drawn to him as a kindred spirit.

It also wasn't lost on him that the newbie might one day be a powerful rival. The question for Martin concerned Curtis's moral fiber. How far would he go to succeed in this place? Right now Curtis's ambition and his lack of experience were weaknesses to be exploited. Granted, inexperience was a rapidly closing window of opportunity, but ambition tended to remain.

Martin would make him walk for his first opportunity. From this position, Curtis would have to cross the long colonnade to reach him. Under the close watch of a superior, that was certain to be a self-conscious. By the time he reached Martin, he would remember who was his better.

But if Curtis was intimidated, he didn't show it. As he crossed the flagstones of the terrace, he returned Martin's gaze. "You had something for me, sir?"

Martin rose to take advantage of his towering height. "While you're barhopping, I need you to check out something for me and report back. It won't take up much time—I just need some general impressions."

"About what, sir?"

"A little town called Nevis. But it's of the utmost importance that you keep the assignment to yourself. I wouldn't want anyone to think I play favorites in making assignments. You're not to ask anyone for assistance. If you do, you could jeopardize something very important. Got it?"

Curtis nodded. "Yes, sir. Anything in particular you want me to keep an eye out for?"

Martin thumped him on the back. "Conscientious—I like that. But don't think too much, Curtis. One of the goals of a trainee soul runner is to develop blind obedience. Thinking can sometimes be a sign of self-indulgence. No," he said, shaking his head. "You just take it all in. Any excessive fraternizing with the locals, or behavior unbecoming one of our station. I can take care of everything else."

"Yes sir." Curtis turned to go.

"One other thing. In your manual, you'll have a list of all your pending transportees—souls nontransportable from the beginning of the retreat until the retreat's moratorium is lifted. Everyone will have one, but you'll also have a second list that no one else will have. It's a master list that details, by soul runner, the identities of all pending pickups."

Curtis's eyes grew wide, and Martin could see fear there. "A second list? Sir, to be frank, I'm not comfortable with any of this. The moratorium … Why isn't it illegal? It appears to be a direct violation of section three-eight-three, which prohibits creating mulligans. We need to transport the deceased."

"Oh, no. None of these should be mulligans. We haven't forgotten any of them. It's a matter of record keeping. We mark each as 'status pending.' As long as they're marked 'pending' in a central file like this, they'll be okay. We've created a stasis. Everything grinds to a halt at the same time. Not one of the deceased will be able to soul-hop into a new body."

Curtis frowned. "Okay, but the master list seems a bit irregular and invasive. Why me? I'd feel much more comfortable if Luke or Hamelin had it."

"Mmm." Martin put his hand out and let some of the drifting fountain spray wet the back of it. "You would think so, but that's what I was told to do. I believe it's a checks-and-balances thing. At any rate, you won't be able to access it except under the direst circumstances. It's almost inconceivable that you would need to step in for another soul runner, but …" Martin shrugged. "Just keep it safe and pray all goes well."

He saw the hesitation and Curtis's inability to meet his eyes. He needed the newbie to buy off on this. He put a hand on his shoulder. "Sometimes, we aren't expected to understand it all. We just accept that it's for the greater good, and move on."

Curtis looked at him, but his eyes were still troubled and full of doubt. "It … it's so much responsibility. How will I know …"

The defenses were crumbling now. Martin gave him a benevolent smile. "If I thought you couldn't do this, I wouldn't have picked you, Curtis."

Curtis offered up his manual. "You take the list, sir."

Martin stared at the book and imagined the possibility of going right to Hamelin's name. If he had created any previous mulligans, they would be listed, too. All his past transgressions. He shoved his hand in the pockets of his vespers robe. "I would if I could, but the list is one of a kind and it's for your eyes only. Another soul runner can read the entries under his own name but no one else's. Rest assured that if the need arises"—and he would do his best to make sure it did—"I will be there if you need me. Now, tuck it away and keep it safe. Soul runners are issued only one book, and God forbid you lose it."

He draped an arm around Curtis's shoulder and began walking him back toward the portico. "Are we good? Because if you really feel that you can't handle this, I can find—"

"No. No, I just had to understand," Curtis said. He slid the manual away inside his vespers gown. "I won't let you down, sir."

Martin smiled broadly. "I'm sure you won't. I see great potential in you, Curtis. Do this assignment well, and I'll make sure you're well rewarded."

Chapter Nine
A Soft Heart with Hard Choices

Hamelin climbed up onto the blue Ford tractor. The engine was still warm and crackling from its morning workout. Before him rolled a green Mississippi field with masses of yellow flowers scattered across the short Bahia grass. Behind him stood a tree line mimicking the curves of the meandering creek on the other side. He put his foot on the tractor's throttle pedal and propped his black book up against the steering wheel. And then he broke a promise he had sworn he would keep forever. He paged through the text to his list of mulligans. Even he was surprised at how many. They weren't numbered, and it wasn't worth doing so, but there were several pages worth. He scanned the names, recalling faces and locations of each meeting in its turn. If there was a pattern to note, it was the randomness of death. Young, old—those suffering and in ill health, as well as the healthy unlucky ones. Sitting here now, he wasn't sure in every case what had motivated him to disobey orders and create a mulligan. The earliest ones had been accidents: late pickups that had resulted in runaway souls who took up residence in the nearest available body—a classic example just as Martin had described it. Those were few, though. Once he discovered that those mistakes could be covered up with creative bookkeeping, he went off the reservation whenever the spirit moved him to pity, sudden affection, or simple fascination. The latter names were mostly done in defiant acts of kindness. Tyler Parson was one of these—a leukemia victim who deserved more than the five short years he was going to get. It wasn't that Hamelin wanted to second-guess God. No, he saw it more as God allowing him to use his free will and humanity to act appropriately. If the soul-collecting process wasn't supposed to include those attributes, then the system itself was flawed and should be replaced. God was merciful—saw all, considered all. If he didn't want soul runners to consider the spirit of the law, he'd see to it that they got the heave-ho. And so far, God seemed content with him.

Little Tyler Parson had been worth it, Hamelin thought as he watched the red-haired youth and his friends riding their bicycles around the cluster of farm buildings. He watched him disappear into one end of the old abandoned chicken house and come flying out the other side with his feet up on his handlebars. He was now a healthy, active boy of ten. Yet Tyler was still in the unlucky category. Hamelin's current assignment list indicated that in a fortnight, he would ride that bicycle out into the street and be killed instantly by a passing car. So Hamelin had a choice. He could take his soul now, fourteen days early, and eliminate the mulligan violation completely, or he could give him the fortnight and risk Martin's discovering one of his mulligans. In that case, a coworker would be immediately dispatched to retrieve little Tyler anyway, and Hamelin could possibly be checking in his baggage with the concierge at Chateau Hell.

Hamelin hated transporting children. Sure, they were quite happy in the blessed realm, but it always brought him back to an earlier time, his first assignment. So many children, and they came so willingly! And then there was the piling-on as parents created a fiction to ease the horror and make some sense of it. They had labeled him a nasty rat catcher, and an abominable stealer of children. As if such an earthly horror would be of his design! That was the last time he hung around and experienced blowback.

He looked away from the giggling, carefree little ones … right into the eyes of another immortal standing next to the tractor. His foot flew off the throttle, and he thumped his book shut. The eyes were kind, but he felt as if he had been caught red-handed at something he hadn't even done yet.

"Sorry, I've startled you." A smile joined the kindly eyes.

Hamelin scrambled down from his perch. "Do we have our signals crossed?"

"No, I'm just observing. Wallace," he said by way of introduction, although he didn't extend a hand in greeting. Instead, a subtle tilt of the chin sufficed. "Who?" he asked, turning back toward the chicken house.

"Red hair," Hamelin said, stuffing his notebook into a hip pocket. "But not yet. I'm just doing reconnaissance, burning a little time before the retreat."

Wallace nodded as if he had often found himself in the same position.

Who was this know-it-all? Hamelin kept his eyes on the children. "Exactly," he said. "It's a holiday of sorts. Chow down on some catfish and cornbread, maybe a beignet or an oyster po'boy a little farther south."

"Aren't you making this more difficult than it has to be?"

Hamelin slowly pivoted toward him. "Come again?"

Wallace's laugh was quiet and gentle. "Relax. I'm not here to judge. Two choices seemingly equal in appeal? I can break that down for you, if you like. Or, if you'd prefer, serve as a sounding board while you reason it out." He cocked an eyebrow and waited.

Hamelin studied the face, trying to get a read on the undercurrent of hostility that seemed to be flowing between them. Then he realized that the negativity was emanating from himself. He tried to rein it in. And then he surprised himself by saying, "I appreciate the offer, but there really is no choice. I'll be back in a fortnight."

Wallace cast another look toward Tyler Parson, who had climbed up on the low-pitched roof of the poultry barn and appeared to be contemplating a jump onto nearby hay bales.

"Wait until he gets a crack at heaven," he said, and chuckled. Then he turned to Hamelin and said, "You said you'll be back again in a fortnight?"

Hamelin nodded. "I have but one choice before me: which restaurant do I hit for lunch? I'm thinking Brown Rabbit. Want to come?"

He wasn't sure where the invitation to sup with him came from. In the span of a couple of minutes, Wallace had gotten him to reconsider his early retrieval of the little boy and elicited a lunch invitation—all without a hearty discussion, threats, or the laying on of hands. Wallace might be a man of few words, but there was a powerful persuasiveness in his low-key demeanor.

When Wallace declined lunch and took his leave, Hamelin breathed a sigh of relief. He wasn't sure which branch of heavenly service the guy hailed from, but he was much more powerful than a soul runner, and no doubt more highly placed than the rest of the managers in the White Corridor.

Hamelin wondered whether the visit was an unspoken warning concerning all his mulligans, or just the child. With all the second-chancers Hamelin had created over the years, why the visit now? The last thing he needed was a fully embodied conscience following him around everywhere.

He scanned his list again. Tyler was the only minor. He zeroed in on a name halfway down the first page: Cyrus Shank. Boston. He was an old geezer, an *oops* mulligan. As Hamelin recalled, he had been a few seconds late in fetching Cyrus. He hadn't meant to be. It was just that he hadn't anticipated that the University of North Carolina's basketball team would be eight points down against Duke with seventeen seconds left and still pull it out. It would have been a dereliction of fandom to skip out on Walter Davis's buzzer tying shot and UNC's win in overtime. In the interim, behold, another mulligan born! With Cyrus now in his nineties, surely Wallace wouldn't begrudge his exit from the mortal plane. Besides, Paul Revere's house museum was in Beantown, and the nearby lobster rolls beat out Pass Christian, Mississippi, oysters any day of the week.

Hamelin circled Cyrus's name and two more located in the same general vicinity. He could make it a trifecta in one quick sweep across the Northeast. And then it was a simple hop down into Nevis, Maryland, to take of business there. If he didn't run into Wallace again, cleanup was going to be easier than he had anticipated.

He stole one last looked at Tyler, who had evidently survived the roof leap and was now playing tag. Tarrying here would invite more temptation. The two-week stay of execution, no matter who had pushed the choice, was a good one. He ditched his lunch plans and headed north.

Chapter Ten

Deep Doodoo and Shallow Solutions

Hamelin's mission to trim his mulligan list was now on a roll. He hadn't run into Wallace again and didn't feel the presence of any other immortal here in Nevis. But as he stood under the brown-and-white striped awning of Sharper's Florists, watching Ryan Thomas drink alone at the beach bar, he was concerned. The man's reliance on booze to solve his problems was a bit disconcerting. Still, there were worse vices to indulge, and Hamelin didn't think it would keep Thomas out of heaven. That was only an educated guess. Decisions about final destinations weren't his bailiwick.

He flipped open his manual. With a spur-of-the-moment pickup in Cherry Hill, New Jersey, Hamelin had whittled his mulligan list down by five. Yes, it seemed a piddling amount, but this was proving easier to do than he had thought. And he could ride the momentum. Ryan Thomas would make it a nice even six.

Then why did he hesitate?

This would be a difficult soul acquisition, for Thomas was one of his favorites. But it was necessary, he reminded himself. Quick and painless. Best for all. He imagined it: a simple walk down one of the town's alleyways, and a quick tap on the shoulder was all it would take to eliminate the greatest threat against him. The mental image was immediately replaced by a high-speed video of Judas Iscariot embracing Jesus on the Mount of Olives. It played and replayed repeatedly in quick succession as Judas backed up and came in again for his treacherous hug. With great struggle, Hamelin finally managed to freeze the vision at mid walk. And a quick glance around confirmed that Wallace had not returned to screw with him. As usual, he was alone.

He looked at Thomas again and heaved a weary sigh of regret. He understood why the first rule of soul runners prohibited fraternization with transportees. Conscience had no place in this work, and his friendship with Thomas was making things difficult. Or maybe it was the inflexibility of the law that was creating the problem. What difference could a few extra years matter in the grand scheme of things? Surely a loving, all-knowing God … Hamelin couldn't agonize over it again. He promised to mull it over later. He crossed the street and headed for Thomas.

***

Ryan had nothing better to do than watch swing dancers lost in the rhythm of Bill Pinkney's "Gonna Move Across the River." He nursed his scotch along with the suspicion that it would be an icy day in the netherworld before Hamelin ever got back to him. The immortal had played him once again. He picked up his glass and turned for the beach. If he deigned to return, Ryan was pretty sure Hamelin could track him down no matter where he got drunk.

Then, apparently, Snowmageddon hit the underworld. Hamelin quietly slid onto the stool beside him. "I thought you were going to wait for me," he said.

Ryan threw him a look that would have frosted Hades over all on its own. "I don't exactly live on the beach. Why did you even bother suggesting you'd be right back? I should have known better."

"Why is it that every time I give you free rein, Ryan James, you blow it all with human stupidity and hubris?"

Ryan slumped back down on his stool. "Huh?"

"Didn't we just agree that Bennie Bertollini was the worst bartender ever and your break in friendship was a blessing in disguise? Why have you invited him back to tend bar at the Phoenix?"

"Somebody else, pal," Ryan said, shaking his head. "That would never come out of my mouth. The relationship was a little bruised, maybe, but we've made amends for perceived wrongs, and he's coming back to Nevis. Where are you going with this?"

Hamelin gave him a cold, hard look. "You need to unamend. It's not the appropriate time to have him here." He took the glass out of Ryan's hand and sent it skittering down the bar top. "Liquid courage is fleeting, Ryan James. Come. I'll walk with you for moral support and wait outside while you invite Delaney back. He'll say yes if you throw a big bonus at him. And then if you still need me, I'll hang around while you phone Bennie."

Hamelin offering moral support? Completely out of character. His modus operandi was terrorizing and bullying—do things his way or he ran over you like a Third Reich Panzer division. Ryan let him walk on a few paces alone before he asked, "What's wrong with you?"

Hamelin tipped his head toward the florist shop. "Come. I'm in hurry. Unlike some, I don't have the luxury of sipping the devil's brew on sandy shores all day long. Rustle that bustle."

Their eyes met, and then Hamelin quickly looked away. His eyes were deep and dark, with an untouchable aloofness about them. Ryan had seen that look the first day they met, when the cold and calculating immortal had tried to kill him and escort his soul into the afterlife. This was all-business Hamelin.

"No," Ryan said. "I'm not going *anywhere* with you."

Hamelin hesitated a moment as if reconsidering, then walked back. He pulled up short, however, and his face fell as Ryan backed up and put three stools between them. "You need never be afraid of me, Ryan James. I always have your best interests at heart."

"Not always," Ryan countered. "What do you really want, Hamelin?"

Hamelin paused a moment as if thinking something through. He wet his lips, and when he looked at Ryan this time, his eyes were warmer, though still deadly serious. "I want you out of here by the end of the day—a nice vacation or a business trip. A couple of weeks, just to be on the safe side. And don't tell anyone—and I repeat, *anyone*—where you're going."

Now, this was the Hamelin Ryan knew and found so vexing—ominous and inexplicable. "Sure. Say when; I'll jump. *Not.*"

Hamelin frowned. "Please?"

Hamelin Russell, the manipulative, always-in-charge immortal, *pleading*? Here was someone he didn't know at all. Was a life-changing experience in a privy even possible? Ryan gave him a closer look. Tall and willowy, with shoulder-length jet-black hair that reminded him of d'Artagnan in a Three Musketeers movie, the immortal looked right. Except for the eyes, which hadn't even a hint of the mischievous gleam he had seen so often.

"Okay, Hamelin," Ryan said. "I might consider it, but only if you give me a good reason, and 'Trust me, Ryan James' is not acceptable. If it's some cockamamie story, I'm going to have one of my burly security people chase you off the beach."

Hamelin cocked an eyebrow, his eyes again a vibrant emerald. "First, threaten me at your own peril."

Ryan laughed uncomfortably. "Really? I feel like I'm already at my own peril! I don't know what new game this is, but I'm not playing. Honestly, you know all you've got to do is tell me where the brunette is."

Hamelin shook his head. "It's not that simple."

"Looks simple enough from here. One name, you're done, I'm out of here. If you can't handle that, then maybe you should take a long hike that way." He pointed to the bay. "And don't come back. I don't need you."

Hamelin remained subdued. "Oh, but you do. As usual, you've got it all wrong about me. You need to heed my advice. Either Bennie goes back to New York, or you need to remove yourself from Dodge."

"You mean 'get out of Dodge'?" Ryan clenched his jaw, and his hands went to his hips. Nobody, especially not Hamelin, told him where to spend his time or whom to hire. He took a deep breath. "You always do this to me, Hamelin. I refuse to be manipulated by you again. There's a storm brewing in that head of yours. What is it?"

For a second time, Hamelin hesitated. When at last he spoke again, Ryan had to crane forward to catch it all. "Enjoying this life of yours?"

Ryan nodded. "Yes, if you'd give me Livia, my wife, back. Let's talk mulligans, Hamelin."

"*Shh!*" Hamelin said, a finger to his lips. "Best think of that 'M' word as having four letters, and keep it to yourself. Don't go looking for trouble. I've no time to spare, Ryan James, so let me plant this nugget of wisdom in that hard head of yours. Did you really think it was just a question of my creating *one of those* and then turning my back and walking away? All would be right again with the world? Those 'M' souls call out every day, yearning for their rightful journey into the afterlife."

Ryan's threw his hands up, stomped off a few paces and then came right back. "Of course, Livia's soul is calling you. It's probably spitting mad by now. If you had left her alone, we would have a happy life together with our son. If you really cared for her as much as I thought you did, you would have let her go. Make your own amends and bring us back together. It's really not that difficult."

Hamelin winced and looked across the bay, where several sailboats with brightly striped sails were tacking into the wind. "Each soul is my singular responsibility, and I care about *all* of them, but you know I have no say in whom they send me to escort into the afterlife. The ones I've left behind haunt me. I talk to them every day—kind and gentle words, reassuring them that I have taken stock and will eventually retrieve them."

"Not my soul, buddy."

He looked at Ryan with hurt in his eyes. "They *all* beg. And every day the begging grows louder."

Ryan gave him a disgusted look. "You make your own problems. Don't expect any sympathy from me. Just tell me where she is, and I'll make her so happy, her soul will never utter another peep."

"The concept you need to grasp is that if a soul calls long and loud enough, a more powerful immortal will not ignore its cry and will come to retrieve it. The soul will be whisked immediately to heaven or hell, without negotiation."

Ryan's heart skipped a beat and stuttered through several more. "Are you telling me that a mulligan's time on earth can be cut short? Sooner or later, the soul will get someone else to retrieve it?"

Hamelin shrugged "Short? It's all relative, but basically, yes, you have it right. It seems that, due to certain circumstances, *your* time may be more limited than I had intended."

"What the ..." Ryan momentarily lost his fear of the immortal and got in his face. "Livia and I are living with a death sentence hanging over us?"

Hamelin remained serene and still, his lips turned up in a slight smile. He pointed Ryan back to his stool. "Did you think you were getting out of this life alive?"

"Well, no," Ryan spluttered. He sat back down. "But with more than a few fleeting memories to press in some celestial memory book. It's a cruel tease, giving us this second chance and then snatching it right back again. You got any clue what it's like to lose someone twice?"

An odd expression, too quick to read and too powerful to stifle, flitted across Hamelin's face. "Maybe," he said, taking a sudden interest in the new band setting up in the bandshell. "All you need to keep in mind is that you are an exception to the rule—the only M I've ever created who realized what he is. And the only one to reconnect with loved ones from his previous life. It's up to you to decide whether that's a blessing or a millstone. If you wish to cling to the notion that you've been wronged, I can fix it all right now. We can leave immediately."

"Where?" Ryan asked, his eyes narrowing.

"Your celestial home, of course."

"I knew you were up to no good," Ryan said, glancing frantically around for witnesses. The bar was now empty. Where was a good bartender when you needed him? "Don't touch me," he said, putting even more stools between them.

Hamelin followed him. "Stop your hissy fit, then. I intend all my mulligans to have long, happy, lives. This is a gift, and I choose carefully who I bestow it on."

"Stop lying!" Ryan hissed. "You were off woolgathering when you got the call to bring my soul in. Oh, no, no," he said shaking his finger. "It was gambling, now that I think on it. Don't turn your misadventures off the reservation into something noble. You're a celestial screw-up!"

Hamelin's head drooped, and he nodded. "I *was* a celestial screw-up, but no more. I've tried to make amends for my failings. And I'm still trying. What we have here is a complicated, unusual situation. Help me help you," he said, beseeching with outstretched arms.

Ryan glanced several times at Hamelin's eyes, but never long enough to be mesmerized by them. They were an emerald green again. The color generally went hand in hand with a certain degree of calm and as much rationality as one could ever expect from the soul runner. But Hamelin was a trickster, with a habit of playing both ends against the middle. Even now he might be engaged in one of the shameless games the immortals played to make their eternal jobs more interesting.

"Not buying, Hamelin. You're getting something out of this. Tell me where Livia is. Then I'll leave town and go to her. That's the only deal I'll make."

Hamelin shook his head. "Not possible, Ryan James." He pulled out his notebook and began thumbing pages. "Should I discuss my professional business, it would be a breach of protocol, with swift repercussions. Have you never heard of HIPPA?"

Ryan's eyebrows knitted together. "Health Insurance Portability and Accountability Act?"

Hamelin rolled his eyes. "The *other* one. Holy Instructions on Portability and Accountability Act—Section eleven." He stopped paging and, with a crack of the stiff spine, spread his instruction manual open wide. "I have certain restrictions."

"*Pffl!*" Ryan said, dismissing the notion with an insolent wave. "When did that ever stop you."

"Certain restrictions," Hamelin repeated. "I'm in an untenable position."

Hamelin over a barrel? Then there was plenty of room for negotiation. Ryan put his feet shoulder width apart and squared his shoulders. "Why am I not surprised? And the answer is no. Sink or swim."

Hamelin looked up from his manual, one eyebrow cocked. "An odd choice of cliché from someone who's petrified of water. If I sink, I'm taking you with me, sir."

Ryan maintained his stance without replying.

Hamelin's expression tightened. "All right, Mr. I'm-only-a-mortal-but-I-know-everything, I can't force you out of Nevis, but you are extraordinarily foolish if you stay. Suit yourself. I will give you this final piece of advice. When they start coming, lock yourself away, preferably at home—certainly not in the Phoenix—and don't come out again until they all have come and gone."

Ryan threw his hands up in the air. "For God's sake, Hamelin, speak English!"

Hamelin gave an exasperated sigh. "I have a beef with someone, okay? And he's out to get me. My Achilles' heel is my creation of M's," he said, drawing out the "S" sound. "To bring me down, he's going to track *you* down—and the others like you—and build an airtight legal case against me for violating celestial law. You'll be dispatched to your permanent destination of eternal repose, and I will be ..." He shook his head.

"So you thought you'd get a step ahead of him. That's what you had in mind when you first got here, wasn't it? You were going to take care of business." Ryan tightened his grip on the stool in front of him. He could use it as a defensive weapon if he had to.

Hamelin let the accusation hang in the air. Then he drew a line in the beach sand with the toe of his black Converse high-top. "If you value your earthly existence, *hide*. If you see me again, *pretend we've never met*. Do it *now,* Ryan Thomas. If you don't, I will be forced to take my own drastic measures. Time is quickly running out for both of us." He took off in the direction he had come, crossed the boardwalk, and disappeared behind Sharper's Florists on the other side of the street.

Ryan sat down hard. God, how he hated the inscrutable immortal! *Who* was coming? And how would he know when they were gone?

"You okay?" It was the bartender, reappearing from God knew where.

"I could have used you a minute ago. Where were you?" Ryan asked.

"Sorry. Restocking," the bartender said, pointing to a bucket full of ice. "I'm running solo here, and I thought you could wing it for a couple minutes. Whatcha need?"

"Shot of Patrón," Ryan said. "No, on second thought," he called after him, "bring the bottle." His legs were quivering, and a mere glassful could not begin to tamp down the wild-eyed demon clawing its way out. Something in his gut screamed, *Heed the immortal soul collector! Take off immediately, anywhere but here!* But his stubborn brain kept whispering, *Call the bluff. Stay the course. Duke it out.* Which side would the liquor feed: emotion or logic? Did he even know which was which? He took a swig and embraced the burn as he studied the bee on the bottle's label. If he kept up this pace, logic wouldn't have a chance. He gave the bottle back.

It wasn't in his DNA to cut and run. Likewise, he didn't think it was in Hamelin's to throw up his hands and walk away. Hamelin was bluffing. Ryan could outwait him. Hamelin would be back for a third round and a better deal—with information about Livia. If not, whoever was looking for him would find him at the Phoenix, where he would be making Bennie so welcome he'd never leave again.

***

Hamelin walked as far as the town green and sat on a wooden bench near the antique carousel. He might have expected Ryan Thomas to be the one to throw a wrench in his plans. If it turned into a real shoving match—and that time was rapidly bearing down on them—was Ryan Thomas's mortal life worth saving? The answer was an unequivocal *no.* Then why give him an out?

Hamelin was losing his edge. If he had really wanted to, he could have lured Ryan off the beach and been done with all the drama. In fact, he should have done it before trotting off down the coastal backroads of Mississippi. *Bam, done, move on!*

This was self-analysis he didn't care to face right now—a sad lesson in keeping business and pleasure separated. With a growl, he fished the manual back out and consulted his list again. There were three second-chancers out west—Denver, Colorado; Winslow, Arizona; and one on a sheep ranch in the hinterlands of Wyoming. Those could all be dispatched easily enough. Then, if Thomas didn't comply and leave town before Hamelin's coworkers arrived, he would most assuredly have to revisit the status of Ryan Thomas's soul. And with the moratorium bearing down on him, he must do it quickly.

One way or the other, there could be no mulligans left in Nevis.

Chapter Eleven
One Big Block Party

Bennie's eyes teared up, and he felt an exhilarating tingle up his spine as he came through the Phoenix's service entrance. He stood a moment and breathed in the faint, lingering aroma of hops and grease—probably from the Tuesday night fried-crab-ball special. It was nothing overpowering, just the suggestion of a cozy, well-remembered relationship. *This* was home, he thought as he looked over the dark wood furniture and paneling of the main room. He wheeled his dolly stacked with plastic totes behind the bar and set to work.

First, he inspected the liquor shelf that ran the length of the bar, shifting bottles, making mental notes. It was impeccably clean, and the variety of stock didn't seem to be out of whack. The stock in the storage room was also passable. He puttered through requisition records in the little cubby near the wall phone, the employee work schedule on the bulletin board near the fire exit, and the keg room that supplied the bar taps. Everything was shipshape and to his liking. In fact, it was as if he had never left—which was a bit odd. Most bartenders who had full run of a bar wasted no time making the space their own. Delaney had seemed gung-ho to set up shop at the Phoenix and, knowing Ryan, would have had a free hand to do so. So, what happened?

He let go of questions about the past, pulled the Tippy invitation out of one of his boxes, and slid it into the corner of the framed mirror hanging behind the bar. Then he stood back to admire it. The prize was within his grasp. He could feel it, and if he proved victorious, he would never ask for another thing in life. The satisfaction would last forever.

The squeak of the service door interrupted his reverie.

"Mr. Bertollini," Ryan called. He put his cell phone on the bar and gave the stout bartender a bear hug. "I never thought I'd see the day!"

Bennie grinned. "Delaney didn't change too much, did he?"

"He was an odd duck. And just so you know, he's going to be running a new place down the street. I've got no beef with him."

"Me, either. He's a decent guy."

Ryan noticed the Tippy invitation. "So this is the contest, huh?" He stepped closer and read it. "Impressive."

"Isn't it?" Bennie felt himself drifting off again into a pleasant daydream of what winning would feel like. He shook himself free. It was a dangerous indulgence that would do nothing to help him win. "How many people you got coming in this morning?"

"Everybody. You never saw such a group of happy people as when I told them you were coming back. We'll spend a moment celebrating, and then we double down and win this thing. And when we do, I'll trot us both down to Fisher's Printing and we'll design a banner for the front window. *Winner of the Tippy Best of Bars Contest.* Great for business."

"I'm good with banners," Vanessa said, coming in from the kitchen. She set a yellow-striped Betty's Bakery box down on a nearby table and gave Bennie a warm embrace. As she did, Bennie's partner, Jean, slunk in behind her in and sat down without comment next to the box.

"Please tell me that's not a cake," Bennie said, looking over her shoulder. "I was hoping for a short organizational meeting without a lot of whoop-de-doo."

"Maybe it's not a cake," Vanessa said. "Whatever it is, it was Ryan's idea."

"I wish," Ryan said, and he stepped aside as a steady stream of coworkers began to arrive and shower Bennie with affection.

***

Ryan tapped a spoon against his wineglass. "Just a few quick words. Bennie's back, he's the best, and there's a cake over there that says both. Thanks for coming back, Bennie. You've been missed, and that's all I have to say. The Phoenix is in your supremely capable hands, Mr. Bertollini." He backed out of the limelight leaving Bennie standing alone and red-faced in the middle of the room.

Bennie walked over to the cake and peered through the rectangular cellophane window on top. "Chocolate. My favorite," he said. "Make sure you get a piece." He stood there a moment, saying nothing as he looked around the room, shifting his weight from foot to foot. "But before everybody digs in, I'd like to say how great it is to be back in Nevis. Working with Ryan and all of you at the Phoenix—well, it's like slipping on a pair of old comfortable slippers. Maybe even ruby ones," he added with a chuckle. "There's no place like home, and that's exactly what this feels like to me. Some of you I know. Some I'll get to know. Together we can make this an enjoyable place and the best pub around."

The staff clapped and whistled.

Bennie raised his hands, and when everyone grew quiet again, he said, "First thing I'd like to share with you is exciting news. I've got a card stuck up on that mirror over there that I want everyone to read before they leave today. It's an invitation to participate in a contest. The Phoenix will accept the challenge."

"Cash prize?" someone in the back asked.

"No, no money," Bennie said. "The Tippy is all about prestige. The Best of Bars competition is worldwide, and for bartenders it's the holy grail. We're talking perfection," he said, and kissed the tips of his stubby fingers. "Everything has to be exemplary: white-glove clean, libations for every palate, impeccably shaken or stirred—or not—responsible serving of alcohol to customers, scrumptious bar snacks. And the ineffable, unfakable X factor: an atmosphere that draws people in and creates a community and brotherhood among patrons. As I said, perfection."

Jean pushed back from her table, her chair scrapping across the wood floor as she rose. Vanessa put a firm hand on her shoulder and forced her back down.

"And you think the Phoenix has a chance?" Vanessa asked, keeping her hand in place.

"Without a doubt."

"Well, okay," she said, glancing over at Ryan. "If you're sure, I'm sure. Get us the rules and when the judges are coming."

"There are no official rules," Ryan said, rejoining Bennie in the center of the room. "And no one knows who the judges are. Right, Bennie? They come unannounced, like the secret shopper. You have to look perfect, giving each patron a genuine smile, at the same time eyeballing them to see who looks suspicious."

"Well, who are the sponsors?" asked a server standing nearest the cake. "I can search the dark web and find out who's going to judge."

Bennie shook his head. "Ryan makes it sound like a crapshoot. It's not. And to answer your question, uh, *Robert,*" he said, straining to read the server's name tag, "I'm sure your computer skills are top-shelf, but nobody knows who sponsors it. Make no mistake, though," he said, "it's all legit." He produced a small black leather notebook and waved it at them. "The only place you'll find out anything is right here. Twenty years of meticulous journal entries documenting every story, every experience anyone's ever articulated about the Tippy. Where this contest is concerned, I'm not leaving anything to chance."

"So you've competed before?" Vanessa asked.

"Never," Bennie said. "You have to be invited, and I haven't been asked to participate, but that doesn't mean I haven't been paying attention. There is no better, more thorough compilation of the ins and outs of the Tippy than what I've got here. It's the definitive work, and other bars would kill to have it."

Ryan reached for the notebook, but Bennie eased it away. "We keep the notes to ourselves and our nose to the grindstone, and we're going to win it. I feel it in my bones."

There was more grinding as Jean scooted her chair closer to her table. "Maybe you should take some ibuprofen and check again in the morning," she said in a loud voice. Then she looked up at Vanessa and whispered, "We moved back here because of an invitation that anyone could have sent, and the word of a shady New York bookie. How reliable is that?"

Bennie looked her way and winced before continuing in a more subdued tone. "The formula is all in here," he said, patting the book. "You're either smart enough to pick up the clues and run with them, or you're an also-ran. As the *Washington Post* used to say 'if you don't get it, you don't get it.' I've checked around. Quiet words about the Tippy are sweeping throughout the bartender community. The contest is on, and invites have been extended. That's as good as the intel gets until it's over. The only ones who know for sure are the ones who get invited, and they tend to keep their mouths shut during the competition."

He put his hands behind his back and walked a few paces. When he began to speak again, he talked as if he were lecturing a classroom with material he knew by heart. His passion spilled out of him. "There are four attributes that a well-positioned Tippy contender must have: location, good drinks, good food, and ambience. Without a doubt, the Phoenix has all of them. Our little town of Nevis, nestled along the bay coast, is lovely and welcoming. If we stick to what we do best, classic Chesapeake Bay culinary experience—heavy on oysters, crab, stuffed ham, and the like—and we stocked the old standbys as well as the great up-and-coming regional brews, praise and reward will come."

Bennie stopped his pacing in front of the cake and stared absently down at it. "We run a clean shop, just like always. The customer is the reason we're here. It's all in our control. We work like the precision team we are, strive to reflect the ambience of this beautiful little town, and treat our customers as family. If we do, this will be smooth sailing. Trust me."

Ryan looked around the room, nodding. "I have faith in Bennie's instincts," he said, "and he has carte blanche to do whatever he feels will make us competitive. I have only one request: promote the Bennie Plenty every chance you get. It'll slay the competition. And speaking of competition, I guess you heard that we've got some moving in down the street. Delaney's. Our good friend Mark Delaney will be running the place. Let's keep things cordial. They won't be involved in the Tippy, so refrain from being petty. No taking potshots. Nevis is a busy enough town for all of us. Oh, and everything we discussed this morning stays in shop. Keep it on the q.t., okay? Especially Bennie's notebook. Nobody talks about it. Nobody consults it but Bennie." He looked at Bennie and got a nod. Satisfied they had covered everything, Ryan waved everyone toward the stack of paper plates, and Vanessa started cutting the cake.

Under ordinary circumstances, Ryan would have no doubt they could win. At times in its brief history, the Phoenix had embodied all Bennie's elements. When things were going right, the pub had heart and could contend with the best—a happy, stress-free port in the storm of hectic modern life. But there was nothing ordinary about the present circumstances. Ryan was pretty sure no other bar owner ever had to contend with an immortal soul runner issuing demands and ominous warnings. The last thing in the world he wanted to see was Bennie's heart get stomped on in a standoff with agents of the afterlife. How on earth was he going to contend with whoever was coming for him, fend off Hamelin, and help win some obscure contest known only to bartenders? Things couldn't be worse.

***

The yellow taxicab rolled past the Phoenix and continued down the block before pulling to the curb. Delaney eased down the window and admired the red and blue neon sign in the large front window. *Delaney's*. It had a certain inviting lilt and flash. The owners evidently thought so, too. They had jumped at the chance to hire him. He glanced back the way they had come—the ornate floral carvings and whiplash curves of turn-of-the-century storefronts all vying for his attention—to the Phoenix, with its simple dark-stained door and unadorned windows. He harbored no ill will toward the rank and file, but the owner was a schmuck. Unfortunately, to bury one, he must bury all.

"Excuse me, Mark Delaney? Delaney's bar?"

Delaney turned to the man with a military-style crew cut, who had suddenly appeared at the car window. His earnest brown eyes immediately put Delaney at ease. "I'm Delaney."

"I was instructed to deliver this to you, sir," the man said. He handed him a white envelope, then strode away before Delaney could respond.

Delaney stared at the envelope a moment. It was addressed to him in the same cursive script as the neon sign, though it didn't elicit the same warm and fuzzy vibe. He flipped it over, noted that it was tightly sealed, and then sniffed it. It was without scent and looked harmless enough, but there was something vaguely unsettling about being hunted down personally for a delivery from a stranger. His new boss was the only person in town who knew where to find him.

There was a tapping on the seat. "Hey, you getting out, or we goin' someplace else?"

"Sorry," Delaney said to the cabbie. He overpaid him with a sawbuck and got out. Once on the sidewalk, he ripped open the correspondence and read the invitation inside.

What on God's little green earth was a Tippy?

Chapter Twelve
Yearning for a Charmed Life

News traveled fast in a close-knit community like Nevis, and business at the Phoenix rebounded immediately. By evening, customers Ryan hadn't seen in months were chowing down and knocking 'em back. That was nice, but there was really only one face he really wanted to see. Unfortunately, Hamelin wasn't showing any inclination to negotiate. And apparently, his insistence that Ryan find a bolt-hole forthwith wasn't as urgent as he had made it seem. At least, Ryan hoped not.

As the hours passed and Hamelin remained a no-show, Ryan sat at the end of the bar and gnawed on the hangnail on his left thumb. He had a growing feeling that perhaps he had misread Hamelin. The immortal was his only hope of finding Livia, and Ryan had stupidly told him to leave and not come back. Pushing him to negotiate a better deal appeared to be a tactical error.

Ryan took a drink of his scotch. He had acted rashly. Ha! No surprise there. The immortal had a knack for pushing all his buttons. If only he had thought to mention who *they* were. Ryan glanced around the pub, checking for the mysterious people who were going to snuff him out. There was a familiar blue-haired lady who drank like a pro, a silver-haired gentleman who liked to take Phoenix silverware with him on the way out, and a bald guy with his nose pierced like a bull's. None looked like a killer.

Ryan got up and went behind the bar, where Bennie was shuttling between several stations. "See any judges?" he asked him.

"Nope," Bennie said. "I never forget a name or face—all regs." He stopped and called to a spry elderly woman as she rose from a nearby table. Her navy cardigan was buttoned up to the chin, and a pair of reading glasses dangled from a chain of fake pearls about her neck. "You doing all right, Irene?"

Irene Mattingly gave him a grandmotherly smile and a wink.

Ryan nodded pleasantly at her. "Just what I wanted to hear," he said, patting Bennie on the back as he swept past. "You just let me know."

Bennie moved to the chalkboard that hung prominently at the end of the bar, and wrote "*Today's Specials*" across the top. "Bad idea, wondering if the judges are out there. Treat 'em all equal, same as ever."

"Maybe we should think about—"

The chalk in Bennie's hand moved to the counter, where it tapped out a soft rhythm on the granite. "Busy hands are happy hands. You want to do this?" he asked, offering the chalk.

"Sorry," Ryan said. "I'll just move it along." He walked to the pub's front windows and stared at Barnacle Bertie's, the bookstore across the street. The strong round curves on the front door reminded him of Bilbo Baggins's hobbit hole. He never saw foot traffic in and out, and briefly wondered whether e-books were doing Bertie in. With luck, increased interest in the Phoenix would give them a boost. He looked down the block at the other small businesses. At this end, it was calm and peaceful: strolling retirees, young mothers pushing strollers, and a mixed terrier of uncertain lineage peeing on a hydrant. Farther down, he saw Walt, with his shopping cart parked just this side of Delaney's.

Ryan had engaged him once—military veteran with a bad back and some troubled ideas about life in general. Thus far, Walt had rejected all offers to help him get off the street, but none of the local business owners were giving up on him yet. Ryan watched a pedestrian give him a wide berth and wondered whether the offers of help were inspired more by economics than by any deep and abiding humanitarian concern.

Ryan's only lifeline was his own personal immortal, and if Hamelin didn't come back into his life, and soon, he was headed for Loonyville. Staying busy was helping him cope, but it was a temporary fix. He couldn't put into words the feelings of emptiness and longing for his wife. And even if he could, who would he unburden himself to? His mother was splitting time between Bennie's quest and Ryan's estranged and recuperating father. And then there was Bennie, effervescing with ideas about a bar contest that nobody knew about or wanted to discuss. In Ryan's small universe, that only left Jean, Bennie's disgruntled live-in girlfriend. He would find small comfort there. She blamed Ryan for the death of her bimbo-brained daughter Marla and wouldn't turn a hose on him if he were on fire.

He shoved his hands into his pockets and absently jingled the contents: change that could do nothing of the sort, a car key to take him anywhere he wanted to go except to her, and a silver charm bracelet memorializing the life of someone who no longer existed. He pulled Livia's bracelet out and set it down on a nearby table, straightening the medallions and chunky charms with his finger: boat, baby booties, diploma scroll, a church. The big clock face on the tower reminded him of St Peter's, not far from where she had studied in Zurich. They were highlights of a life he had been cheated out of sharing—a life too precious to forget, yet too painful to remember. Every time he looked at it, heard it jingle, felt its weight in his pocket, it was like opening a Pandora's box of pain. But to put it away somewhere meant giving up on her. Grief enveloped him like two huge hands wrapping around his chest and squeezing all the joy from him. He shoved the bracelet back down in his pocket. And then he retreated, just as he had done every day for the past six months, back to his office and the refuge of mindless paperwork.

Delaney would have let him be, but not Bennie. He stuck his head in the door. "You're not having a good day, are you?"

"I'll be all right," Ryan said, massaging papers around on his desk.

"Well, I didn't mean to make it worse by being difficult. Ignore me for the foreseeable future. But one more thing before you tune me out. It'll make your bad day somewhat brighter." He jerked a thumb toward the main room. "Guess who's popped in?"

"Judge?" Ryan hotfooted it to the door and stuck his head out. Three patrons were at the bar. A 1970s tree-hugger type in a blue and green tie-dye T-shirt sat at the far end. In the middle, a prim woman in a gray business suit was chowing down Old Bay fries. And on the stool at this end was a guy in a Washington Nationals shirt and a curly "W" cap that hid most of his shockingly red hair. Ryan locked on like a smart missile to the baseball fanatic.

"Hamelin Russell!" Bennie gushed. "How serendipitous is that! Best bluesman we've ever had at the Phoenix. I'll try to talk him into doing a set for us—you know, because great live music makes this the *perfect* bar."

Ryan elbowed past Bennie and headed for the Nationals fan. "Hamelin. Long time no see," he said, unable to take his eyes off the flaming locks."

Hamelin tapped his brow in a lackadaisical salute. "Mr. Thomas.

Still have a nice bar here."

"Pub, not a bar," Ryan said. "I was hoping we'd see you again. Got a free moment?" he asked gesturing toward his office.

Hamelin gave him a heated look, then rose without complaint and followed him. They entered the dimly lit office furnished simply with a desk and a few straight-backed wooden chairs.

"Ah, memories," Hamelin said, skirting a mound of dark clothes piled on the floor. At the window, he raised the venetian blinds and peeked outside at the brick facing of the building across the alleyway. "And the most important of those would be that you didn't pay any heed to what I said. Why is it that every time I give you instructions, you ignore them? One: I told you to not acknowledge me the next we met. And two: Why haven't you shown even the faintest scintilla of the self-preservation instinct and fled Nevis?"

Ryan could handle any verbal abuse Hamelin might dish out, but he thought it wise to keep out of striking distance. He could never ignore the immortal's power to drag someone off to hell at the tap of a shoulder, and he couldn't shake the feeling that Hamelin had been up to no good last they met. He kept the desk between them.

"Because you always talk over my head, Hamelin. But I've had time to reflect, and I've come around. I'm ready to deal, and I'll accept the original terms. Tell me where she is, and I'll leave immediately."

Hamelin turned humorless eyes onto Ryan. "I never so much as intimated any such deal."

Ryan studied the grave expression. Somewhere in the scary immortal known as Hamelin Russell must lie some weakness he could exploit. "I, uh, realize it was just a verbal commitment, but please don't renege now. I knew you'd come back, and I've made arrangements to leave town. Let's stick with the plan. It's a sound one. Where is she?

Don't leave me here crushed and without hope. There's no telling what I might do …"

"One would suppose there is an actual name to go along with that vague pronoun?"

Ryan's jaw clenched. "Don't get smart with me. *Livia Williams.* You know where she is, don't you?"

Hamelin raised a hand and looked skyward. "In the arms of a loving God."

"Don't bullshit me. You left enough clues for me to know you didn't take her to heaven. She's a mull—"

"Tut-tut," Hamelin said, wagging a finger at him. He stepped toward the desk.

Ryan slid two steps to his right. His attempt to control the situation was obviously heading in the wrong direction. "Whatever the current term is, then. You reincarnated her in someone else's body, just like you did me."

"Reincarnated?" Hamelin chewed on it a moment. "Not so much. On most occasions, the 'M' word is fine, but not right now." He removed the lid from a glass dish on the desk and scooped out a handful of M&M's peanuts. "M's," he said, looking at the candy. "Did you buy these to taunt me?" He popped one in his mouth and shook his head. "I've no clue where she is."

"Yes, you do. You know everything."

Hamelin raised his index finger. "I know everything that I *need* to know, which, at this particular point, doesn't involve Miz Mc—" He shoved the rest of the handful into his mouth.

"Aha!" Ryan said, slamming his hand down on the desk. "Now we're getting somewhere." He picked up a yellow pad of sticky notes and a pen. "Miz Mc*Who*? And she's a *Ms,* so not married."

"'Ms.' doesn't necessarily mean *not* married."

"To an old-fashioned soul like you, sure it does." Ryan put pen to pad. "What's the last name, Hamelin? Where in Saint Paul? That was the boat's home port."

Hamelin put a finger to his lips. "Keep your voice down! This is a very dangerous time for M's, and you obviously haven't reflected on things." He fished around in the M&M's and selected two green ones cemented together like conjoined twins. He held them up for Ryan's benefit. "Has it not occurred to you that she might be happy as she is now? That she may not want or need you to go stalking her? Think, for a moment, about what she may want, which may not be the sweet reunion you've been fantasizing about. Contacting her could have unwanted consequences." As if to emphasis his point, Hamelin split the candy apart and ate the pieces separately.

Ryan watched Hamelin's eyes flick to the closed office door and then back to him again. "Stop trying to freak me out," he said. "If I were really under siege, you wouldn't be scarfing food. Nobody cares what's going on in here. Meeting Livia again won't be a problem. It'll all come back to her, just as I remembered everybody important in my life. She'll want me. And that's something you can scribble down in your little black book."

Hamelin put the lid back on the dish and brushed off his hands. "See, here's the thing. *She,* not you, has to initiate all of that. You are a bystander in her life until she makes you more than that. You can throw whatever little tantrum you want, but that is something I *do* know. It's in the notebook."

"Fibber. What page?"

Hamelin patted his breast pocket. "Page eighty-seven, Appendix F."

Ryan decided to go for broke. Hamelin would have to tell him or kill him. He came around the side of the desk. "Show it to me and I'll leave you alone."

Hamelin smiled. "Can't. Page seventeen prohibits the direct sharing of written materials. You just need to be a man of faith, Ryan James. Be happy. How is your son?"

"Oh, that's another thing you can fix," Ryan said. "You assured me I'd get custody of Mattie. Didn't happen. My son is still with Livia's parents."

Hamelin frowned. "Oh, that won't do. What got monkeyed up there?"

"You're the only one I've seen monkey up anything around here. *Fix* it. And don't try to change the subject."

"I've got your back, bud," Hamelin said. "Don't give it another thought." He offered his hand.

Ryan took a step back. "Ah, ah, ah. No handshakes of doom."

"Relax. While in some respects that would solve a whole lot of problems, I find that it would be most foolhardy to conduct any official business with you at the moment. I just want you to know how sincere I am." He reached out and pressed his finger into the middle of Ryan's chest.

Ryan closed his eyes and shuddered. When he opened them again, he was still alive and still standing in the Phoenix office. Hamelin still stood mere inches away, staring. "You … you can control that?"

"I think it speaks for itself."

Ryan batted his hand away. "Stop toying with me. Everything's just a game to you. Same old unreliable, unrelatable immortal flake. It's clear I'm not going to get anything of value from you. Get out. You're not pestering anyone else here. I have enough information now. I'll find Miz McWhozit on my own!"

"Oh, I'm not about to leave. I said I didn't have any business with *you*. That doesn't mean we don't have a vested interest in being here."

"*We?* As in *them*? Oh, dear God." Ryan scattered the heap of dirty laundry as he plowed his way to the door. He peered out. The two patrons he had seen at the bar earlier were still there. "*Dangerous immortals?*" he whispered. "They look more like entries in a Halloween costume contest."

Hamelin's answer sounded more like a hiss than a yes. "And why do you mortals insist on labeling things?" he asked.

Hamelin was so close behind him that Ryan could feel his breath on his neck. He tried to pull away from him without spilling out the door.

"If I told you they were here for *her,*" Hamelin whispered, "and the only way you could save her was to leave town, would you listen to me and just slip out the back door without any further discussion?"

Ryan glanced over his shoulder at him. "No. Because nothing you do is selfless. You somehow have a cut in all this." He resumed sizing up the immortals. Bennie was holding court with them as he dried barware.

"*Everybody's* got a cut in this. I gave the two of you a fighting chance, but if you keep hanging about and making a hullabaloo, you're endangering her life, too. Why won't you work with me, knot head?"

"Well, obviously I can't lead them to her if I don't know anything, now, can I? You wanna see a hullabaloo? I'll make your life miserable; then you'll give me what I want."

He darted out of the office, arms flailing. "Get out," he shouted at the immortals. "Gotta close early. *Out.*"

The hippie and the legal secretary scrambled off their stools. Bennie's beer mug hit the floor and shattered. And the rest of the house fell silent as every face in the bar seemed to pivot toward the commotion. The ambience of cheery bonhomie evaporated.

Ryan froze in mid stride. He turned sheepishly toward the packed house. "Private joke. Please, stay as long as you want. Next round's on the house." Then he swung back around to the duo and jerked his thumb toward the door. "Out," he whispered.

"Gerard, Rebecca, let's go." Hamelin motioned his associates toward the door, and as he brushed by Ryan, he whispered, "I believe you're what we used to call a *donkey's rear* (though often in coarser terms). Know your friends from your enemies, son. We'll talk, but you might want to reconsider how you treat your customers. Especially the ones who would have done you no harm. Not a good first impression for the Tippy."

"*Tippy?* Wait!" Ryan dashed after him, but Hamelin ignored his plea and disappeared out the entrance with his two fellow immortals. Ryan halted at the door. There was no use chasing and further antagonizing him. He cut his eyes at the rest of the clientele. Most had gone back to their own business. Bennie stood rooted in place behind the bar, his eyes downcast and his cheeks flushed.

Ryan walked back to him. "Did you hear all that?"

"No," Bennie said. "Just the loud, embarrassing part—along with everyone else in here. Those were decent folks, Ryan. Just for future reference, what was your beef?"

"I'm sorry, Bennie. Mistaken identity." He joined Bennie on the floor as he stooped to gather up the shards of glass. "Get up, please," he said, gingerly picking up a large piece. "I'll get a broom and clean up the rest. Then I'll clear out. The last thing you need is someone screwing with your contest. And don't worry about Hamelin. He said he'd be back."

Bennie shook glass out of his bar towel into the trash can and pointed to a stool. "Sit," he said, taking the next seat. His voice was quiet and soothing, which made Ryan feel even worse. "You're making this too complicated. Relax. All we need at the Phoenix is a normal, chill environment. Good vibes—you know, what we usually have when we're not worrying about what kind of vibes we have. A place everyone wants to come and feel their problems float away for a while. Okay? All you've got to do is let those problems drift away. Can you feel them drifting, Ryan? Close your eyes and let 'em drift."

Ryan had to squeeze his eyes tight to keep them from fluttering. "Yeah," he said, nodding. "I feel it. I'm drifting." He sneaked one eye open. "I'll take this good vibe into the back and turn on some Enya or something. Thanks, man. And I'm really sorry."

***

In the privacy of his office, Ryan yanked open the full-length cabinet near the door, pulled a book off the top shelf, scanned its cover, and tossed it to the floor with a bang. Several more books followed. *Bang, bang, bang.* "I know it's in here," he muttered.

"I hope it's in there," Bennie said, coming up behind him, though not close enough to get elbowed. "But I don't think Enya's going to do it. Seriously, what can I help you with, Ryan?"

Ryan side-eyed him but kept hauling out books. "Phone book. Saint Paul. Didn't we have one?"

"Across the bay? Check the one for Saint Michaels. They're both small towns—might be rolled into one book."

"How did I ever manage things when you were gone?" Ryan dropped to his knees and sorted through the pile on the floor. He chose the one on the bottom, stood up, and began flipping: *M, Ma, Mc* ..."

"Dialing information four-one-one might be faster."

"Yeah, but I don't have the whole name … 'Mc' something." He sat at his desk and picked up the phone. "Damn. Did he say 'Mic' or 'Mac'?"

"You gonna dial all those 'Mic-' or 'Mac-' somethings?"

"Oh, er, no. I'm good here. I'm sure I'll recognize the name when I see it. He lowered the phone and looked at Bennie. "Have I said how great it is to have you back?"

Bennie nodded. "Multiple times. My business is back out front, so I'll just shut your door and let you be. But if you can find that Enya—even some Ravi Shankar …"

Ryan nodded and watched him leave. It was all coming into focus now. Obviously, Hamelin had bet big on the outcome of the Tippy—in some sort of heavenly currency, no doubt, or favors with a heavenly bigwig. Maybe Bitcoins. *Something.* And the unnamed people Hamelin had warned him about? Tippy judges. Everything Hamelin was feeding him about mulligans was horsefeathers. Hamelin needed him out of the way so he wouldn't make any scenes in front of the judges. Well, he'd just fixed that. Why did Hamelin hate him so much?

He picked up his pen and, beginning with "McAdams," marked the handful of "Mc-" "Mac-" listings with female first names, and those designated only by initials. He could find her. And if he couldn't, he would keep pressing Hamelin, only not in the Phoenix. Bennie deserved more respect than that.

Chapter Thirteen
Cousins

Ryan dropped the phone directory on the floor with the others. There were as many Mc's and Mac's in Saint Paul as in a midsize Scottish town. He'd never find her. If he had to start knocking on doors, they would arrest him for stalking long before he located her. Foiled no matter how he went about it. He sneaked out the rear service entrance and headed home.

He gunned his black Porsche Carrera up Bayside Avenue, briefly easing back at the top of the hill. He didn't need a friendly chat with the omnipresent policeman running radar from a lawn chair underneath the crepe myrtle there. Then he cut the black beast loose and barreled south on Route 4, past the hamlet of Mutual Consent, past forking rural roads named for this or that wharf. He spent the last mile on blacktop that narrowed considerably, navigating a series of S curves that snaked around large tracts of farmland owned and worked for generations by families who settled there in colonial times. At the top of the last rise, he broke out of the trees and descended between planted fields to a yellow house on the bank of the Patuxent River. This was his refuge.

Without anyone to unload his frustration on, he decided to thumb his nose at all the homeowners' associations rules that had ever cramped his individuality. He pulled onto the middle of the lawn, near the mailbox, and parked.

Once inside the sparsely furnished bungalow, he tossed the junk mail in the garbage can, and a new round of bills on the kitchen counter, right next to an open package of deli ham, a mangled head of iceberg lettuce, and a glopped-up paring knife balanced precariously on top of a Dijon mustard jar. Definitely not how he had left the place. A burglar stopping to make lunch? He ducked behind the kitchen island with the knife.

"Mr. Thomas?"

Ryan popped back up. "Mrs. Mattingly?" He intercepted his elderly neighbor, dressed cozily in a lavender gingham house coat and fuzzy pink bedroom scuffs, as she shuffled into the kitchen from the living room. "Something amiss?" he asked. He glanced at her and then out the window, toward her white farmhouse next door.

"No-o-o-o," she said, drawing the word out as if she hadn't quite decided. "Didn't know if you were expecting company, so I thought I'd sit with your cousin and chat until you got here. I hope it's okay," she whispered, motioning toward the counter. "He made himself right at home."

"Cousin?" Ryan asked, frowning. The high-pitched whine of a motor drew his attention through the sliding doors to the backyard. There on the edge of his swimming pool, sat Hamelin. He appeared to be sailing a remote-controlled boat around in the pool. "Oh, *that* cousin. It's fine, Mrs. Mattingly. Would you like me to walk you back home?"

"No sir. I may be old, but I'm not dead yet," she murmured. "Let me know if you need me, son."

"Thanks, I will." Ryan walked her out and headed for the pool, where he sat down at one of the patio tables. There was no advantage in entering Hamelin's orbit before he could determine his mood. As soon as he opened his mouth to speak, Hamelin sent his little speed boat roaring across the water at full throttle.

"*Cousin?*" Ryan shouted above the engine noise.

"We're all related if one goes back far enough," Hamelin yelled back. "Besides, she needed reassurance. I'm good at that."

"Yeah, I feel it whenever we're together." Ryan drummed his fingers on the table until the noise subsided. "Are we good? Because you know I'm sorry I created such a commotion earlier. Believe me, it wasn't my intention. I insulted people I don't even know. And poor Bennie was beside himself."

Hamelin kept his eyes on the boat. "You have done an unbelievable job of screwing up things, Ryan James. It could have been so simple, and everyone would have benefited. Now ..."

Ryan slid forward in his chair until his elbows were resting on his knees. "It's just that you're all over the place, man, and I can't keep up. Quit playing with your toy and talk to me. And I mean *really* talk. When you came back to the beach bar, I got the distinct impression that if you could have gotten me off the beach, you would have, er, conducted *a little business* with me. Then you seemed to make a correction midcourse and ordered me out of town. And *then,*" he said, ticking this one off on his ring finger, "you come to the Phoenix, and you're all wrapped up in this random Tippy contest. As if that weren't enough, now you're on to not-a-care-in-the-world-Hammy-boy, and I find you playing in my pool. How in the ..." He threw his hands up in the air. "You have my head spinning like a whirlybird. Which iteration should I run with, huh, Hamelin?"

"It's all business, of a sort. We don't have what you would call *vacation*."

Ryan looked from Hamelin to the boat and back again to Hamelin. "Oka-a-ay. So this moment is not about me. You're transporting someone."

"Do you really want to know?" Hamelin asked, sending the speedboat skidding toward the deep end of the pool again.

"Maybe. I don't think you're here for me. Please don't tell me its sweet old Mrs. Mattingly."

The whine of the boat engine modulated as Hamelin steered the toy into a gentle curve and brought it barreling back toward them. As it drew near, he cut the engine and let it drift. He looked toward the old woman's place.

Ryan turned and saw her disappear into her house through a side door. "Oh, dear. When?"

"Not yet, but soon. After the moratorium." He looked up at the sun. "Which began right before we hit the Phoenix. Lucky you."

"What moratorium?"

"It's not important."

"I bet it is to her."

"Well, then, I'll take it up with *her*." If Hamelin could have collected souls with a withering stare instead of a handshake, Ryan would be halfway to heaven.

"As indifferent as you can be, even *I* don't think you're callous enough to lounge around here like a one of those hideous black vultures circling roadkill. If that's what it is, you should go."

"It's not like it's a death sentence."

"Come again?"

Hamelin huffed and got to his feet. "When one door closes, another one opens. Not a bad cliché, really. Consider me a doorway that leads to so much more. Surely, you've wondered about what they're doing *up there.*" He rolled his eyes up at the cloudless azure sky. "Do they know what you do? Watch you take a leak first thing every morning? Intercede on your behalf?"

"It's crossed my mind, but—"

"No *buts* about it. They've experienced it all—the loveliest sunrise, the exhilaration of soaring with eagles, the most comforting embrace. If mortals really understood …" He looked at Ryan a moment, and his expression softened. His sigh was a gentle one. "The best you can do is try. Someday, you'll get it."

"Hopefully when I'm old and gray."

"What is that monstrosity?" Hamelin asked, changing topics. He pointed to the blue behemoth anchored out in the middle of the channel.

"Dredger. Soft-shelled clams. There used to be a wharf out there at the end of the property. When they offloaded oysters, it wasn't neat and clean. A natural reef formed from the spillage. They tell me that back in the good old days, their reefs built up so close to the surface that veering too far out of the channel would get you grounded pretty fast."

"So what's—"

"Enough about fishing, Hamelin! What do you really want? How do you even know about the Tippy?"

Hamelin scooped his toy out of the water and began tinkering with the motor. "You know you almost blew it for Bennie. Did he shoo you off?"

"No. And Bennie will be just fine," Ryan said. "Tell me what you know, but be brief, because you know this isn't what we really should be discussing. You immortals are involved?"

"It's our contest and there's nothing random about it. The Phoenix is in the running, but it's not about you, the owner. With all due respect, Bennie is the one bringing magic to the place. We nominate a list of bartenders, visit their bars, and then vote on which is the finest. It's a nice little team-building exercise, a great outing, and the bar gets bragging rights."

"Does he have a chance?"

"Bennie was looking good until you bounced part of the judging committee out on their ear. You need to leave town and give Bennie a fighting chance."

Ryan gave him an exasperated look. "Nice try, but you know I'm not leaving until you give me what I want. And why should I help you out with your gambling? Bet a bundle, didn't you? But I'm onto you now, so suck it up, buttercup!"

Ryan held his breath as Hamelin got up and moved toward him. He hooked a foot around the only other chair at his table and pulled it tight against the table, forcing Hamelin to choose another seat.

Hamelin smiled and sat down at the other table. "Then we are at an impasse, my poor delusional friend. This has nothing to do with betting. It's a matter of self-preservation. And contrary to what you may think, the Tippy is currently central to everything that means anything." Hamelin stretched out his long legs and leaned back in his chair, looking like a bored king obliged to hold court with his inferiors. "I am rather surprised that you aren't grasping all this. I thought you were one of the smarter ones. Must I hold your hand through everything?"

"Don't ever try to hold hands with me," Ryan said, pulling his off the table and onto his lap. "I learned that trick of the trade long ago. Since neither of us is happy at the moment, Hamelin, why don't you explain it all. But go slow, 'cause you know us mortals."

"One last chance," Hamelin said, pointing at him. "You just don't seem to get the bigger picture."

"Because you're not giving me the bigger picture."

"Shh!" Hamelin said, pressing the finger to his lips. "Listen, for a change. You are correct about our meeting on the beach. That date should have been the one etched on your memorial stone. My existence is currently threatened by the continuation of yours. I should have terminated you. Let's just say something complicated the situation and I didn't. Now, with the moratorium in effect through the end of the contest, and other immortals in town, it's too late. I'll have to wait until after—kill two birds with one stone, so to speak. Or—and this is the part you don't seem to grasp—you can leave town and spare us both a lot of heartache."

Ryan stood up. "I think I need a drink."

"Drink away," Hamelin said, sweeping his hand toward the outdoor kitchen behind them. "Unfortunately, liquor is the way you approach all your problems. How's that been working?"

Ryan murmured something dismissive as he walked past the brick barbecue and minibar. "Yeah, well, having conversations with dead people is a little hard to handle." He pulled out a bottle of Bacardí dark. His hand shook as he splashed some into a glass and baptized the counter with most of the rest. He waved the nearly empty bottle at Hamelin. "Seeing as how you don't drive, how about one for the road?" he asked hopefully.

"No alcohol for me, thank you. Water, straight, no lemon."

"A teetotaling immortal giving a bar owner advice, and participating in a bar contest where everybody drinks but you?" Ryan pondered it a moment. "Doesn't make sense. Is the Tippy a required assignment?"

"Something like that. And the Phoenix is a pub, not a bar," Hamelin reminded him. "At least, that's what the pompous owner keeps reminding everyone."

Hamelin's little barb struck Ryan as more of a deflection than a personal slight. Why didn't Hamelin drink? Other immortals were imbibing. Was it that Hamelin didn't *like* alcohol, or that Hamelin couldn't *handle* it? Ryan studied the rum bottle. "No water. Faucet's broken," he said. "If I'm going to drink, you should at least look the part. Coming right up, one *virgin* strawberry daiquiri for my very strange *cousin*."

"Virgin?"

"Yeah, zero alcohol. Trust me when I say you're in good hands. Bennie's a great teacher." As Hamelin studied the dredger out in the channel, Ryan added a healthy portion of rum to the daiquiri. "Virgin daiquiri coming right up." He gave Hamelin the drink and sat down across from him. This could be both educational and fun.

If Ryan felt any guilt over hoodwinking Hamelin, it would come later. For the moment, he was enjoying Hamelin enjoying his drink. By the way Hamelin was hoovering the daiquiri, information would soon be tumbling off his lips. "Might want to slow down, bro. I don't know if immortals experience pain, but an ice-cream headache can be a doozy." He took a long draught to hide the smirk he could no longer stifle.

"Excellent," Hamelin said, setting down his glass.

"Yeah. How 'bout that *virgin* daiquiri?"

"Actually, it reminds me of something," Hamelin said, tapping the side of the glass, "but I can't quite put my finger on it." He frowned and took another swig.

"So tell me, Hamelin. How long does this Tippy contest last? After we negotiate something between us, I still need to know when you'll be back for Mrs. Mattingly. I can do a welfare check so she just doesn't lie there …" He winced at how cold and clinical he made it sound.

"This year's is expected to last five days, so we'll shoot for three days of merriment and two extra days to clean up any messes. It's a bit fluid depending on the length and success of the managers' retreat."

"Ah, yes, of course. There's a hierarchy in the afterlife. And who, exactly, is management? Jesus and the twelve?"

Hamelin rolled his eyes. "Don't be ridiculous. Saint Peter is the figurehead, but day-to-day activities are run by individuals you've never heard of. They're all good people, but sometimes they can be just a little too into it."

"Somehow, it doesn't seem like heaven would be a democracy."

"Oh, it isn't. But that's not what we're talking about here."

"Not a . . . Wait! You're not in heav—"

Hamelin's eyes flashing a warning to back off. "Speak less, listen more." He swished the dregs of whipped cream and fruit puree around in his glass. "Every organization has an organizational structure, and smart CEOs delegate, don't they? When I refer to 'management,' I'm talking about *middle* management. They occasionally break for corporate retreats to reenergize and assess where the organization currently is and what direction it should go in the future. Admittedly, it's a conservative group. Direction relates more to administrative management than the core mission statement. Those in charge pick a fancy place—warm and cozy in winter, outdoorsy for the summer months. They go off to eat, drink, and amuse themselves on the corporate dime. Meanwhile, their underlings have their own party and then wait patiently and loyally for them to return and make everything perfect." Hamelin sucked air through the bottom of his straw and began chasing the cherry around the bottom of the glass.

Have another?" Ryan asked, reaching for the glass.

Hamelin shook his head, reconsidered a moment, and then handed him the empty glass. "All right. But virgin."

"Just like the first one," Ryan said, reaching for the last of the Bacardí. "So the bar contest is running while management is off learning about how to throw around fish, discover who took the mouse food, and learn whatever management theory is currently in vogue?"

Hamelin nodded. "The latest training module centers on making your business into a Mr. Rogers-style neighborhood. Everyone gets a cardigan at registration, and I believe there is a breakout team-building session on knitting."

Ryan caught the twinkle in Hamelin's eyes. "You're lying."

Hamelin shrugged. "Why would anyone make *that* up?"

Ryan gave him the second drink and sat back down. "Because you love to entertain. I can already hear the bluesy little ditty sliding off your guitar strings."

"Pffft." Hamelin downed a third of the new drink. "The sad part? Everybody puts so much energy into looking progressive, yet nothing ever really changes. After a few hundred years, the troops get jaded. We know our work best. We make our own changes. They get to party in a nice place; we party wherever else. Everybody blows off a little steam—more than enough happy to go around." He looked at Ryan with glassy eyes. *"Capisce?"*

Ryan shook his head. "Not really. The last time I saw you, you were struggling to get off Saint Pete's naughty list and having to make deliveries to the hot place. I would assume after you sent my parasitic twin Ryan Llewellyn Thomas winging off to the netherworld that you were rewarded with a heavenly route. But here less than a year later, you're jaded enough to organize little party jaunts while the bosses are in training. I thought the afterlife was supposed to be a happy place. So why aren't you happy?"

"I'm not organizing anything. Martin's in charge."

"Martin?"

"Shh! Don't make it sound like an invocation."

Ryan grew thoughtful for a moment. "The tree hugger in the Phoenix? Did Martin always look like that?"

"That was Gerard. Martin is elsewhere."

Ryan nodded. This was the chattiest he had ever seen Hamelin. He put his own drink aside and shifted forward in his chair to make sure he didn't miss a morsel. "I thought besties hung together."

Hamelin chuckled. "*Besties?* Look at you, all young, hip, and ridiculous. You should act your age."

"Maybe you should act *your* age. You're what, eight billion years old and still running around participating in bar contests? Now who's looking ridiculous? I hear there's a wet T-shirt contest down at Cap'n Petes on the weekend. You don't want to miss that one."

"I know that place," Hamelin said as a sly smile creased his face. "No, as I told you before, he's not my *bestie.* We parted ways years ago."

Ryan waited a moment. "And?"

"There is no *and,*" Hamelin said, refusing to make eye contact.

"Oh, I bet there is. You were dragging people to hell for a time, right? Punishment for stepping out of line on something. Was Martin involved, perchance? Aiding and abetting? A tear-jerking story of besties forced to separate for the good of the work unit?" Ryan paused for a reaction, but Hamelin remained stoical. Considering how heavily he'd spiked the daiquiri, Hamelin seemed to be doing a yeomanly job of holding it together. "You can't look me in the eyes, so I'm close. Let me think."

Hamelin dismissed the idea with a fluttering of fingers. "Think away," he said.

Ryan took a swig and studied him. "Got it!" he said, snapping his fingers. "He wasn't complicit in your antics. He's the one who *busted* you. Do tell, Hamelin. If barhopping is acceptable while management is away, then what, pray tell, would have been egregious enough to reduce you to making runs to hell?"

Hamelin trained his now dark and heavy-lidded eyes on Ryan. "Be careful, my friend, not to misjudge your place in the scheme of things. Don't expect to find your wife by snooping through other people's closets." He licked his lips and frowned. His impeccable posture had developed a slouch.

"Yes, the real reason you're here. You promised you were going to help with that," Ryan lied. "Where is she?"

Hamelin waved him off. "Oh, please. The clues were so clear."

"No, I agree, all excellent clues," Ryan said, nodding. "But the one with her last name was so clever, I couldn't decipher it. What was the answer to that one?"

Hamelin eased out of his seat. "It's important for you to leave town. At the moment, I can't remember why, but you need to do it *now*. Don't head back to town. I can't protect you."

Ryan watched Hamelin sway. "From Martin? Is he the one?"

Bleary-eyed and looking confused, Hamelin stared at Ryan as if he were speaking Old Aramaic. He put a hand on the back of his chair and steadied himself. "What did you put in my drink?"

"Jeepers, Hamelin, you can't even handle a virgin drink? I'll bet it's jet lag. Would you like to lie down?"

Hamelin's knees buckled. He went down, clutching at the chair in a futile attempt to remain standing, and when his knees hit the paving stones, he put his head down on the chair seat. "Get me some water, please."

Ryan made a move for him, balked, then darted to the minifridge. When he turned back around, Hamelin was gone.

Was Hamelin capable of flying, teleporting, or hailing a sweet and low-swinging chariot while under the influence? The only thing worse than an immortal riding your case was a cocky immortal loaded and missing in action. Ryan sat down with the bottled water and pondered a very troubling future.

Chapter Fourteen
Putting a Spin on Things

As he knelt on the Phoenix's hard ceramic floor in a rare moment of self-flagellation, Ryan embraced the pain radiating up from his knees. What, he wondered, was the penalty for poisoning an immortal? He poured Drano into the floor drain. Could a soul runner die twice? All his past troubles paled in comparison with what Hamelin would do when he sobered up and hunted him down.

The sound of snuffling and the squeak of rubber soles brought his head around. "Hamelin! I've been frantic," he said, scrambling to his feet.

"*Et tu, Brute?*" Hamelin said.

Ryan gave him a quick up-and-down wellness check. Except for the sniffling, things looked fairly normal. "What happened to you? Was it food poisoning?"

Hamelin ignored the inquiries and, in an inexplicable move, tore a page from his little black book.

Not normal. Mutilating heavenly property was way out of character. Ryan searched Hamelin's eyes and saw a guarded, hurt look there. Was payback going to involve a horrid guilt trip? Painful as it was bound to be, it would be much better than Hamelin pulling life support.

Hamelin offered him the page. "Four dozen of my coworkers will be passing through town at various times in the next few days. Don't come to work during these hours. Destroy the list when you've memorized it, and not a word to anyone."

Ryan took the list. The dates ran pretty much all day long—not a particularly taxing memory exercise. "And this date at the bottom?"

"The time I have set to retrieve your soul should things spiral out of control. This is goodbye, Ryan James. I shan't be bothering you again. It's been a pleasure making your acquaintance."

Ryan stared at the date and then at Hamelin. To see one's own death date was sobering enough. To see the steely intent of a soul runner was a thousand times more terrifying. He wadded up the paper and launched it at the trash receptacle.

Hamelin's hand swept out and intercepted the shot in a move rivaling Willie Mays's famous catch in the 1954 World Series. "I said *destroy,* not toss in the garbage."

Ryan took the wad back, pulled off a piece, and shoved it in his mouth. And when he had chewed sufficiently, he swallowed it.

Hamelin sighed wearily and shook his head. "I don't know why I bother with you. I'm off now, as if you would really care. If you don't know already, the new bar down the street, Delaney's, has also received an invitation to compete. Local competitors are never a good thing. They tend to take pot shots at each other, which kills off all the good vibes in both establishments. Goodbye, Ryan James. Heed the list, or get started on your own. Make it a *bucket* list."

"Wait!" Ryan said. "I owe you an apology. I'm a self-centered sinner, Hamelin—really not worthy of your friendship. I'm truly sorry," he said, striking his breast in repentance. "I don't know what came over me at my house. I only wanted to loosen you up a bit."

Hamelin slid his book back into his pocket and fixed Ryan with a scornful look. "We're not friends. And I don't judge the sins of others. Don't think for a second that this is about you or yours. I merely need you to clean up your act so I can protect my back, hide my impulsiveness and missteps. This is your last chance before I am forced to do something you won't like. You're a smart man. Choose wisely."

Butt-hurt Hamelin with a bit of toddler thrown in. Had the negotiating phase really ended? Ryan tried to channel Bennie's patience and wisdom. "I understand. Each man for himself. But I really hate to see us part under these circumstances." He pulled out a chair. "Wouldn't you like to sit a moment before you go?"

Hamelin shook his head. "Absolutely not. I want you to know how very much you've disappointed me. Why did you have to betray my trust in you? All you had to do was ask in the right way and I would have told you about Livia."

Ryan gaped. "What? Listen, you, you … you *fibber*! I've done nothing but ask you."

Hamelin put his hands behind his back and began to pace from one end of the kitchen to the other. Ryan wasn't quite sure what emotions were bubbling up, but he decided to take Hamelin's advice and not indulge the mortal obsession with labeling things. When a volcano threatened to erupt, you ran like hell and saved the questions about geology and seismic activity for later. Unfortunately, his feet wouldn't obey, and he stood transfixed, waiting for all-powerful karma to pronounce sentence against a man who had the cheek to ply an abstinent immortal with liquor.

Hamelin suddenly halted his pacing. "How do I make you understand the … the *nuances*? This isn't a *you* problem. It isn't even a *me* problem. It's an *us* problem, and it *s*eems to grow thornier by the day. Bennie would do fine in a fair fight, but right now that is not in the cards. Extra bars were added to the Tippy on the pretext of making the competition more interesting, but it's merely subterfuge to aid in Martin's vendetta against me. He's throwing out a dragnet to identify all the mull—er, *irregular situations*—he thinks I've created. He's casting about wildly, but dead-on with Nevis. Adding another bar keeps everybody in town longer and ups the chances of one immortal or another figuring out that you are, um, a *problem.* And if Martin pays a visit to Nevis and *you're* here? You and I are both history. As I said before, if push comes to shove, I'll have to transport you myself. Nothing personal, as I hope you'll understand. If I hadn't intervened, you would have succumbed to your injuries in that car crash five years ago. I gave you five extra years." He looked at Ryan with pain in his eyes.

Suddenly, he lunged at Ryan, grabbing him by the shoulders. With unassailable strength, he shoved him between the last kitchen cabinet and the utility tub, pinning him against the wall with his weight.

"Not yet, please," Ryan said, trying to twist free.

"Sh-h-h!" Hamelin hissed, clamping a hand over his mouth. His pupils had all but disappeared into murderous, flashing green, and his firm grip threatened to cut off the circulation to Ryan's arm. Ryan stopped fighting. Hamelin loosened his hold but didn't let go. He stood listening. Ryan heard nothing except the drip of the faucet in the tub.

"Close your eyes," Hamelin whispered.

Ryan raised an eyebrow.

Hamelin's grip tightened again. "It would be preferable."

Ryan closed his eyes and felt himself spinning off into space.

Chapter Fifteen
Outing

He spun but a moment, but when the motion stopped, Ryan was nowhere near the Phoenix kitchen. He opened his eyes to a dimly lit room filled with haze, loud music, and indistinct voices.

"Still with us?" Hamelin asked, studying him closely. He scooted a glass toward him. "Water. Take a sip so your head will stop whirling."

Ryan squinted, trying to regain his bearings through a miasma of smoke—reefer, by the smell of it. They were sitting at a pub table near a crowded dance floor. He eyed the glass suspiciously. "Dear God, is this … hell?" he whispered.

"I seriously doubt the smokes are this good in Hades," Hamelin said, appraising the blunt in his hand. He stubbed it out in the bottom of his glass and left it to soak there. "I thought you might like to see the fifth bar on my list. Everybody else is at the first, so we won't be bothered. We also need to have a frank discussion."

"Finally! Thank you, Jesus," Ryan murmured. He looked out on the crowded room. The couple at the next table really ought to get a room, and a curvaceous va-va-voom at the end of the bar was glancing seductively at him. They were in a seedy pickup bar. "Aren't there any *nice* pubs on your list? This looks like the red-light district. A libertine angel—now I've seen it all." He noted Hamelin's reefer. You can't drink, but you can get high?"

"It's Amsterdam," Hamelin said with a shrug. "Any libertine tendencies I might have had were leached out of me long ago. And, if you call me *angel* one more time, I'm going to leave you here to fend for yourself. This is the Bull Dog Café. I didn't pick it," he added with a huff, nodding as the waiter handed him a menu. "It's in the contest, and I thought you might like to get out and about. Shall I order you a nice fat spliff? Probably do an uptight straight-lace like you a world of good."

That last one hurt. Ryan had always considered himself a social liberal. He swung off his stool. "No thanks. I'm getting high just breathing. "I'll wait for you on the curb."

"Suit yourself. Door's that way." Hamelin pointed past the disc jockey in the center of the room, through the throng of bodies pulsing to techno dance music, to the double glass doors on the far side of the room. "Hang close to the building. The harlots outside can be aggressive if they deem you a pushover."

Conservative *and* a pushover? "That's what you think of me?" Ryan climbed back up on his stool.

Hamelin's head disappeared behind his menu. "What say to *patat frites, bitterballen,* and a refreshing *jenever* to wash it all down?"

Ryan yanked the menu away. "Who's at the Phoenix that you don't want me to see? A bill collector? Martin? *My wife?*"

"You already know she's in Saint Paul. And lucky for you, Martin's still somewhere else. Now, enjoy the moment and stop being difficult."

Ryan tossed Hamelin's menu onto a nearby vacant table. "You're a piece of work, Mr. Russell. Constantly plotting and maneuvering, but always scrambling. What bill haven't *you* paid?"

"I don't need that," Hamelin said, dismissing the menu with a look of disdain. He called the waiter back over and ordered something in a language that Ryan assumed was Dutch. When he turned back to Ryan, his eyes were dancing. "I love this place."

"Show-off. I'm sure they would have gotten it just fine in English."

Hamelin shrugged. "When in the Netherlands …"

Raucous laughter broke out at a nearby table as a beer chugger tipped over in his chair.

"Well, I've paid all my debts," Ryan said, trying to shut out the craziness. "I appreciate the bonding experience, but take me home."

Hamelin lit up another blunt and blew a little chain of smoke rings in Ryan's direction. "As long as you're here, you may as well make the most of it. Enjoy; then I'll take you back."

"Stop it," Ryan said, batting the smoke away. "What's at the Phoenix, Hamelin?"

"AWAB," Hamelin said, his head bouncing to the beat of some atrocious, grating electronic noise masquerading as music.

"I'm not guessing," Ryan said, shaking his head. "And you probably wouldn't hear the half of it anyway. Isn't there somewhere quieter we can go?"

"It means *apprentice with a bullet*," Hamelin said, ignoring the request. "All new immortals arrive in the afterlife as equals. They're placed at the bottom of the work ladder and climb up according to their talents and virtues. With his skills and sensibilities, AWAB won't be on the bottom rung long. He'll rise quickly to more rewarding responsibilities. 'Management' seems to be written all over him, but there are certain characteristics that need to be tested. When placed in a position of power and influence, does AWAB make the right choice, or give in to residual base mortal instincts? All immortals face that ultimate test, and it certainly determines whether one progresses into the higher planes of … how well he does in the great beyond."

"What's his name?"

"You can call him Curtis."

"So Curtis is an opportunist. That's why you're afraid of him."

"Not him specifically. He's Martin's fair-haired boy, and it's what he could report back to Martin that has me worried. And to go back to what you said earlier, no, you haven't paid all your debts."

"And he'll know I'm a … er, you know, a second-chancer? And he's hunting down Livia, too?"

"Not much chance of them finding her. I put her in a 'pending' file, tagged it with an extenuating circumstances code, and shoved it as far back in my filing system as it would go. There's no chance anyone will stumble across it unless they are rifling through my affairs and have my notebook. Or unless you are with her and they track you down. You're the weak link in all this. Your life is still owed, and if you set off any alarm bells with AWAB, he'll report back to Martin that something isn't kosher. And boomerini! Next thing you know, we've got Martin showing up. He'll know you're a mulligan, and you'll be history. Me, too—called on the carpet for freelancing and insubordination."

Ryan rubbed his forehead. "There isn't some mark on my face that will tip him off, is there?"

Hamelin laughed, but there was no mirth in the eyes—only a darkness that reminded Ryan of deep, churning water. "We are soul runners," he said. "Our entire purpose is to seek out souls ready for their defining journey and escort them to their appointed place. There are no marks, just a beacon-like signal as the soul calls—a sort of cosmic transponder, if you will. Homing in on a soul is a natural immortal tendency, but we don't just pop up fully formed and functioning, like Athena from the brow of Zeus. While a newbie can sense the soul they are sent to retrieve, their senses are not sufficiently refined to zero in on souls charged to another immortal. But Martin? He's been bouncing around the universe for eons, and experience has made his senses keen. He need only hit town to know there's a mulligan nearby. If both you and Livia were in Nevis, it would lay her circumstances bare. Both of you in the same bar together? Much too close. Thank your lucky stars that he has an assignment that will keep him busy elsewhere." He chuckled to himself.

"You think that's funny, huh?"

Hamelin grew serious. "Of course not. It's just ironic that Martin tried so hard for this promotion, and now it's going to keep him from being here and finding you."

Ryan gave him a sour look. "Why in God's good name have you been in Nevis at all? You shouldn't even have nominated the Phoenix. Now you're scrambling to keep from getting caught with your pants down after making a mulligan."

Hamelin nodded in agreement. "Because Martin is a coy one, and he sprang this machination on me unawares. I entered Bennie in the contest at Wandering Joe's, not the Phoenix. Fate, or karma, has dealt a new card in sending him back to Nevis. Martin's last official act before we broke for the retreat was to lecture the group about creating mulligans. I believe it was directed specifically at me. He suspects something happened during my visit to Nevis last summer. At best, all I can hope to do is keep you away long enough for the contest to move to the other bar entries so he doesn't have the opportunity to confirm his suspicions."

Ryan ran his finger along the rounded edge of the table, considering Hamelin's explanation and his past behavior. "It's *your* bad karma," he said. "Either you help me find her, or I'll tell Martin what you've been up to, because I'd rather die than live like this: no wife, no son, no nothing. I appreciate your concern for me, I really do. But please, take me back to Nevis. Or my house. Can you do that? Then, I swear to God, I'll be out of there as fast as I can get in my car and head across the Bay Bridge to Saint Paul." He reached out and touched Hamelin's sleeve. "Please, Hamelin. I can't live without my wife."

Hamelin dropped the butt of the second blunt in to join the first. Then he looked at Ryan with kind, understanding eyes. "You wouldn't sacrifice her like that. I know you."

Ryan clenched his jaw and narrowed his eyes in a pathetic attempt to appear steely. Of course, Hamelin knew him, but now was not the time to let him know just how well. For a moment, they engaged in a staring match, Hamelin earnestly searching as Ryan put on the best poker face he could muster. If soul runners could read hearts, Hamelin had him dead to rights.

Ryan prided himself in reading faces. It was a life-or-death skill he'd learned in the criminal underworld, where trusting the wrong person might be the last bad decision one ever made. He saw no resolve in Hamelin's mug, only the wheels and gears of indecision grinding uselessly away. Unless the immortal was picking up a soul, he was clueless—living in eternal light yet bumbling in the dark.

The wheels ground to a halt, and Hamelin's expression relaxed. "I believe you. But you are an obstinate, misguided fool, Ryan James. I don't know everything, but I can assure you beyond a whisper of doubt that violating the sanctity of her new life contract will have grave consequences. And it will affect me, so . . ." He leaned away as the waiter set his order down on the table: a cardboard cone piled high with thick, chunky, french fries covered in a thick white sauce, a bowl of breaded, fried balls of some sort, and two bottles of pale ale.

Ryan ignored his ale. Through flailing, swaying bodies he watched as a husky bouncer escorted a drunk, belligerent patron to the door. "What are the odds there are other immortals here?" he asked, assessing the Bull Dog's crowd.

Hamelin dug into the *patat frites.* "Little to none right now."

"Then it wouldn't matter if I stood up and announced to the world that I'm a mulligan?"

"Shush!" Hamelin said between mouthfuls. "A needless risk. Remember, this bar may not be first on the list, but it's still on there."

"Mulligan," Ryan said a little louder.

Hamelin set down his fork. "Enough, foolish man!"

Ryan stood up. "Mulligan, mulligan, mulli—"

Hamelin doused him in jenever. "Sweet Jesus, for the love of all that's holy, cease and desist!" He tossed a napkin at him and surveyed the room. Not a patron in the house had turned their way—liquor flowed, dancers gyrated, and couples continued to flirt. He pushed his half-eaten food away and signaled the waiter. "Very well. I will give you what you seek, but the price will be high."

Ryan wiped gin off his face. "I'll pay it," he said. He reached over and pulled a miniature pencil and some sort of survey card from an acrylic holder on the table. "Question mark, 'Mc,' question mark," he murmured as he wrote in the card's free space. He slid it across the table. "Just fill in a few blanks. If I guess it, go to the next word. Okay?"

Hamelin closed his eyes a moment. He was either praying or jerking Ryan's chain for dramatic affect. At this point, Ryan didn't care. It was just a matter of time until he had what he wanted. He watched Hamelin scribble something.

Ryan looked down at the four numerals and two letters the immortal had written, and frowned. "What's this? Some sort of code?

'One' for 'A,' 'two' for 'B'?" He began to count on his fingers.

"Boat."

"The *registration* number? Good Lord, you *can* give when you want. Letter," he demanded, pointing back at the paper.

Hamelin crossed out the second question mark and added the letter "G" after the "C."

"McGowan?"

Hamelin sighed and shook his head. He added an "al."

"McGalla—"

"*Silence!*" Hamelin hissed. "Nod if you have it."

Ryan nodded and gestured at him to continue.

Hamelin drew a line through the first question mark and wrote "Ma."

Ryan took the pen back and added an "r."

"Yes."

The addition of a "y" got a nope, as did "g" and "c." He jotted down an "ie."

Hamelin snatched up the paper.

"Marie McGallagher?" Ryan mouthed. His heart suddenly began thumping in sync with the hard-driving beat of the music. "Take me home."

Hamelin sat there looking thoughtfully at Ryan. "You're quite sure? It's a noble idea, but you are foolish. Having a name solves only one problem. This will end poorly."

"*Now,* Hamelin. This is going to turn out okay." Ryan squeezed his eyes shut and braced for the angelic Tilt-a-Whirl. "Just don't let go of me. I don't want to end up someplace like North Korea." As he waited for Hamelin's magical touch, he heard a quiet sigh of resignation.

"Very well. And, Ryan James, what I said earlier about our not being friends—it's still true. But if I were ever to have a friend, it would be someone like you."

Before he could respond, Ryan felt himself spinning off to God knew where.

Chapter Sixteen
Hope and a Little Crosby

Ryan took his eyes off US Route 50 and sneaked a glance at Hamelin, riding shotgun. He was sitting ramrod straight, eyes closed, his aura shimmering a delicate ethereal blue. Ryan wasn't sure whether Hamelin was asleep or merely meditating. The vogue response *I'll sleep when I'm dead* ran through his head. Ryan swerved the Carrera onto the shoulder and back onto the road again. The immortal's eyes popped open, and the aura vanished.

"Aren't your drinking buddies going to be looking for you?" Ryan asked. He immediately regretted the phrasing. If Hamelin didn't have any friends …

Hamelin didn't seem fazed. "Doubtful. I come and go as I please. One of the perks of tenure," he said, overemphasizing the "K" sound. He seemed happy and free for a change.

"I really think you should go back to Amsterdam or wherever the next bar is on the list. When I asked you to bring me back, that wasn't an invitation to tag along. You're going to be fricking beacon for Martin."

"Nope. All eyes will be on Nevis. I'll catch up at Cheltenham's Summerbee's Royal Oak. It's, as you used to say, a win-win. You're out of Nevis, and I get a road trip." He gestured out the window at the cornfields flitting by. "Where is this, and how much longer?"

"Maryland Eastern Shore near Stevensville, and ten minutes less than the last time you asked. If I can't get rid of you, then maybe I should sing you back to sleep. Your nonstop travel commentary is getting on my last nerve."

Hamelin twisted around and looked at him. "And miss all this? Not a chance." He shook his head. "I just gave you everything you've been clamoring for. Why aren't you happy?"

"You've as much as told me that my quest is going to fail. After all the gloom and doom you've been dumping on me, shouldn't we be asking why you *are* so happy? Make up your mind. Which Hamelin should I be paying attention to?"

"I never told you any such thing. I merely warned you that there would be a high price to pay. It's a bit like shoplifting—the thrill of stealing, but the agony of arrest and prosecution. Although I've never done that," he quickly added. "I love an underdog, and your enthusiasm is rubbing off on me. You just might get away with this. So relax." He rolled the window up and reached for the radio on the dash.

Ryan pushed his hand away. "I hate country."

Hamelin shrugged. "We have a narrow window here, in which to bond before I need to get back. It'll be like Hope and Crosby in *Road to Morocco*. Only we should forget the girl. That always caused problems."

"*The girl* is the whole point here. I'm Crosby and I get the girl." Ryan realized he was tailgating the vintage Cadillac in front of him. Driving was a full-time job, just like Hamelin. He tapped his brakes. "Tell me something, Hamelin. If it weren't for the contest, and Martin sniffing out your *creations*, would you ever have come back to Nevis?"

Hamelin shook his head. "I leave it in the able hands of the Almighty."

As they approached the traffic light at the Queenstown outlets, slowing traffic prevented Ryan from turning to read the degree of sincerity in Hamelin's face, but it was a pat answer if ever he heard one. He persisted. At worst, Hamelin would get annoyed and return to Amsterdam. That would be a win-win-win. "Never want to take a peek? See, for instance, if Livia's all right in her new life? Seems kind of odd considering you were kinda sweet on her."

"She was a charming woman with honesty and depth. I'm sure she's doing just fine without any interference from me. I care about all my charges, but it all comes down to faith."

Like some Christian Chatty Cathy doll spewing empty religious platitudes, Hamelin was still sound-biting him. "But that's not really what I asked you, is it? The fact of the matter is that it's *you* who can't approach her. That page eighty-seven that you're so fond of quoting from your little DYI manual? It refers to what *you* can't do, not what applies to others. Your hands are tied. It was no accident, you telling me that her current last name begins with 'Mc.' Just as it was no coincidence that I saw her down at the War of 1812 celebration, getting into a boat registered in Saint Paul just across the bay."

Hamelin chuckled. "Page eighty-seven? And here I thought you never took in a word I said."

"You *want* me to find her—do the legwork you can't. It's like one of those classic vampire movies where the monster can't cross the threshold until he's been invited into the house. You can't search for her, but if someone else should bring her into your orbit, you can get involved. Something like that."

Hamelin let out a little huff and glanced out the window. The view had changed from furrowed fields of soybeans to a commercial strip of car dealerships, fast-food restaurants, and a Walmart the size of a community college. "It would be a falsehood to say I haven't wondered. But we'll meet again. I eventually transport all my charges—even you."

Ryan sighed in frustration. Hamelin wasn't giving anything away. He shifted subjects. "Last time you inserted yourself into my life, you admonished me to get my act together. So where, exactly, am I on my little choo-choo ride to the next life? And what's the destination, by the way? Is my ticket punched to eternal bliss or unrelenting regret?"

"Don't ask me things I am unable to tell you." Hamelin closed his eyes, and the door on any further inquiries. The air around him began to shimmer and hum.

Ryan began to hum the theme music for *Road to Morocco.* Hamelin was absolutely wrong about unhappy consequences. Once he found Livia, Ryan anticipated the train ride being long and smooth. And the sooner he found her, the sooner he could be shed of his looney passenger. He pulled out into the left lane, punched the accelerator, and didn't acknowledge the raised middle finger of the Caddy driver as he passed.

***

Saint Paul was the Little Town with a Big Heart, or so it said on the pocked and peeling road sign. If ever an entire town was on the wrong side of the tracks, this was it. Ryan side-eyed his passenger, who had been blessedly quiet for the past half hour. He coughed to shake Hamelin out of his reverie.

"Hamelin, we're here!" Ryan said. "There used to be a ferry around here somewhere. Saint Paul to Nevis. Once the railroads came in, Sollars Ferry and Saint Paul went straight to life support. The longer land route became quicker, and this became one dead little place without much to offer."

"Except your wife."

"Exactly. That's what I'm saying. I don't think there will be much over here to entertain you. This might be the perfect time for you to rejoin the Tippy. I'd hate for you to miss out on all those great bars." Ryan didn't venture a look, but he could almost feel Hamelin's eyebrows arching.

Hamelin stretched and yawned. "What could be more delightful that a little town with a big heart? If I trusted you less, I would assume you were trying to ditch me. No need to give me the bum's rush just yet, though. I might end up being helpful."

Ryan muttered and slowed to get a look at downtown. In a moment, he breezed through the commercial zone with its single stoplight: a series of shabby storefronts advertising tee shirts emblazoned with slogans such as "I got crabs in St. Paul" and "My Johnson is bigger than your Evinrude, and an assortment of bait, tackle, and booze shops. He half expected the sign on the far side to say *F*** You Very Much, Come Again.* He hated the thought of Livia being here, sleepwalking through her existence selling suggestive bumper stickers and Styrofoam cups full of bloodworms. He made a U-turn and pulled into the McDonald's, the sole fast-food joint on the main drag.

Hamelin opened his door. "Is this my only choice?"

"Don't get out," Ryan said, scrolling through his phone. "Your only choice is to follow me around or go get plastered with the rest of your folks."

"Fair enough." Hamelin closed the door. "Picking up souvenirs, or are we going to reconnoiter now?"

Ryan glanced back down Main Street. "I wouldn't even buy *bait* here." He went back to scrolling. "Way ahead of you. I put out feelers before we left. Just checking intel."

Hamelin's countenance brightened, but it wasn't quite a full-blown shimmer. "How about I drive and you can *feel* all you want. Much more efficient."

Ryan chuckled. "Never happening, dude. Why don't you keep an eye out for the coppers? The last thing we need is to end up in the pokey in a two-street town."

"Coppers," Hamelin mumbled. He rolled down his window, apparently content with a new game.

Ryan opened a message from his favorite snoop, Jerry I-can-get-you-anything-for-a-price Pernell: *"The boat is registered under the corporate name Ahoy, Inc. Recently relocated. Company still in St. Paul somewhere."* He looked up from the message and glanced around. They were surrounded by residential bungalows, bungalows converted to commercial use, boats, and piers. "Somewhere" could be any one of these podunk little flotsam-trap inlets, or any of the small marinas in "greater" Saint Paul. He put away his phone and turned to Hamelin. "So the question would be, does Livia actually own *Ahoy,* or is it just another brick paver on the path of her new life?" He pulled a road map out of the center console and began unfolding it.

"No, just a rental," Hamelin said as he watched a fisherman on a nearby pier.

Ryan threw the map at him. "Dag nab it, you son of a something. You knew about *Ahoy* and didn't say anything? If you weren't dead, Mr. Russell, I'd kill you right here and now."

Hamelin turned preoccupied eyes toward him. "No, just intuition." He deftly folded the map and handed it back. "If you must proceed in contacting her," he said, "you must do it now." His voice was strangely quiet and emotionless.

"Intuition?"

Hamelin nodded. "Where does your intel say she is?"

"Ahoy Inc. owns the boat, and it's berthed in Saint Paul. That's all Jerry could give me. Let's take a minute to get a burger and let me decide next steps." He pulled into the McDonald's drive-through lane but stopped short of the ordering window. Instead, he turned to Hamelin and said, "If you have anything else that would be helpful, now would be a good time, you know, to speed things along."

Hamelin told him no, and for maybe the first time ever, Ryan believed him. He ordered cheeseburgers, fries, and two sodas—diet for him, regular for Hamelin. As they waited at the pickup window, he quizzed the soft-spoken employee on the town's biggest marinas. If they couldn't find her at one of those, they'd be back for apple pies and further leads.

Chapter Seventeen
Wild Goose Chase

Ryan stabbed the burnt, stubby remains of cold french fries into the last of the ketchup as he studied Joe's Marina at the water's edge. He was to start inquiries at the boatyard and, if that didn't produce results, work his way across the parking lot to some of the smaller stores: Those would be the shack-like Bobby's Bait Shack (which, indeed, it was), a 7-11 clone called Rita's Quickie Mart, and the Amoco gas station near the byway. And if none of those panned out, there were two more large marinas on Bay Street heading south.

He saw no large boats moored at these docks, but what was here looked pampered, fast, and impressively expensive—from the state-of-the-art communications antennae and paraphernalia on the roof over the captain's chair, to the berthing for six below the waterline. This was a haunt of the weekend warriors who traversed the Chesapeake Bay Bridge from west to east during the warm seasons, bringing their noise, pollution, and money along with them.

The boatyard was busy. The cavernous blue and white steel boat warehouse was a hub of activity, its huge doors thrown wide for a forklift pulling a pleasure craft out of storage. It looked like a major operation. Ryan decided to hit Rita's first. He could always circle back to the warehouse.

You stay here," he said to Hamelin as he shoved trash into the empty

McDonald's bag. "Unless you can manage a decent Eastern Shore accent. I'm much more likely to get help if they think I'm local." Problem was, he didn't sound like someone from the Eastern Shore, Western Shore, or anywhere in or around Maryland, for that matter. As soon as he flapped his gums and his New Yorkness seeped out, eyes would narrow and friendliness would dry up. While he might get a pass to buy T-shirts, asking for personal info would probably cross the line.

Hamelin dropped his toy helicopter back into the Happy Meal box and gave Ryan his full attention. "Perhaps. Let me hear yours."

The only Eastern Shore accent Ryan had ever heard was Tilghman's, the guy who delivered blue crabs to the Phoenix during the height of crabbing season. Unfortunately, the big guy wasn't much of a talker. Ryan cleared his throat and tried to channel him. "Good afternoon." That wasn't even close. He cleared his throat and tried again.

Hamelin gave him a quizzical look. "If Donald Duck's cousin is a waterman, you'll be fine. I'd say stick with what you know, Yankee. I'll stay here in the getaway car. Give me the keys and I'll have us rolling at a moment's notice."

Ryan kept the keys and entered the marina's store with the confidence of a fish stick on Good Friday. He didn't know the first thing about the water or boats. Unless you threw in a goodly amount of Jack Daniel's Single Barrel, he had no use for either. He bypassed the fishing rods, ship-to-shore radios, and sailing wardrobe and headed straight for the chips-and-soda section. He pulled the latest Coke variety out of the cooler, and some Old Bay chips off the endcap and took them to the ponytailed teen at the register.

"Nice place," he said. "Worked here long?"

"Forever," the girl said, her eyes glazed over from boredom or reefer—maybe both.

“I’m trying to find a friend. He invited me down to see his new boat, and I’ve lost the directions he gave me. The boat’s called the *Mulligan.* Heard of it?”

She shook her head and put his stuff in a bag. This was a time waster. He rolled his eyes right into the impassive face of the shopper behind him in line: a solidly built guy, bald as an egg, with a gap between his front teeth that he could drive the boatlift through. Ryan offered a weak smile. “You know the boat I’m talking about?”

Obviously not a big fan of New Yorkers, the guy walked to the exit door and swung it wide open. Ryan assessed his size, which was formidable, his demeanor, which was annoyed, and Ryan’s getaway driver, who was probably too engrossed in his new helicopter to help him out. It would take the Fighting Irish’s Four Horsemen to get past this brute.

“Can’t show you if you’re gonna stand way over there,” the man said.

Ryan released the breath he had been holding. “Right, then,” he said. And grabbing his bag, he double-timed over.

“Your friend was here ’bout half hour ago. Bought ice. If you’re lucky, might still be docked.” Baldy stepped out the door and pointed to the main drag. “Back out here and turn right; then take the third left, just past Lofter’s Grill. There’s a Lotto sign in the window. Park in their lot. Third pier down, right side. Boat’s there.”

Four dollars and eighty-three cents—it was the cheapest Ryan had ever left for a tip. If it was good, he’d spring for a Lotto ticket before he left town. Maybe a house, too. Because if there was the remotest chance she could be here, he wasn’t leaving.

He climbed back into the car. “I need you to count left turns,” he said to Hamelin as he headed out of the lot. “We take the third left.”

They crept down the main drag, keeping an eye peeled for Lofter's, and the other for bored police officers chowing down Krispy Kremes in their cruiser. There were no more businesses in this section of town. The pothole-riddled street was lined with an endless array of single-story cottages, looking a lot like Nevis.

Much to Ryan's surprise, there really was a second traffic light in Saint Paul, and he hit it red. Unless the dude in the marina was counting parking lots, the third left should be coming up.

Hamelin stirred. "Are we there?" he asked.

"Close. How many, Hamelin?"

"Nine and a half, if you count alleyways, turnabouts, and private drives. Twenty-two if you include the bay-front properties stacked double-deep with houses, mother-in-law suites, and freestanding garages."

"Helpful," Ryan mumbled. The light turned green, and he eased off the brake.

Hamelin's left hand shot out and grabbed the steering wheel as his right pointed at a Canada goose just beginning to cross the street with five fuzzy goslings in tow. "Wait," he said, and refused to relinquish the wheel until they had waddled across the road. "Now," he said, letting go.

Ryan accelerated. Just as he cleared the intersection, he glimpsed a lottery sign in the window of a business buried deep in a cluster of storefronts. He slammed on brakes. The pickup truck behind him laid into his horn, and the goslings disappeared one by one through the bars of an over-sized storm grate.

Ryan waved the pickup around him, made a U-turn, and then did a quick right into the Lofter's Grill parking lot. A small crowd of people had already gathered around the drain. A few were on their hands and knees trying to pry it up as the distraught mother circled and honked from a safe distance.

Ryan left it in the crowd's able hands and walked over to the restaurant. Lofter's was tucked behind Atlas Tires and Ken and Betty's Grocery. It looked like a nice, clean place. On the waterside, a walkway connected the restaurant to a pier that had boat slips reserved for diners. Its outdoor patio had a bustling lunch crowd.

A heavy vault door from somewhere deep inside Ryan swung slowly open, and a surge of molten grief surged up and engulfed him. The memory was raw and clear: Livia leaning over the rail of the bridge at Point Benedict as a Boston Whaler passed underneath. He wanted to reach out and capture her blond hair as it twirled around her, see her face as she gushed about combining boats and food into a twenty-first-century curb service. He winced as he remembered how mean and dismissive he had been. He had made an art of denying his attraction and pushing her away. Too late, he'd realized that she was the love of his life. When he found her, he would never take his eyes off her again, and he would buy her the moon if she desired it.

He pushed the door shut with a mighty heave and looked at the pier again. Then he considered the others that lined the water's edge as far as he could see. Which would be the third? "So, Hamelin, do we count this pier connected to the restaurant, or begin with the next one?"

Hamelin was gone. Apparently bored with restaurants and negligent geese, and harder to keep track of than a toddler on a sugar high, he had moved on. Ryan located him way down past the next pier. He took off after him.

Pier number two—or one, depending on how you counted—leased slips for a variety of boats: double-decker sleepers, speedboats with tall mounted captain chairs, and a couple of flat-bottom wooden bay-built craft. Ryan decided to count it as pier number one. He walked two more piers down and stopped next to Hamelin, who apparently had counted them the same way.

Hamelin gave him a smug look, sat down at the end of the pier, and propped himself against one of the posts. "Your turn," he said. "How bad do you want it?"

Ryan looked across the pier. Halfway down hung a dark-blue sign with white block lettering that read "Ahoy, Inc." And next to it bobbed a small white speedboat. It was the *Mulligan,* and a few paces beyond it stood a guy coiling a boat rope. He wore long khaki shorts, new Top-Siders, and a blue T-shirt—probably a weekend warrior.

Ryan studied the distance from shore to the boat, the lapping of the water against the bulkhead, and the rise and fall of the vessels as they rocked in the wake of a passing runabout. He shuddered and watched the pier. It was wide, but he'd still be able to see the water. Potato chips and diet soda shifted in his gut.

"Can I help you find something?"

It was the rope coiler. Ryan stayed where he was, and watched with relief as the man came his way, wiping his hands on a rag as he came. His shirt was emblazoned across the chest with the Ahoy logo in big letters.

"I'm looking for someone who works with Ahoy, Inc. I'm interested in that boat," he said, gesturing toward the *Mulligan.*

"That'd be me. Donovan Palmer, owner," the guy said, thrusting his hand out. "But if you're interested in a charter, we're all booked up."

"Oh, yeah? Congrats on the business, but no good for me. A few months back, weren't you over in Nevis for the tall ship festival?"

"No, didn't make it."

"I ... uh, your boat ... Didn't I see it when the *Kalmar Nyckel* passed up the coast? Across the water." Ryan pointed in the general direction of Nevis.

"Yeah, I know where it is. Been there plenty, only not that day. The *Mulligan* did go out as a rental that weekend, though. We had such a demand that these little boats were going out as fast as we could clean 'em up and send 'em back out. Good money. Did you have a complaint about the renter? Damage your boat, pier, crab pots? We can fill out paperwork. I have insurance." He gestured for Ryan to follow him.

Ryan remained firmly rooted and shook his head. "No, nothing like that." He gave an uneasy laugh. "I'm interested in the girl who was on the boat."

Donovan tossed his rag into the nearby trashcan. "Look, man, I don't run a dating service, and I'm kinda busy." He turned and walked back toward his pile of rope and other gear.

Ryan scrambled after, focusing on the center line of the dock and its wood planks. "No, that's not it. I'm an investigator. My, um, client is looking for his sister. They were separated growing up and ended up in different foster homes. Lost touch. He's desperate to find her."

Donovan stopped and crossed impressively muscled arms across his chest. "Oh, yeah, what's her name?"

"Uh, Livia. Her brother's not sure of the last name. That's all I have to go on."

"Get off my pier."

"No, seriously, I'm not bs-ing you." Ryan fumbled for his wallet and pulled out a laminated card and waved it at him. "Licensed investigator," he said, giving silent thanks for a business not even off the ground yet. "I really need to find her, and you're my last good lead." *Last lead...only lead...whatever.* Even Hamelin couldn't justify dragging him to hell for that one. Ryan gave him the most pleading look he could muster.

Donovan silently mouthed the info on the card, then handed the card back. "Look, dude, I rent to lots of people. Don't know who she was. Now, if you don't mind ..." He turned and continued toward the *Mulligan.*

Ryan stayed on him. "Tall, leggy, long brown hair. She was on your boat in Nevis when the tall ship *Kalmar Nyckel* came through for the 1812 enactments. Maybe she has a connection to the *Kalmar.* There was somebody else in the boat, dressed up like a reenactor."

"Best ask the *Kalmar,* then." Donovan began tossing flotation jackets out of the *Mulligan,* onto the pier. "Look, bud, it sounds like you've got a big job ahead of you, but it's not my problem." When Ryan didn't budge, he pulled his cell phone out and began tapping. "How about you discuss it with the police?

Ryan put his hands up in surrender. "Okay, okay, leaving." He scooted back down the pier. Hamelin was in the same spot he had left him in, *in the zone* again. Ryan prodded him with his foot. "Come on, swami, dead end. You're good with those. Says he doesn't know her. Now what?"

Hamelin got up slowly, stretching out his long frame in unhurried movements that reminded Ryan of a cat. "No surprise there. Let's drive."

Ryan swore an oath as he wheeled around on him. "You *knew*? You let me come all the way over here, and the whole time you *knew*?"

Hamelin threw him a look of warning as he waltzed past. "You wanted to find Ahoy, and you did. One less thing on your list. Don't throw away life's smaller moments, Ryan James. It was a nice ride and we got to share some much-needed bonding time." He headed for the car at a brisk walk. "And you're safely out of Nevis."

"You demon's spawn!" Ryan said, scurrying after him. "I'm not driving anywhere unless it's going to help." He imagined his hands around Hamelin's neck and liked the way they fit. For about five seconds. Hamelin's payback might be hell. He stopped chasing and pulled the local listings out of a nearby Realtor's box. "I'll leave you here," he said, waving the colorful pamphlet at the immortal. "Year-round rentals!"

Hamelin didn't seem inclined to spar. When he reached the car, he jiggled the handle on the locked door a few annoying times and waited without comment.

The buzz of Ryan's phone preempted his next biting remark. He considered ignoring it, just like the rest of his calls this morning. He checked the caller ID. It was Bennie.

"What's up?" he asked, still fuming as he climbed into the car.

"Where are you, Ryan?"

There was a discomforting tone in the question. "What's wrong?"

"Other than not knowing where my boss is, when he's coming back, or what I should do about Delaney opening up a new bar down the street—which, by the way, is said to be competing for the Tippy … You picked a bad time to check out, Ryan. You've asked the right question, though. *What's wrong?* We need some direction back here, that's what's wrong."

Patient, even-tempered Bennie being testy? Guilt descended. "Yeah, I'm sorry, Bennie. It's complicated."

"Life generally is. Are you due back soon, or do we need to schedule some Skype time?"

As Ryan began backing out of his parking space, a vintage Volkswagen Beetle zipped behind him, cutting him off. "Crazy drivers," he muttered, adding a few other choice words. "What, Bennie? … No, crazy drivers … No, sorry, you have my full attention. Nothing's panning out here. I'm coming home."

He checked traffic and resumed backing. "Be there in a couple—"

He dropped the phone as Marie McGallagher hopped out of the little red Beetle.

Chapter Eighteen
More than Life Itself

She was every bit as beautiful as he remembered her. Tall and willowy, she moved with the ease of someone who was aware of how beautiful she was but didn't care. Ryan snapped a picture as she made her way toward the *Mulligan*.

There were now two guys tending the boat. Marie gave lying Donovan a quick hug and then planted a lingering wet one on the new guy. Ryan fought the urge to go punch the guy's lights out as she let his hands roam to places where only the intimately acquainted went. They were a mismatch if Ryan ever saw one. Mr. Touchy Feely was your average desk jockey with a long commute and no time to work out. His long gym shorts and plain dark T-shirt screamed "landlubber and computer nerd." There was something vaguely familiar about him. The reenactor driving the boat that first day?

Hamelin cleared his throat. "Ryan James."

Ryan ignored him and opened his door.

Hamelin piled out the other side and intercepted him halfway around the car. "Look at me!" Hamelin said.

Ryan stopped, dragging his eyes away from her to engage him. "Quick," he said, "before she disappears again."

"She has a happy new life, and a loving one by the look of it,"

Hamelin said. "Walk away and let her be. You haven't done anything egregious yet, but we are at a crossroads. If you interfere, this will not turn out well."

"Then you shouldn't have given me her name."

Ryan tried to look away but was unable to break loose from the intensity of Hamelin's stare. The winsome and preoccupied Hamelin was gone, in his place the focused, demanding immortal who couldn't be pushed around.

"Please, Hamelin," he said gesturing helplessly toward the boat. He felt his tongue cleave to the roof of his mouth as Hamelin's control on him intensified. He pleaded with his eyes.

"Nevis is now crawling with my coworkers. I couldn't let you stay there. Amsterdam showed me that you're willing to give up your life to reunite with Livia, so I needed some way to keep you out of town and keep you from doing something stupid. If you love her as much as you say, you'll sacrifice what you think you want, for the security she needs. It's that simple. Now, get back in the car."

Ryan flashed through the past few hours: Hamelin's good mood, his *helpfulness*—and all of it just part of a web of manipulation and deceit. "I should have known it was too easy. Is there anything real and true about you? Just curious."

Hamelin didn't respond, and they stood for a moment locked in a silent emotional tug-of-war.

"The moratorium you spoke of," Ryan said. "It's in force now? Death the same as ever, but no procurement of souls? No deliveries to heaven or hell?"

"You are correct."

"Then the force of law is against you, your threats are empty, and you are powerless to touch me." Ryan squeezed his eyes shut. The mesmerizing effect of Hamelin's gaze broke like the snap of a dry twig. "Get out of my way." Ryan shoved past Hamelin and started for the pier. He took three steps and stopped short. The dock was deserted. The only activity was the *Mulligan* pulling away from the dock and heading out into the channel. At the helm sat Donovan with Marie beside him, and the nine-to-fiver draped all over her.

Ryan took off at a run, shouting, arms waving. No one in the boat seemed to notice, and as it slipped farther away, Ryan ran out of pier. Without hesitating, he took a flying leap out into the bay, hit the water like a cannonball, and sank like a concrete block.

The cold water sent a jolt of reality through him. He couldn't swim. He struggled toward the light at the surface and momentarily pulled his head above water, sputtering and gasping for air. He saw Hamelin, frozen in place on the dock. Just watching. He went under a second time. Somehow, he had always known that it would be by water. Even when one had his own personal soul runner, death was not a negotiation. No one cheated fate.

***

As he watched Ryan go under again, Hamelin cursed the devil and all things unholy. Should he save him or let life—and death—take its natural course a second time? He slowed time ever so slightly, pulled out his manual, and consulted his list of postmoratorium pickups. In just a few earthly hours, it had grown substantially. But there was no Ryan Thomas listed there. Likewise, there was no listing under his pre-mulligan name, James Hardy.

Hamelin looked up briefly and noted Ryan taking another dunk. A bit of a pickle. Was Ryan on someone else's list, or had fate dictated that Hamelin should save him? Or had the soul fallen between the cracks of recordkeeping, never to show up on anyone's schedule?

He looked away from the water and turned his senses deep within. He caught not a glimmer of another soul runner remotely connected to this death. He looked out across the murky water again. Ryan was nowhere in sight, and the ripples where he had been a moment ago were beginning to dissipate and smooth. *God, help us all.* He tossed his notebook onto the decking and dived into the water.

Reaching Ryan, Hamelin grabbed him by the collar and hauled him up to the water's surface. Then he threw an arm across Ryan's chest and towed him to shore, where several frantic bystanders helped pull him onto dry land. He watched silently as the bartender vomited up bay water. He would never understand mortals and the discomfort they visited upon themselves. When he seemed to be finished, Hamelin knelt beside him.

Ryan looked up at him with tired, haunted eyes. "Why'd you wait so long?" he whispered. "You *know* I can't swim."

"We are this close to getting things under control," Hamelin said pinching his thumb and forefinger together, "and you try to off yourself. Perhaps, I should have let you finish it."

Hamelin left him to suffer and went off to retrieve his notebook. It was exactly where he had left it, which was good. Possession by a mortal was forbidden, its use potentially catastrophic provided said hypothetical mortal survived long enough to try. He decided to check his transportee list to make sure Ryan still wasn't on it. At least, that was his intent. Try as he might, he could not get the book open. He shook it, dug his fingernails into the gilt-edged paper, and tried to will it open with the mighty force of his immortal will. But alas, to no avail. The manual remained sealed as the pages held fast to their cover and each other.

He took a deep breath and turned the notebook over, examining it from front to back and end to end. It looked the same. And since no acrimonious chastisement echoed in his ears, and no slighted soul runner hung about waiting to chew him out for interrupting his assignment, Hamelin was positive this wasn't Ryan Thomas's time to cross over. So why had they locked him out of his book?

He glanced over at Ryan and the crowd he was attracting. Sudden insight clubbed him like a Neanderthal fending off a rival. He was *so* wrong. Whether Ryan Thomas's name was on one of the lists or not, his time had indeed come. And passed. Instead of transporting his soul, Hamelin had saved his life by direct divine intervention—a clear violation of Section 3: *Interfering with Mortality, and Related Issues.* He looked up at the storm clouds that had suddenly begun to roll in, and half expected a lightning bolt to take them all out and erase this whole sordid little affair. They needed to get off this pier.

He hurried back to Ryan—who was now sitting up and talking—and shooed away the gawkers. Then he hauled him to his feet and walked him back to his car.

"How far did she get?" Ryan asked as he dried off with a T-shirt from his trunk. He took several faltering steps toward the pier.

"Gone. Give me your keys," Hamelin demanded, holding out his hand.

Ryan ignored him and climbed into the driver's seat. And there he sat, thinking, vegetating—Hamelin wasn't quite sure which.

"Drive," Hamelin growled, "or I will remove you by force and chuck you into that poor excuse for a back seat."

Ryan responded by coughing up disgusting brown liquid and spitting it into the hem of the T-shirt. When he finished, he wadded the whole mess up and tossed it into the back. "Don't you have any compassion?" he asked, reclining his head against the headrest and closing his eyes.

"More than you realize." Hamelin tapped his fingers on the door frame. He needed cooperation even more than he needed to lecture. He looked down at the manual lying uselessly in his lap. "Your dive into the water has inexplicably set things in motion. And in ways that I cannot relate to you. Start this car or else I will leave you stranded with a malfunctioning Carrera and a hitch-hiking thumb bent like the lowercase 'r.' Marie is headed for Nevis, and if we don't head her off, she's a dead woman."

Ryan's eyes popped open. "No more tricks?"

Hamelin ran his hand down the cover of the book that defined the very purpose of his existence. "None. We are in a most serious dilemma."

"Now you're talking." Ryan took off with the conviction of someone with an angel as his copilot.

Chapter Nineteen
Coat of Many Pockets

Ryan had never farmed, but he was pretty clear on the concept that if one didn't put in the work, there would be no harvest. So as they barreled westbound on Route 50, he ploughed through all the facts as he knew them, turning them over one at a time, trying to make sense of it all.

"We were standing right there. She had every opportunity to walk over to us," he mumbled. "No need to go all the way back to Nevis." And then louder, 'If her soul is calling to you, why didn't she hunt us down in the parking lot?" The question was more rhetorical than anything else. Since they left Saint Paul, Hamelin had refused to engage in any conversation. And Ryan was fairly certain he hadn't shifted in his seat once in the past hour.

"Nevis had a stronger pull. It's overrun with soul runners."

"What kind—"

Ryan swerved to the right, shot across two lanes of traffic and came to a skidding halt in the gravel of the shoulder. He slammed the Carrera into park and put on his hazard lights.

Hamelin didn't so much as flinch. "I don't believe we have time for Cracker Barrel," he said, turning to gaze at the local businesses strung like beads along the service road to their right. "Do I need to drive?"

Country cooking was the farthest thing from Ryan's mind. In his brooding, he had almost missed the highway sign: "Last exit before Chesapeake Bay Bridge. Slower traffic right lane." He stared at the sign for a moment and then looked past it to the electronic billboard an eighth of a mile down the road. One lane on the three-lane westward span of the bridge had been designated as eastbound. The westbound span now ran two-way traffic. It was a daily occurrence to accommodate the flood of rush-hour commuters fleeing to the idyllic Eastern Shore from the burden of jobs in Washington, DC, and the Maryland Western Shore. He had enough trouble crossing the four-mile bridge during nonrush, when everyone around him was traveling in the same direction. Now eastbound rush-hour traffic would barrel past him, and his heart palpitated. Ahead lay four miles of a gephyrophobic's and aquaphobic's worst nightmare: narrow bridge lanes, no shoulder, and vistas that invited endless speculation about the almost two-hundred-foot fall to the choppy water below.

"Not your time," Hamelin said as if reading his mind. "Now, either drive or I leave you. And if you can't man up by sunset, call the Maryland Department of Transportation and have someone drive you across. It's a lovely service for chickens like you."

Ryan felt his shirt sticking to him and could hear the pounding of his own heart. Every second counted. If they didn't make it across, who would help Marie? "No wonder you have no friends," he mumbled. "Please don't go anywhere until we're on the other side." He inhaled deeply and accelerated back into the lanes of traffic.

As they ascended to the bridge's summit, the decking rattled under the weight of traffic, and Ryan felt the steel structure sway. To avoid eastbound traffic sweeping past his left shoulder, he stayed to the far right. He could hear Hamelin's fingernails tapping on the window glass, but the immortal refrained from commenting on either the irritation he was feeling or whatever had caught his attention. Ryan ground his teeth together and kept his eyes glued on the live chickens in the blue and yellow Perdue semi in front of them.

"That one's caught the breeze nicely!" Hamelin suddenly announced.

Spiders ran up Ryan's arms, and he tried to squeeze the steering wheel into submission. "Shh! This is hard enough without you remarking on what's *down* there."

"Calm yourself. We're on the downside."

Ryan peeled his eyes from the bumper in front of him and sneaked a glance around. The bridge span was flattening out, and they were nearing the broad beach of Sandy Point State Park, stretching off to his right.

Ryan loosened his grip, and when they hit the Western Shore, he floored it. The Carrera zipped through the congestion in Edgewater, muscled its way around the traffic circles in Lothian and Friendship, and barreled past Sollars Wharf on the outskirts of Nevis. Soon, they were flying past the ruins of collapsed warehouses on the bayside, and tidy bungalows on the other.

Ryan knew this road well, but he still struggled to keep the Carrera tight in the curves. The road would soon fork: Boyd's Turn heading away from the shore toward higher ground, and Sollars Wharf Road hugging the shore as it became Main Street. "Which way, Hamelin?" Ryan asked.

Hamelin pushed up in the seat. "Slow down. I'm not sure."

Ryan took his foot off the accelerator. "You don't know? You have the capabilities of a freaking GPS. Open up that notebook you've been hugging for the last two hours and give me something definitive. Otherwise, I'm heading downtown."

Hamelin slid the notebook inside his jacket. "To know for sure, I'd have to change her status from pending to active. That, in turn, would put her on the activity report and make her mortal existence even more obvious. I do believe that to be at cross-purposes to our goal. The soul is already calling like a beacon in dark waters. Amending her status would ramp that up considerably."

Ryan checked his rearview mirror and braked to a crawl. "Yeah, well, I've been pondering that very thought while you've been sitting there pouting. Something's not right here, Hamelin. If her soul is already pitching a hissy fit, why didn't she approach you at Lofter's?"

An exasperated sigh floated over from the passenger seat. "Because something else is at work here, and it's inexplicably driving her this way." Hamelin unbuckled his passenger restraint, and the seat belt alarm began to chime. "Pull over."

"Martin?"

Hamelin grunted. "Suffice it to say that we are being attacked on many fronts, Ryan James. It will take both our efforts to find and protect her as well as ourselves. And it must be soon. Now, let me out. I need a quiet place."

"You've had the last two hours of quiet ..."

Ryan didn't need to look to know that Hamelin's eyes were now all over him with a searing heat he could feel through his shirt. "I'll let you off at Vanessa Hardy's. Remember that, right? Where you deserted me? Remained outside while I was trapped in my unconscious battling my black-hearted alter ego Ryan Llewellyn?"

"Certainly," Hamelin said, shifting in his seat. "A necessary activity and satisfactory outcome, as I recall." He pointed out his window to the bungalows they were passing. "Here will do."

Ryan raised a palm to hold him at bay. "We're almost there. You'll seek me out at the Phoenix when you have something?"

"Too risky. *Go home.*"

Ryan reached over and pulled his cell phone free from its Bluetooth adapter. "Take this. You know how to use one of these things, right? Power button here—"

"Why do I deal with you?" Hamelin pulled it out of his hand, and it disappeared somewhere inside his coat.

I have no idea, Ryan thought. He also wondered how many pockets Hamelin had. Probably many, like a magician or a professional shoplifter. With Hamelin, nothing was quite as it seemed, and even now he didn't fully trust him.

As they rolled toward the heart of downtown, the once widely spaced bungalows bunched closer together, and low-rise commercial buildings began popping up. Hamelin was mumbling, and it sounded at times as if he were arguing with himself. Ryan let him be and concentrated on pedestrian traffic.

They were to Chestnut Street, three blocks from the center of town, when Hamelin's hand shot out and grabbed the steering wheel. "Here," he said, swerving the car toward an old brick building with stately white columns.

Ryan slapped his hand away and pulled to the curb. "Damn it," he said, turning on him. "What is *wrong* with you?" Then he *really* looked at Hamelin. The immortal was pallid, his gaze unfocused. "My God, what's wrong, Hamelin?"

Hamelin ignored or missed the question. He hopped out, circled behind the car, and struck out toward the waterfront. Head down, shoulders drawn up as if a cold wind were buffeting his ears. Ryan watched him quickly disappear down the boardwalk.

A tidal wave of helplessness washed over him. He was now a

benchwarmer in a cosmic game he had no business being associated with in the first place, yet he was positive he would fully experience the euphoria of victory or the misery of defeat.

He looked at the columned building next to him. Probably once a bank, it had relinquished any semblance of dignity long ago. Gone were the days of money deals and saving for the American dream. The place served cheeseburgers to the great unwashed. He went inside. *They* would never find him here.

Chapter Twenty
Separating the Tick from the Tock

Hamelin followed the beachfront promenade until foot traffic disappeared and the retail trade petered out. And when the pathway narrowed into a planked walkway with handrails, he followed that, too. Sprawling private homes dotted the coast, perched high on the bluff overlooking the Chesapeake Bay. At the end of the walkway, he took stairs down to a secluded beach. A prominent blue and white sign proclaimed, "*Brownie's Beach. No glass or littering.*" It also included an image of a dog with a diagonal red slash through it. More rules. Was there no reliance on common sense anymore?

Sitting down on dry sand just above the jagged line of wave-polished pebbles left by the high tide, he tried again to open his notebook. It may as well have been cast of stone. He wanted to hurl it out into the surf—just throw it away and wait until someone came and got him. And they would. And he didn't care. Much.

His official notice of suspension had been short on details. There was no direct accusation and no directive to come home. He feared leaving, for if he returned home to plead his case, he might be forbidden to revisit earth. That would leave his remaining mulligans easy pickings for zealots like Martin, and in all good conscience, he couldn't do that. *Conscience.* The more of one he developed, the more contrary he became, which got him into even deeper trouble. Should he go running back to the comforts of the deeper collective soul, confessing sins and showing contrition? What were the consequences for not doing so?

As if he were unfolding wings, he stretched his arms out with palms up and raised his face to the sky. The strong summer sun worked its heat deep into his being, and the soft breeze made it feel as if he had taken flight.

"Luke?"

Nothing. He searched again. Silence. He could almost feel the barrier bouncing his plea earthward again. It seemed that even his friends had turned their backs to him. He dropped his arms.

If that was the way it must be … He tucked his manual away and contemplated a short, sweet life on Brownie Beach, free of responsibilities. High overhead could be heard the faint piping of a solitary bald eagle as it lazily followed a warm wind current. Nearby, a cluster of brown and white speckled sandpipers stalked, tails a-bobbing as they picked through the wet sand for midges and snails. Hamelin watched a thin sheet of water slide across the sand, chasing them back. Its foam-tipped edge reached an unspoken boundary and then withdrew back into the bay. It was the natural order of things. All creation knew its role and limits—except humankind, who lived in discord and unhappiness as it struggled vainly to expand its niche, reap perceived entitlements, and achieve its full *potential.* As if the divine plan could be improved upon. He sadly shook his head and looked around. As lovely and serene as this was, he knew he would grow bored here.

Had he reached beyond his own limits? Was he trying to improve on the plan? Was there to be no discretion and compassion in administering the law? It seemed that would be the higher order of understanding. The elaborate and highly mechanized soul-collecting system had proved to be no better than anything he'd seen designed by mortals. Designed by an order of beings evolved beyond the mortal—but not yet fully immortal—the system failed to discern the intricacies of the human condition and respond accordingly. If God wanted to end a life, why all these hoops and hurdles to fetching and delivering?

The discordant cawing of crows disrupted his thoughts. Some distance down the beach, two figures walked near their squawking and fluttering. The shorter one, in heavy, dark clothing, trudged along the surf's edge sand with a fishing pole slung over his shoulder. The other, in billowy white, took the higher ground and appeared to carry no burdens. Hamelin considered how the land narrowed and tailed off into the water at that point, and the steepness of the timbered shoreline. Where had they come from, and how had he not seen them earlier?

Hamelin desired no companionship. He got up, brushed the sand from his clothes, and turned to leave.

"Wait! Don't let me chase you off."

Hamelin looked back. Where there had been two, now he saw only the man with the fishing pole. Hamelin's eyes flitted to the spot where he had just seen both people together. The stranger's languid movements were somehow deceptively fast, or he had increased his pace. Hamelin nodded to him. "No problem. Have a blessed day."

The man continued walking toward him until he stood right next to him. "And you as well. And I apologize; you were deep in thought." He turned to gaze out across the bay. "It's a wonderful place to solve problems."

"No problems," Hamelin said, taking a better look at him. His clothes were loose and ill-fitting, but the toned arms hinted at a youthful vitality and fitness. "Do I know you?"

"Morgan Kant," the stranger said, extending a hand.

Hamelin looked at it and shook his head. "I shake hands only on business deals."

"And who says it isn't?" Morgan replied. He walked a few steps up the beach away from the surf and sat down cross-legged on the sand. One of the crows that had been following him flapped down nearby. He gave it a look, and it joined the rest of the flock in a nearby pine tree.

I don't make a habit of intruding," Morgan said. "Generally, people figure things out for themselves, but even back there"—he pointed in the direction he had just come from—"I could see you going around in circles. Duty can be an honor or a burden. If it's of any value, here is the question I see you struggling with. Do I follow the *letter* of the law, or the *spirit* of the law? Is soul running an *end* that should be accomplished as a rational act without question? Or is the transportation of souls a *means* to an end? And if so, whose end? The soul's? Yours? The powers that be?"

Hamelin shifted his weight from one foot to the other and laughed uncomfortably. "What?"

Morgan picked up a handful of sand and let it slowly spill through his fingers. "Did it ever occur to you that they're holding you back? If you were allowed to operate on your own, wouldn't you develop the requisite compassion and wisdom to get you out of where you are now? I mean, it's a bit naive to think that if you merely do what you're told, you'll somehow eventually transform into a higher state of being."

"Who sent you?"

"It's not so much an issue of being sent. It's more a matter of going where I'm needed. I was out fishing, and when I realized you were distressed, I thought I'd offer support."

Hamelin studied the fishing pole. "Where's your bait?"

"I've spent it all," Morgan said.

"And your catch? Your creel?"

"It's more the satisfaction of getting the nibble." Morgan dug his heels into the sand as he stretched his legs out to their full length.

Hamelin studied him a moment, rubbing his thumbnail across his lip as he took the man's measure. "I see. No nibbles here, spawn of evil. Go fish somewhere else. I don't need the likes of you screwing with my head."

Morgan smiled as he studied the horizon. "Are you sure? Hell can be shockingly unpleasant."

"How do you know I'm going to hell? Redemption is possible to the very end."

"You've said it yourself. Why would anyone expect an immortal to change? *Really* change. It's a bit like marrying a flawed person with the expectation of changing them. Doesn't happen. And how do I know about you? Because you're near the end. Every soul—even yours—is on someone's list. Why is it you've never heard of a fellow soul runner taking another soul runner to the unholy void? We both know that some end up there."

"You run souls—"

"For every tick there is a tock," Morgan said, rocking his index finger back and forth like the pendulum on a metronome. He chuckled to himself and got up. "I've said my piece. I'll leave you to think about it. If you're going to go down in flames, why not put your heart and soul into it, Hamelin? At least know that you tried your best, even if no one else was willing to. See you soon, my friend."

As he watched Morgan climb the stairs, Hamelin felt an aching hollowness. Had he fallen so far that evil personified had personally come trolling for him? He might be in deeper trouble than he thought. He turned back to the water and closed his eyes, letting the water's ebb and flow disconnect him from his physical surroundings. "Luke," he thought, reaching out again to his closest friend. "Luke?"

This time Luke responded immediately. "For the sake of all of us, where are you? Scratch that. I don't need or want to know. I'm just going to tell you where you should have been. Nevis. A mandatory meeting. They're asking about you, and I heard they're pulling your union card."

"I don't know about that," Hamelin said. "Is that all you've heard?"

"Just rampant, terrible gossip. What have you been doing?"

"Nada. If you hear anything legit, let me know. I'm really flying blind here." Hamelin got up and walked down to the water's edge and then back up again to a steeply rising bank covered in switchgrass and little bluestem. "Where are you now? Because I really need you to head back to your office and do something for me."

"Your request smacks of *sneakery,*" said Luke. "No can do. We're under a work moratorium, remember?"

Hamelin walked out far enough to the water for the approaching wave surge to kiss the tips of his black Nikes. "This is not about work. I'm trying to do the right thing here. I need you to pull up a list of Martin's—"

"Whup, nada—"

"… assigned transports for the last year and cross-check it with—"

"There is no way to cross-check with arrivals. You know that. If it could be done, you'd be out on your ear by now."

"… travel itinerary."

There was a moment of silence; then Luke laughed. "Wait. Are you suggesting you can't collect a soul that you can't touch?"

"Exactly! Smart boy." Hamelin put his hand protectively over the useless notebook in his pocket. "I'll bet my book he doesn't follow through on everything he's assigned. If he's supposed to pick up a soul in snowy Cleveland, he can't very well do it from a ski slope in Vail. I'm wondering, what kind of lazy trail of mulligans has *he* left behind?"

"Aha! You're good, Mr. Russell."

Hamelin thought about the angler's prediction. He felt pretty sure he was more in a gray area, with decided leanings toward the dark, corrupt side. "I'm in a hard place, Luke. Help me. I've got to make things right, and it can't wait."

There was a momentary silence. "No. Just because I admire your scheming from an intellectual point of view doesn't mean I'd jump off a bridge with you. This is a pissing match with Martin, and I've told you to let it go. That's still the best I can do for you. Do you really comprehend the trouble you're in, or have you decided you're above it all? You can't blow this off."

"Jeez Maries," Hamelin said, turning to gaze at the decked-out minimansion above him. "I'm not under any false impressions or sense of grandiosity. They've suspended me, okay? I can't get the book open, and I have no other information. I'm defenseless. I'm in Nevis, but if I leave, I might never get back. There are good people here, and they don't deserve to be picked off like flies by our self-aggrandizing, hypercritical leader. Please. You're my lifeline, man."

"Nevis? Then why couldn't you get yourself to the meeting, dude? Sorry, no."

Hamelin could almost see Luke shaking his head in frustration. He stepped on an oyster shell tumbling in the receding surf and picked it up. "I hate to do this, but remember that tear we went on last spring in the Adirondacks?"

"Bastard."

"Brother."

Luke sighed. "How much time?"

"Don't know, but make it quick, okay? AWAB has been skulking around, and I feel it won't be long before they nail me for nontransportation and the "M" word that shall not be named. I need a bargaining chip." Hamelin could feel the tension between them and visualized Luke rolling his eyes. "Come on, Luke. I just had a visit from temptation himself. Even Beelzebub thinks I'm ripe for the picking. Yes?"

"Oh, God have mercy." There was quiet on Luke's end, and then, "All right. But this makes us even on the Adirondacks thing." Luke broke the connection.

Hamelin tossed the oyster shell high up into the air and watched a nearby seagull dive toward it. If Luke didn't come through, no one could.

He looked in the direction Morgan had gone. Had he moseyed on, or was he waiting farther along the way? Hamelin decided to scale the hillside. There would be no "see you soon."

Chapter Twenty-One
Screw Them All

Curtis stood on the sidewalk admiring the flashing red and blue neon *Delaney's* sign. He stepped back to get the whole affect. The curve of the neon tubes mimicked the tendrils of vine carved into the stone lintel above the door. Nice touch.

He looked down the street. The Phoenix, first bar on the Tippy list for Hamelin's group, was down there somewhere. Group members were hitting that one hard. That was where Martin wanted him. Truth be told, Martin's obsession with what went on in this bayside community was a little unsettling. In fact, this whole contest thing was an embarrassment—immortals running around debasing themselves with liquor.

His eyes returned to Delaney's. He liked the neon. And he hated the condescending way Martin had approached him. As if he needed to kowtow to someone like Martin to get ahead. Screw him, screw impartiality, and screw the whole newbie bonding-experience rigamarole. Maybe he'd visit the Phoenix, but he was going to throw his weight behind this bar and see how much he could sway the contest, test his influence. Who would know? Certainly not Martin. He was up to something else.

Curtis entered the building. Despite the promising neon sign, his initial impression was disappointment. The entrance was a nearly empty storefront barren of pizzazz and warmth. He walked past a series of wooden bookshelves that lined the wall facing the street, and up to a wide reception counter at the far end. "Big wheels keep on turning," he said to the beefy gentleman sitting there.

Heavy-lidded eyes studied him a moment over the rim of a Styrofoam coffee cup. It was not quite four in the afternoon—a little late to be shaking off sleep, and much too early to be calling it a day. The bruiser grunted once, put down the cup, and moved to the shelf nearest the counter, where he pulled out a yellow-covered book. The big guy's solid build and enormous biceps suggested he wasn't a bookish sort, so Curtis wasn't surprised when the right half of the bookcase swung smoothly out to reveal a doorway. Curtis nodded and stepped inside. The bookcase closed behind him with a quiet swoosh, and a white-shirted waiter ushered him into the only speakeasy in Nevis.

"Bar or table, sir?" the young man asked.

Curtis's eyes swept the place, settling on the slim brunette in orange sitting at the far end of the bar. Now, this was more like it. "Bar's fine," he said. He ordered a local beer, bartender's choice, and settled down near the attractive woman. He might be dead, but his urges weren't. He couldn't seal the deal, of course, but a little titillation never hurt anyone. She returned his smile but showed no particular interest in conversing. He leaned in her direction. "Buy you another?" he asked.

"Sure," she said. Her squeaky voice destroyed his sensual fantasy.

He sighed to himself and took a second look around. There were two intriguing areas. The smaller room was closed off behind glass. It appeared to be a sports bar with a moatlike countertop in the center, surrounded by high-top tables. Several flat-screen monitors were playing in various corners of the room. Curtis was in the larger, main room, with an equally impressive bar and linen-covered dining tables. It was modern and glitzy: chrome, mirrors, and clean lines. The sweet notes of Billie Holiday singing softly in the background gave the place a grounded, earthy feel. A nice change from the ethereal afterlife. Curtis paused to identify the song—"All of Me," if he was not mistaken.

There were few patrons in the main room, but the murmur of voices and clink of silverware and glass gave it a subdued, cozy character. Impressive. And bonus points for Holiday. He mentally tallied a tentative bar score for the contest. And then the bartender slid him a can of beer and a glass. Curtis studied the clock face and yellow black-eyed Susans on the label. Then he lopped off twenty points for serving him a metal can.

Before a comment could tumble out of his mouth, the waiter said, "Watershed Moment, from Jailbreak Brewing. Not many bars can offer it. It's limited batch, with profits going to restore historic Ellicott City after the flooding." He paused a moment and then added, "but if you'd like something on tap …"

Curtis dismissed the offer with a wave. "Distinctive. I like it." He took a sip of the excellent Belgian ale and added the points back. Over the top of his glass, he watched the approach of a tall man in a dark sports jacket.

"Delaney, at your service," the man said, thrusting out a hand. "I pride myself on getting to know all my patrons, and I don't believe we've met. First time? May I ask where you got the password? Just so I have a feel for which of my advertising platforms is working," he quickly added. His eyes were guarded despite his smile. Curtis silently deducted five points from hospitality.

"Name's Curtis. Curtis Merriweather," he said, returning a firm handshake. "And you have me dead to rights. I'm a newbie. The password was just a case of knowing the right people. I tried the place down the street. The Phoenix? Too manic. I'm searching for somewhere I can have a quiet pint. Leave the pressures behind while I work on a big project." He scanned the room, nodding. "This place fits the bill."

"Local?"

"No place too long. You name it, I've been there. Just hit town. Like what I'm seeing."

"Doing something for the town?"

Curtis bobbed his head. "You might say. Right now, it's all about bars."

Delaney cocked his head. "The Tippy? I thought you looked familiar! You gave me the invitation."

Curtis smiled and picked up the menu. "Why don't we start with your signature dish and another Watershed to wash it down? Then we can talk. All right?"

Delaney let out a sharp whistle. "Fred! Mr. …"

"Just Curtis."

"Give my friend Curtis whatever he wants." He turned back to his customer. "Will there be other judges in town?"

"Sh-h-h." Curtis tipped his head, beckoning Delaney to come closer. "I'm expecting another one anytime now from the Phoenix, your closest competitor. Tall drink of water. Dark, wavy hair. He's one to watch—a senior judge with lots of pull."

Delaney scratched his jowl. "Haven't seen him. He'll make his way here?"

"Most definitely," Curtis said, nodding. "And others. But if they don't stay long, forget it. You don't have a ghost of a chance. The duration of the visit reflects your chances of winning. In fact, there's a formula for it all—something inversely proportional to something else. And at some point, that number is divided by pi."

Delaney sat down beside him. "You don't say."

"Oh, absolutely." Curtis eyed him over a fresh ale. The bar owner was licking his lips. "Yeah, I never was good in math, but I know the rules inside and out."

"Anything you want, man," Delaney murmured. "On the house."

"Sorry, Delaney, couldn't do that. It'd be cheating." Curtis put down his drink and surveyed the joint. The clientele had decreased by one, and the music had moved from "All of Me" to Jimmy Dorsey's "Green Eyes." "How long you been open?"

"First week. Doesn't seem too fair to include me in a contest when we just opened."

"Fair? You're misunderstanding the situation. You weren't even in the initial field of competitors, but the powers that be felt that your potential was off the charts and that it would be a shame if you weren't included. Actually, you're one lucky son of a gun. What's your handicap?"

Delaney looked puzzled. "Handicap? Not following you, sir."

Curtis slumped back in his seat, looking suitably astonished. "Someone really should have explained all this. If you're new, they gave you a handicap to make things more sporting. What's your number?"

"I don't have any number. If you gave me the invitation, aren't *you* supposed to do that?"

Curtis stiffened. "Oh, no. That's not my job."

"Well, who should I be asking?"

"No one. You'll never win if you make a nuisance of yourself. As it is, I've gone out on a limb telling you this much."

Delaney's face fell. "Then it is what it is: an uneven playing field."

Curtis chuckled to himself. Delaney was trying to be cool, but he wanted this bad—bad enough to cheat. And he was vulnerable enough to let himself be jerked all over the place. A fun one. Curtis let him twist a bit. "Unless you had the book . . ."

Delaney perked up. "I have Amazon Prime. What book?"

Curtis smiled benevolently. "Bennie Bertollini, the bartender down at the Phoenix. His book. Stuff he's compiled over the last twenty years. It's everything you need to know about the Tippy. Why, anyone who had that would have the Bible on how to win. You know Mr. Bertollini?"

"Not directly. He referred me for the job I got at the Phoenix, and I got fired on short order when he decided he wanted to come back. No way he's gonna talk to me about what's in his book."

"I get it. Resents you setting up shop down the street."

"Bertollini? Heck, no. He's decent to everybody. There's no reason for bad blood between us, but anybody who's been keeping notes on a contest for twenty years is serious about winning. Our bars are competing against each other, so …" He shrugged.

Curtis nodded and appeared deep in thought. "No doubt about it. That's a tough one. Can't think of anything I could tell you that wouldn't be construed as cheating. If they found out, they'd immediately disqualify you." He scratched his head, then winked at Delaney. "Tell you what. You've been so hospitable, maybe I can offer you a tidbit. Go down and smooth things over; reestablish some ties with this man. See if you might catch a glimpse of what's in the notebook. It's black, about yea big." He motioned with his hands. "He keeps it close, though I've seen him leave it on the counter. But not for long."

"*Steal* it?"

"Oh, heavens, no! Let's not get ourselves into legal trouble. The term would be '*borrow.*' You're going to *borrow* it. If you're smart about it, you might temporarily acquire and then return it with Mr. Bertollini none the wiser. But it would take a deft hand."

Delaney's eyes flickered a moment. "You don't say."

"Oh, I *do* say." Curtis pointed across the room toward a door marked "*Office*." "You have an assistant?"

"Looking at him."

"There you go. There is something I can do for you without getting either of us in hot water. You can't get this place off the ground all by yourself. I can point you in the right direction to get an experienced assistant who could do all the little things you can't get to or don't want to get involved in." Curtis thought a moment, then dismissed the idea with a wave of his hand. "No, even better, I'll get you one. How would you feel about that? No rule-breaking involved."

Delaney eyed him. "What do you want in return?"

"Nothing. Consider it a gift from a fan."

"I'll take all the help I can get."

Delaney tried to shake on it. Curtis ignored the gesture, and his gaze shifted to the brunette as she tucked a bill under her empty glass and slid off her stool. There was nothing overtly suggestive about her demeanor, but she was his type, and she was silently sending out some interesting signals. Newbies weren't instantaneously scrubbed of all temptation when they arrived in the hereafter. Continuing the process of purification and working one's way into heaven was generally a long process. He didn't fight it, but he did work at reducing it. He followed the regulations in his St. Peter-issued notebook to the letter of the law—unlike Hamelin Russell and some others who bucked the system.

For whatever reason, they didn't seem to understand that playing by the rules could work to their advantage. Following the letter of the law was like receiving a "Get Out of Purgatory Free" card.

Curtis caught her attention and smiled. She returned it. He turned to Delaney and said, "Settled, my new friend. And I'm afraid it's time for me to go." He downed the rest of his brew and reached into his pocket.

"On the house," Delaney said. "Not staying for your meal?"

Curtis gave him a wink. "Not necessary. You have been most accommodating, and Delaney's will receive an excellent rating from me."

Curtis followed the woman out. Leaving the bar was much easier than getting in. Curtis pushed through a clearly marked exit and found himself in an alley—narrow but immaculate. The woman was gone, but as he suspected, she had turned right and headed up onto the main street. He located her heading in the general direction of the Phoenix and followed at a discreet distance. It was a little too soon to be hitting a second bar, but if she did, he was a firm believer in fate and he would consider hitting it, too.

Chapter Twenty-Two
Cutting Out the Middleman

Curtis trailed her all the way to the Phoenix, and the vibes between the two of them were flowing. He watched the exaggerated sway of the woman's hips. Her coyness was a real turn-on. It brought to mind a song from his youth: "Poetry in Motion." Back then, there was a song for everything. Or maybe it was just that back then, you could understand the words. A feeling of something lost pecked at him. He stifled the memory and reminded himself that carnal urges could never be acted on and that greater things awaited in the spiritual realm.

When she reached the Phoenix, the woman suddenly stopped. She put her hand to her wrist, where a watch might have been, and then looked back at him. "Would you have the time?" she asked, turning and walking back toward him.

Curtis locked eyes with her and offered an arch smile. "Daytime?" He drank her in from head to peep toe and then met her eyes again—deep blue and sparkling with titillation. "Curtis Merriweather," he said, offering a gallant half-bow.

She laughed. "Helen Warner. It's a little early to be barhopping."

"That's a bold statement for someone who doesn't even know what time it is. And I wasn't barhopping. I was following you."

For an instant, her eyes widened, and then she seemed to master her surprise. "Now who's being bold?"

"I wouldn't label it as such. But I will admit that if you were to sit down at the bar in there and there was an empty stool next to you, that's the first place I'd go. Buy you a couple?"

"It's a public place." She entered the Phoenix and took a seat at the bar. The bartender was at the other end, dispensing cold IPAs and warm advice. He acknowledged her with a nod and held up his forefinger in a be-with-you-in-a-moment gesture.

Curtis claimed the vacant seat next to her, but his interest immediately shifted to the stocky barkeep. Bennie was the polar opposite of Delaney. He was short and stocky, patient and wise, and had the perfect grandfatherly demeanor for his occupation. Curtis assessed the Phoenix an immediate ten points.

"Forgotten me already?" Helen asked, placing a hand on his arm.

"Heavens, no," Curtis said with a wink. It suddenly occurred to him that Delaney might not need a full-time office assistant. What he needed was an outgoing social director like Helen— "How about introducing me to your friend the bartender over there, and we get this party started?"

Bennie cruised to their end of the bar, busing an empty glass as he came. He acknowledged Curtis with a nod and then looked at Helen. "What'll it be?" he asked.

She ordered soda water with a twist of lime. "Is now a good time, Bennie?" she asked.

"No, hon, not yet." He looked at Curtis. "Don't believe I've had the pleasure. New to the area, or just passing through?"

"Couple days. Nice town."

"Well, then," Bennie said with a wink, "let's make it memorable. I'm Bennie, by the way. What can I get you?"

"How about a local Maryland beer?" Curtis said. "Bartender's choice." Helen was really turning it on now, twittering in his ear, but he was zoned in on Bertollini. Where was the notebook he'd heard the other immortals whisper about? If the man had dedicated years to compiling it, Curtis couldn't imagine it being far from reach. He perused the shelves stocked full of Gray Goose, Johnny Walker, and a goodly selection of what were probably regional brews. Nothing but bottles up there. Nor did he see it lying around on any of the work counters. It had to be on him. He checked Bennie's apron for any large pockets he might have stashed the book in. There were two: one side flat and empty, the other weighted and bulging. A pulse of energy raced through him. Could he artfully lift it undetected, or did he need Bennie to take the smock off?

"Double Duckpin from Union Craft," Bennie said, setting Curtis up with a glass of dark-orange brew with a thick white head. He slid a bowl of crab chips their way. "Got crab balls coming out in a minute. You gotta try 'em."

If Bennie had intended to make small talk, he didn't get the chance. He immediately excused himself and moved toward someone hailing him from the opposite end of the bar. Curtis watched with curiosity as the newcomer walked behind the bar and poured himself a double shot of Maker's Mark. The owner, perhaps?

"You seem to know your way around," Curtis said to Helen. "Who's the new guy?"

Helen leaned past him to get a better look. "Behind the bar? Ryan Thomas. He owns the place."

"Curtis!"

Curtis turned to find Hamelin hovering behind him. His countenance was dark, and he seemed hurried. "Hamelin! I was beginning to wonder if you were still making deliveries."

"No, just fixing loose ends," Hamelin whispered. He took a quick look around. "I see we're here in force."

"Seem to be." Curtis patted the empty stool beside him. "You don't look like you're in the groove of things quite yet. Have a seat and an IPA. Crab balls are coming out shortly."

"Sure, give me a minute. "Restroom?" Hamelin asked Bennie.

Bennie lit up like a sixty-watt bulb. "You're back! Same place as before," he said, pointing past the bar and around the corner. "And a place for you right here when you return. We still need to talk about open-mike night." He turned to Curtis, pointed to the empty stool next to him, and said, "Tilt that up against the bar."

So the two had met before. Fraternization was inappropriate under Tippy contest rules. Curtis's interest intensified as he watched Hamelin disappear around the corner with the Thomas fellow right behind him. He leaned toward Helen and said, "I have a couple of errands to run before I can actually give you all the attention you deserve."

She paused and put her drink down. A long tangerine-hued fingernail tapped out her displeasure on the side of her glass.

"No, really, hon. And you could help me immensely with one of those errands. What do you say?" Curtis reached out and began tracing a pattern on the back of her hand with his finger.

Helen stopped tapping and said "Maybe," but her eyes were sparkling again.

"Delaney. You know, from down the street? He needs me to pick up something here and run it back down to him. But I also have to make a bank deposit. I had enough time to do both before I came in here. Now I'm short on time. Two places, only one person. It sure would help if you could run the package back to him. Then we can meet back up and spend some quality time together."

Her eyes mapped his face. It didn't take a lot to buy her affection, but he could see he didn't quite have her hooked. His mojo was a bit rusty, and his sense of masculinity began to erode.

"You're talking about *today*?

"Oh, absolutely," he said, wrapping his hand around hers.

"Well, all right" she said, starting off her stool. "I'll ask Bennie and take it right over."

"Oh, no," Curtis said, sliding his hand up her arm. "You can't ask Bennie. The matter is a little more delicate than that. It's something personal. Delaney left a diary here, and Delaney wants to get it back with no questions asked and his privacy intact. He thinks he might have left it behind the bar … or maybe in the owner's office." His eyes trailed off in the direction Hamelin and the bar owner had gone. "No, on second thought, I believe he said it was in the office. Yes, that's right—in the office."

"Oh, I can't get in there."

Curtis absently rotated his glass around on the bar top. Hamelin was most assuredly cheating. But the only way he could prove it was to catch Hamelin and Thomas in a tête-à-tête.

"Back in a second," he whispered, and headed for the restrooms. When he rounded the corner, he ignored them and went to the door across the hallway. It was shut, but he could hear voices on the other side. He put his ear up to the door and listened. Hamelin and someone else were in a heated argument about something.

He stepped back and thought a moment. This was what Martin suspected? Fraternization and cheating? His orders had been clear. Curtis was to report back to him on anything suspect, and Martin would decide what to do. But there was nothing ambiguous here. It was dishonesty and fraternization, inappropriate by any measure. It should be reported immediately through normal channels, like any infraction. If Curtis let Martin formalize the complaint, Martin would also reap the accolades. In some cases, that would be okay. Martin could do a lot for him, but Curtis would never get ahead if all his major accomplishments went on someone else's tally. No. Hamelin was a tenured soul runner, and this one was too big to give away. He would catch them red-handed and get the credit himself.

He returned to the door, put his hand on the knob, then hesitated. On the other hand, what were the repercussions of misinterpreting things? He couldn't afford to incur Hamelin's wrath. He had a reputation as a screw-up, but the man had standing nonetheless. No, there would be no barging in on them. He needed to *stumble inadvertently* into the middle of things. He should exploit the weak link—in this case, the mortal. But manipulating a mortal was a major no-no, every bit as egregious as fraternization. So what was he left with? Manipulating something that *wasn't* a mortal.

Curtis closed his eyes and began pulling in the latent energy around him, slowly at first, directing his efforts through the door into the room on the other side—pulling the oxygen out of the space. Conversation on the other side of the door ceased. In his mind, he pictured the pub owner turning blue and flailing in a frantic attempt to draw a breath. When he heard Hamelin cry out, and a crash from within, he shook free of the force, staggering backward several steps into the wall. He flung open the office door and rushed in.

The pub's owner was in a heap on the floor, amid a scattering of papers that he had pulled from the desktop as he fell. Hamelin was leaning over him.

"Help!" Curtis yelled. "We need help in here. Somebody!"

The room quickly filled with people. Bennie rushed past Curtis and fell to his knees next to Hamelin. He put his hand to Thomas' chest. "Ryan, can you hear me? What happened?"

"I don't know," Hamelin said. His hands hovered over Ryan but did not touch him. "As I came out of the bathroom," he lied, "I saw him in here leaning against the desk, gasping for breath. Then he went down like a ton of bricks. He seems to be breathing easier now." His eyes flickered toward the doorway, where Curtis, Helen, and a few others stood transfixed. He held Curtis's gaze a moment before turning back to Ryan.

Curtis ignored the suspicion he saw in Hamelin's eyes. His own eyes were on the small black notebook now lying on the floor between Hamelin and Bennie. The scene was better than he could have hoped for. He moved closer, pulling Helen along with him. "I used to be an EMT," he said, kneeling behind Hamelin but within arm's reach of the notebook. "I think you should call nine-one-one. We'll keep an eye on Mr. Thomas."

Hamelin shifted his body so it was between Curtis and Ryan. Bennie stood up, fumbling for his phone.

"Wait, Bennie. His eyes are opening."

As Hamelin looked at Bennie, Curtis scooped up the notebook and passed it to Helen. She promptly shoved it under her arm and firmly against her ample bosom.

"We'll get out of your way," Curtis said, rising and pushing Helen through the throng of gawkers toward the door.

"Is this Delaney's?" Helen asked, pulling the book out.

"Yes, but not here," Curtis whispered. He took her by the elbow and ushered her out onto the sidewalk. Once outside, he checked over his shoulder, and when he was satisfied that Hamelin wasn't following them, he continued. "If you don't mind, take it right to Delaney. Tell him the notebook is from Curtis. He'll understand."

As she began to protest, he put his finger to her lips. "I'll be right here when you get back." Then he turned her about and gently propelled her toward Delaney's. She was smitten, and if he showered more attention on her, he could probably get all kinds of dirt on what was going on at the Phoenix. Unfortunately, he didn't have the time. He headed off in the other direction.

***

Ryan rejected all the well-meant but unhelpful ministrations and got up. "Fine. I'm fine." He turned to the gawkers at the door. "Sorry for the hubbub. Everything's under control." He shooed them out and locked the door behind the last of them. He turned to find Bennie still on the floor, crawling around on all fours and peering under the desk. Ryan needed him out. He wasn't fine, nothing was making sense, and Hamelin needed to start explaining why. But he found Hamelin similarly occupied in a search of the office, peeking under piles and around Ryan's assorted tchotchkes collecting dust on his cabinets. He didn't think he had been out of it that long. "What did I miss?" he asked them.

Both turned to him with panicked faces. "My notebook," each silently mouthed.

***

Helen found Delaney at the end of the bar in the great room. He was engrossed in paperwork. "Curtis said to give these to you," she said, offering him the notebooks.

He glanced up at her, and there was recognition in his eyes. He looked at the books and frowned. "What?"

Helen's cheeks flushed. "Uh, well ... I have no idea. He said you'd understand. Please ask Curtis." She set them down and fled.

Delaney watched her exit. Was this the office assistant Curtis had promised? The last thing he needed was someone unloading more paperwork on him. He studied the books. If Curtis thought he was going to read these . . . He reached out and flipped open the top one. *Tippy. Tippy. Tippy.* The word jumped out at him down the length of the page. He pulled it closer.

He skimmed through what proved to be a detailed multiyear history of the Tippy contest, with each year demarcated by a colored tab. Each section contained a basic summary of the contest that year, thoughts, and tips for future years.

Delaney closed the book. This had to be a joke. He glanced around for the camera crew of some funniest-video television show.

He took a longer second look. Dates, locations, bar highlights. Holy moly, it really was Bertollini's book! Delaney shoved it underneath the liquor order he had been writing. Getting implicated in a theft was much more serious than starring on some modern variant of *Candid Camera.*

He contemplated the second book. More of the same? It seemed like overkill. He slid it over and pulled at the cover. It wouldn't flip open. He turned it over and searched for some sort of lock or band that held it tight. There wasn't one. He ran his thumb along the gilt fore edge and tried to work a fingernail in between the pages, but it was as if someone had glued them shut. If Curtis was playing with him, he didn't get it. He tossed it into a trash can under the bar.

But this one, he thought as he picked up the Tippy book again—this one he *got.* Curtis had advised him to borrow the book, and now, as if by magic, here it was. Delaney didn't suppose a little borrowing would hurt anyone. And Curtis seemed to be high up in the pecking order of contest judges. It wouldn't do to offend him. How long could he borrow it before *borrowing* turned into *stealing*? And after that, how he would get it back to Bertollini? He buried the notebook in his stuff and headed for his office. He had some serious reading to do. Then he would make Curtis take it back.

Chapter Twenty-Three
Out of My Hands

Curtis made it about ten paces before Hamelin came thundering down the alley after him with a fury that raised the hair on his arms. Although an immortal doing violence to a fellow immortal was rare, it happened. Curtis considered a run for it, but that would be like grabbing a slicker and a bumbershoot to weather a hurricane. Curtis turned, squared his shoulders against the coming onslaught, and waited. Why such upset over a few bumbling mortals?

In seconds, Hamelin was on him, nose to nose, a deep and terrifying power flashing in his eyes. "Where's my book?"

"Your book?" Curtis repeated, frowning. Then his eyes grew wide with understanding. "As in *the* book?"

"Don't play dumb. That might work with the higher-ups, but it's wasted on me. I had it next to me on the floor. What did you do with it?" Hamelin put his hand to Curtis's chest. The touch was slight, but it was warm, and growing alarmingly warmer by the second.

Curtis took a deep, uncomfortable breath. This was not going to be a battle of wits. Unfortunately, he didn't have anything else to work with. "Why on earth would you even put it down?" He tried to step away, but Hamelin matched him step for step.

"Because you took it upon yourself to screw around with a mortal.

You were the only one. Give it to me. *Now.*"

"W-why would I take yours when I have one of my own?"

"A little above your pay grade, *AWAB*. This was Martin's doing, wasn't it? If I hadn't caught you, you'd be in his office right now with it."

"*AWAB?* You've lost me there, Hamelin. Please, if you'll remove your hand ..." He managed to reach into the left side of his jacket and take out a notebook. Then he showed him there was nothing on the right side. Finally, he patted down his empty trouser pockets. "Did you try the bartender? He was there as well."

Hamelin yanked Curtis's book out of his hand and tried to open it. Despite vigorous attempts, his thumb slid uselessly down the gilt pages. Curtis stood speechless, his gaze ping-ponging back and forth between his book and Hamelin's face.

Hamelin uttered an oath. "Obviously, it's yours. Why did you hurt the mortal, in direct violation of Section Eighteen? A most grievous transgression, I might add. As your team leader, I can't let this slide. I've half a mind to send you home. What do you have to say for yourself?"

"I, er, I had no idea that would happen, sir. When I came looking for you, to see if you were ready to push on to the next competitor, I heard you talking. I thought I'd prank you, sir. I had no inkling there was someone with you, let alone a mortal. How was I to know you were in private discussion with the bar owner? The door was closed, and we have a no-fraternization policy."

"There was no fraternization," Hamelin said. "Furthermore, I don't have to explain myself to you. But just to ease your troubled mind, Mr. Curtis, I mistook his office for the lavatory, and he walked in before I could gracefully exit. I was as surprised as anyone. Quite frankly, I find your thinly veiled accusation offensive—"

Curtis raised his hands in protest. "Oh, no, sir. Somehow, that came out all wrong. I didn't mean to …"

Hamlin's eyes flashed, and he seemed to grow even taller. "Stop being concerned about what others are attending to. I'm leading this team, and that's my responsibility. Have you checked the premises for order, vision, and cleanliness? How can you vote if you're not thorough? Stop merely going through the motions, and take your own responsibilities more seriously."

Curtis bit his tongue and nodded. From the little he knew of Hamelin, he had no discipline, his vision was limited to immediate gratification, and his current motives seemed dirty as hell. "Order. Vision. Cleanliness. Got it. That's the last time you'll have to tell me that. And I do apologize." He dropped his head and studied the discarded cigarette butt at his feet. "Are you sending me back, sir?" He held his breath as Hamelin took his time answering.

"Not if you shape up." Hamelin said. "As for this conversation, it never happened. Not a word to anyone, understand? And if I find you've lied to me about the book, there will be no place in the universe too remote, nor benefactor too powerful, to save you." He shoved Curtis's book back at him and stalked back the way he had come.

Curtis waited until he was sure Hamelin wasn't coming back, and then opened his book to the center seam and began thumbing through it. Actually, he wasn't sure he understood any of this. He might be new, but he was pretty sure the manuals were not person-specific. And what in the world was an AWAB?

Martin could probably tell him, but he'd most certainly want to know the full course of events. Curtis would look inefficient and foolish. Unless perhaps … maybe … Curtis could try to track down

Hamelin's book before he did and take it to Martin. Then any criticism leveled at him by Hamelin would appear merely spiteful.

It could work. He closed his eyes and pictured the office in the Phoenix, and all the players. Then he slowly replayed the chaotic office scene in his head, reenacting each player's movements, and everything configured as closely as he could recall: the seating, the desk and how it had been swept clean, the papers and books on the floor. Halfway through the review, he saw it. There were two books on the floor, one Bertollini's and the other Hamelin's, stacked one atop the other. And he had sent them both off with Helen.

He turned his attention to the celestial realm. He would give Martin a quick tease that he was coming with something of value. And then he was off for Delaney's.

***

Hamelin charged back into the pub. Three people had been hovering near him on the floor: Curtis, Ryan, and Bennie. If Curtis hadn't taken the notebooks, one of the others had. He entered Ryan's office with a storm raging in his head, his fingertips tingling with a powerful urge to smite anything in his way. He found Bennie sitting at the desk, head in his hands, and Ryan standing in the middle of the room, hugging an armload of papers.

"... brought the notebook in with you?" Ryan asked Bennie.

"Where is it?" Hamelin demanded, looking at each of them in turn.

Ryan shook his head. "We've turned over everything in here."

Bennie ignored the question. Instead, he walked out of the room, past Hamelin, returned seconds later, and walked straight to the spot where Ryan had collapsed. He dropped to his knees. "Right here," he said, slapping a hand down on the carpet. "I can still picture the book right *here.*" He dropped back onto his butt and shook his head. "Twenty years, and gone like that."

"Twenty years?" Hamelin asked. "Are you discussing my b—"

"*Bennie's* book," Ryan said. "It's gone."

Hamelin took two quick steps in Ryan's direction, obliterating his personal space. "I don't have time for histrionics," he hissed. "*My* book is gone. Now, there were only two of you close enough to take it. *"Who?"*

Ryan shuffled backward. His heels hit the chair behind him, and he plopped down hard into it. "What can I tell you, Hamelin? Neither book is here."

Bennie got up slowly. "There *was* someone else. Helen. She was right here. With that new fellow who was sitting next to her at the bar. They left at the same time."

"Curtis," Hamelin said.

"Oh, dear God," Ryan said. "AWAB was here?"

Hamelin nodded and motioned for Ryan to follow him out into the hall. "Of course he's here. I told you the town was crawling with *us.* And I also knew you couldn't stay away from here."

"I got tired of lousy cheeseburgers, okay? And Marie will be drawn here. She knows this place, and you have all this soul-beckoning going on. I couldn't let her walk in here cold." He paused and gave Hamelin a considered look. "You do look somewhat better. Tell me you've worked things out, that you can solve all this. Give Curtis the what for."

"At the moment, I'm not interested in your mortal take on things," Hamelin snapped. "Curtis and I have already had a little chat. He doesn't have the book. Where would Helen go?"

Ryan shrugged. "Hamelin, I'm not her keeper. If she's not with

Curtis, she could be in any of the booze joints around here. Think about it, though. Why would she walk off with either book? She isn't the reading type, if you catch my drift."

Hamelin paused as a wandering bar patron located and disappeared into the men's room. "Because Curtis gave them to her. I can't imagine the loss of Bennie's book being anything other than collateral damage. Curtis must have inadvertently scooped up both books. He's a shallow opportunist looking to please Martin."

As much as Hamelin wanted to swiftly put Curtis in his place, his power and options were limited without his manual. Not that he could open it even if he possessed it. "Called on the carpet for doing a good deed," he said suddenly, reliving Ryan's water rescue. He shot a look at Ryan, who was now staring at him, confusion all over his face.

"I don't care about your personal dramas," Ryan said. "Just Marie. Has she gotten to Nevis yet?"

"Without the book, I have no idea. She's completely off my radar at this point. And that's the honest-to-God truth. As I was telling you before Curtis's little prank, I've been dealing with much more pressing issues."

"Since I've got you in a rare moment of honesty," Ryan said, his voice thick and shaking, "when exactly did you lose track of her? Because I thought that's what you scampered away from my car to do—long before you lost your book."

"When I dived off the pier and saved your life, I altered things. To be specific, I violated Section Three: Interfering with Mortality and Related Issues."

"Altered things," Ryan repeated. "So there's no reason to believe that she's in Nevis now? Damn it, Hamelin! You said she was headed here. It's one lie after another with you. You should just go back to wherever you roost, and get your comeuppance." He pointed toward his office. "The honest man who needs my help is in there."

Hamelin grabbed Ryan by the shoulders and pulled him close. "Look! A funny thing happened on the way to pulling you out of the drink. I've been suspended, okay? Even if I had my book, I wouldn't be able to access it. The only way I can resolve the issue is to return home and meet with my superiors. An immortal losing his book is beyond the pale. If I return without my reference materials, they could boot me out entirely. Bad for me, bad for you, bad for Marie. And bad for the several other mulligans I didn't get a chance to take care of."

Ryan frowned. "Where would they boot you *to*? I thought you were already immortal."

Hamelin pushed him away and took off through the service door. He was halfway across the parking lot before Ryan managed to scurry abreast of him.

"What *are* you?" Ryan asked, grabbing Hamelin by the arm and spinning him around. "You're not a mortal, not an angel …"

"What I am is *screwed*!" Hamelin growled at him. He cast a withering gaze at Ryan's hand still grasping his biceps. "I am immortal, and you should never forget it. Touch me at your own peril, *mortal.*

Ryan released him at once and backed off, putting his hands up in a defensive posture. "Yes, of course. I meant no offense. You said you were suspended, so …" He shook his head. "Never mind. What I wanted to ask is whether such a book is specific to the immortal it was issued to. Because if not, we could trick Curtis out of his. Get that karma thing going for us."

Hamelin shook his head. "I thought I put the fear of the Lord in him, but he's played me all too well. Certainly, he's already fled home. And probably directly to Martin."

"Then that's even more reason to stick it to him."

Hamelin put his hands on his hips and looked beseechingly skyward. "The books are initially standard and then they individualize according to the possessor. But Curtis's will do me no good. I couldn't get it open, either."

"Maybe not, but you could use it as leverage. Without his manual, he'll be up the same creek as you. Make him *want* to return yours." Ryan paused a moment and then added, "I'd hate to see you serve time because of someone like Curtis. Whaddaya say, Hamelin?"

"*Serve time?*" Hamelin laughed. "What we're talking about is a good deal more permanent than that." He scratched his head in frustration. How could he say just enough …?

"It's like this," he said in a tone he usually reserved for children or the slow-witted. "I can't get my powers back without going home and appealing the suspension. However, it will be tricky to maneuver my way through a hearing without my written regulations. Locating the book when I'm not operating at full strength will also be difficult."

He paused and cocked an eyebrow. Ryan nodded that he understood. "Any mortal possessing the book is in grave danger," Hamelin continued. "As long as the manual is locked, no one, mortal or otherwise, can use it. But if I should win the appeal, the manual becomes usable again, *immediately,* by anyone strong enough to understand and wield its contents."

"So you can't go home until we find it."

Hamelin smiled at the use of "we." "Correct. They haven't summoned me home yet. I guess they figured l would be upset enough to return on my own. I have no intention of doing that. I have only a small window of time to search. I don't want them to send someone for me. While they're here, they might take it upon themselves to hunt down the book. In the hands of an unsympathetic immortal, I'm, uh—*we* are—*toast*. Now do you get it?"

Ryan nodded a second time, but from his knitted brow, Hamelin could still see confusion. "You have to understand the book. It contains not only rules of law, but also a of every action I've taken as an immortal. Every indiscretion I've ever made is recorded there, including a meticulous list of all souls I've put in a pending mode. And all future pickups I've been assigned, as well. So think hard, Ryan James Thomas. As if your life depended on it. Because it does. Tell me about this Helen."

Ryan closed his eyes, and Hamelin could almost see the synapses firing double time. The first words out of Ryan James's mouth were going to form another question. "No more specifics," Hamelin admonished, shaking him gently. "Take a deep breath and relax."

Ryan's eyes popped open, and they were wide with panic. "Let go. I can't think with your hands on me."

Hamlin turned him loose. "Just spit out what's going through your head. I can sort through it faster than you can."

Ryan pulled in a deep breath, then blurted out, "You're a nasty piece of work and probably deserve this." And then in a second rush, "Bennie sent her down to Delaney's earlier today to spy—"

"Delaney's? Now it all makes sense. They're going to give him a tactical advantage in the Tippy. Fine. Let's go."

Then, suddenly, Hamelin's face contorted. He raised his index finger in a sign to wait a moment. It was the moment he had been dreading. His time had just run out.

He turned to Ryan, his manner terse and deadly serious. "Change of plans," he said, already moving in the opposite direction. "*You* go get the book back."

"*Me?* Why me?" Ryan said, following him. "You're a lot better at arm-twisting than I am. Delaney would be a damn fool to give it back. Also, he's a lot bigger than I, and he already hates my guts."

Hamelin halted. "The worst has happened, Ryan James. We no longer have choices. I've been summoned home to appear before a magisterial review board on charges of misuse of authority. I am required to appear. And if I'm to save myself, I must first take care of Curtis. If he's headed back to Martin and has kept the book, I need to intercept him before he hand-delivers the very means to destroy us."

"But—"

"No buts. Use that wonderful intellect God has graced you with. Welcome Delaney to the neighborhood if you have to. Whatever it takes. Even if you don't get it back, you'll be able to discern whether he has it. Then he'll have to answer to me. Now, go!" he said, and waved him off.

Satisfied at last that Ryan was doing as he was told, Hamelin headed for the nearest alley. Disappearing into thin air was damaging to mortal witnesses and invited awkward questions. He called upon Luke as he walked. "I know I'm pushing, buddy, but please tell me you have something for me. It's now or never."

Luke's response was most unholy and not reassuring.

Chapter Twenty-Four
Inviting Trouble

Ryan's breath hitched when he saw Helen sashay out of Delaney's alone and empty-handed. Then he caught sight of her brown leather handbag, which was big enough to hold five notebooks and his pet toy poodle, Hoffa. He might not be too late.

He fell in step as she drew abreast. "Twice in one day? Either you couldn't do all your reconnaissance in one quick visit, or you've developed a crush on our competitor."

She shifted her bag to the shoulder farther from him and kept walking. "Not my type," she said with a sniff, "and I'm done with all men. Just finishing up a little business. Some very unpleasant business." She gave him the once-over and smiled. "Were you looking for me?"

"Yes, actually. I need to tap your memory. We can't seem to find something. When I passed out on the floor and you were kneeling next to me—do you remember a notebook?"

"Sure do, hon. Don't give it another thought. I brought 'em both down here and gave 'em back to Delaney, just like Curtis asked. But don't spread that around. Curtis said it should be done discreetly."

Ryan stopped. "*Two* books?"

"Yeah," she said, shaking her head as she looked off into the distance. "That was the only confusing part. Curtis never said there would be two." She waved at a passing bicyclist before turning back to Ryan. "Anything else I can do for you? I really need to report back to Bennie about what Delaney's bar looks like inside. Now Bennie, that's a good man."

"He's the best," Ryan said. He took her hand in his and stopped on the sidewalk. "Delaney has the books?"

She nodded. "Although I don't think he appreciated it. That's the odd—"

He let go of her hand and sprinted toward Delaney's.

"Big wheels keep on turning!" she yelled after him.

***

Curtis stood under the dark-green awning of Bolt's Ice Cream Emporium. He closed his eyes and shut out his surroundings.

"Martin?" he said softly to himself. There was no response. Not surprising, for Martin was a busy man. He would try again after he had Hamelin's manual back.

He stepped off the curb and then right back up again. Ryan Thomas and Helen stood directly across the street—she looking miffed and he looking hurried. Obviously, Hamelin had discussed his missing book with the mortal. Curtis shook his head in disgust. This was so against protocol. He pulled out his manual and quickly scribbled an entry in the back. *Disclosing confidential information* went right under *fraternizing.*

Curtis cast a glance around. Where could he cross over to Delaney's without being seen by them?

He didn't need to decide. Their encounter ended abruptly as Thomas bolted toward the speakeasy and Helen slunk off the other way. Curtis admired the sway in her gait for a moment and then shook his head. She was indeed an alluring woman, through and through.

"*Nice,*" said someone behind him, giving voice to feelings that Curtis was trying to tamp down.

Curtis started and then stepped away from a shabbily dressed man with a fish creel at his hip, and lust shining in his eyes.

"I remember that poetry in motion," the derelict continued. He fumbled in his dirty coat and pulled out a dark-hued business card and shoved it at Curtis. "Fish is my game. If you're interested …"

Curtis's flesh crawled. He didn't recall seeing the guy earlier in Delaney's. And even if he had, his thoughts about "poetry in motion" had been just that: thoughts.

He took the card to shut the man up and moved away. A quick look over his shoulder told him the bum was already heading the opposite way. Curtis took off at a run for the service entrance of the speakeasy, bending and pushing the time-space continuum before him like pushing a giant, bulging soap bubble. He could get to Delaney long before Thomas gained admittance into the speakeasy.

With his hand on the door handle, Curtis changed his mind. He turned away and walked briskly across the rear parking area. Once on the opposite side, he stopped and faced the building so he could see the door. "Martin?" he asked, speaking softly to himself.

"Where are you?" Martin asked. "I thought we were meeting."

"At the moment, a parking lot—"

An impatient huff cut him short. "Why aren't you *here*? I thought you were bringing information to the magisterial meeting this afternoon."

Curtis hesitated. He needed a little freedom. "Oh … Well, I was on my way out of Nevis when something came up. At the moment, it's awkward for me to just pick up and leave. I need to attend to something. It won't take me long. I'll call you back."

"Absolutely not. Something special has come up. I need you back here now, on a very important matter."

Curtis's eyes returned to the door. So far, no one had entered or exited.

"Curtis?"

"Martin? Are you still there?" Of course he was still there. In a cozy office with his feet up on his desk, no doubt.

"Yes. Come straight to my office."

Curtis clenched his fists and was suddenly reminded of the bum's business card still in his hand. He flipped it over and read the gray lettering on the matte-black card.

B. Bub
Life Counselor
Day or Night
Just Holler

Curtis smirked, started to flick it aside, and then, for no reason he could name, dropped it in his pocket.

He found Martin's tone less amusing than the card. Martin was a whiney user. *Well, not this time.* Curtis would reach the pearly gates only if he cast aside the bushel basket covering his own light. He needed Hamelin's manual.

"Martin?" he asked. "What's that, Martin? Can't hear … interference … later?" With that, Curtis tuned him out and shot back toward Delaney's.

The service entrance was unlocked. He entered and threaded his way around food prep, dishwashing, and fast-moving wait staff. In the whir of activity, no one gave him so much as a second glance.

Delaney's bar was a dark horse in the Tippy competition, but the place was bustling, and its bartender now had in his possession what was effectively a manual for winning the contest. Curtis had no taste for gambling, but he knew a good bet when he saw one. As soon as he found Hamelin's book, he might place a small wager on this little horse that could. Later, he could figure out what one did with a heap of cash in the afterlife.

Curtis felt a wave of shame roll over him. What a horrifying train of thought! Where had that come from? Such desires and machinations were beneath an immortal aspiring to a higher plane of being. But surging adrenaline obliterated the thought before it went any further, and propelled him into a great room of shiny brass fixtures, booze, and tantalizing bar conversations. So many temptations …

Chapter Twenty-Five
Thrust and Parry

Curtis was the shrewdest newbie Hamelin had ever met, so he wasn't overly surprised when he couldn't find the guy anywhere in town. Meanwhile, the overriding emotion that he felt was one of panic building toward sheer terror. The magisterial review would be it for him. He wasn't ready to face his own final judgment. He left Nevis and headed home with a lump in the pit of his stomach.

This shuttling back and forth between the immortal and mortal realms was a bit like riding the metro system in any major city on earth: a constant stream of nameless faces, each quietly wrapped in its own thoughts or hiding out inside a carefully constructed bubble of nonsocialization. At the moment, Hamelin felt more common cause with the latter group. Even as his mind raced with thoughts of eternal damnation, he pulled out his lovingly dog-eared *Guide to the Western Nebulae, Part Two* and projected a look of calm engrossment.

At the appropriate moment, he put away his prop and slipped through a portal into the celestial realm. As he headed for the large conservatory in this wing, he continued his slow burn over getting hoodwinked by Curtis. AWAB was no lone wolf. This was Martin, pulling his protégé down a very dark road. But Hamelin suspected that AWAB wasn't as bright a rising star as everyone supposed. Goodness shouldn't be so easily subverted. There had to be some dark tendency, some grayness, to begin with. Which made perfect sense. Otherwise, Curtis wouldn't be stuck soul running with the rest of the probies while he tried to work his flaws out. He would have vaulted right into paradise.

Hamelin turned left at the first bank of elevators and continued down one of the many corridors housing business offices. This particular one, referred to as the Masters Hall, was lined with religiously themed paintings by some of the most gifted artists that Earth had ever produced: Rembrandt, Raphael, El Greco … Hamelin seriously doubted they had tarried long in this immortal weigh station long, if ever. He had spent much time here admiring their work. But today he kept his head down and powered past them. When he reached the end of the hall, he glanced up briefly, unable to resist the pull of Berlinghiero of Lucca's exquisite Madonna holding her son, the Divine Infant, protectively to her. She stared soulfully out at Hamelin. The painting drew him in with its interplay of the human and the sacred—reminding him of where he had been and where he needed to go. There was so much Hamelin wanted to confide in her. How hard it was. If his father had been a more enlightened man, Hamelin would have been one of Berlinghiero's greatest pupils. Of this he had no doubt. Hamelin pulled his eyes away and walked on.

He cut down an intersecting hallway—shorter than the last, its walls unadorned—and headed for the glass doors halfway down. When he reached them, he double-checked whether he was alone. Satisfied, he pushed through and was immediately assaulted by a thick wall of humidity and the heavy scent of honeysuckle. This was one of many conservatories tucked around the office complex. They were open to all, though he visited them infrequently. When he needed a moment to reflect or commune with nature, he sought the true outdoors. He passed through the various color-themed plantings of vibrant red tea roses, striking yellow frangipani, and cool white gardenias, to a more private garden tucked away behind a wall of blue hydrangeas.

He found Luke there, waiting with his back to the entryway. His feet were propped up on the rim of a fountain tinkling water from a Grecian urn into a broad, low basin. From the forward tilt of Luke's head, he appeared to be dozing. Hamelin walked up beside him and tried to ease free the papers he held loosely in his hand.

Luke leaped up from his chair, and the papers went sailing out of his hand and into the fountain. "Holy mother!"

"S'okay, s'okay," said Hamelin, snatching the papers out of the water and wiping them across his sleeve. "Do you have it?" he asked shaking the pages.

"You're holding them. Not here, though. People float in and out all the time. I know a better place." He lightly rolled the documents into a tube, and they left through a nearby door.

They passed no one, but Hamelin knew there were many busy workers behind the closed doors on both sides of the hall. He read each bronze door plate as they passed, but as expected, he didn't recognize any of them. These were not the rank and file he associated with.

They crossed two intersecting hallways. At the third, Luke turned and stopped at a door. It was unmarked. And locked. He put the laminated access card hanging around his neck up to the reader and admitted them. On the other side, they took an ornate spiral staircase down deep into the library stacks. As he drew his fingers down the carved detail of the handrail, Hamelin marveled at the beauty of all things placed here—even to the slightest details of a staircase hidden from the eyes of all but a chosen few.

No amount of light could ever sufficiently illuminate all the dead ends and carrells tucked away in the lower levels of the Saint Peter Memorial Reading Complex, the innermost sanctum of the afterlife think tank, known simply as the RC. As in the conservatory, the air here was thick with scent—not of flowers but of musty ancient books—their pages foxed and yellowed by time and wrinkled by eons of use. Hamelin thought it the perfect quiet place to plot the downfall of a lofty figure like Martin—or perhaps the swift demise of two very foolish soul runners.

After a few twists and turns among the stacks, Luke seemed content. He holed them up in a corner space and motioned Hamelin to sit at the desk there.

Surrounding them were shelves holding all manner of recorded knowledge: books, scrolls, CDs, cuneiform tablets, and other gizmos that Hamelin couldn't even begin to name. "You're much more connected than I assumed," he said. "I should have asked for help sooner."

"From what I'm hearing, you're going to need all the help you can muster. How did you get yourself suspended?"

"Huh?" Hamelin said. He never thought it would stay a secret forever, but … He shook his head.

"It's not common knowledge, and yes, sometimes it's good to be connected. For those reasons, this is the limit of what I can do for you. I don't want to be labeled a co-conspirator in some cockamamie scheme and end up on the outs—or just plain *out.*"

"No scheme, cockamamie or otherwise. I just want to reveal the creeping malignancy otherwise known as Martin Westwood Cobb."

"Well, that would please more than a few of us, but we're not crazy like you." Luke spread his research on the desktop and squatted down next to Hamelin's chair. "There's enough here to hang him—a definite mismatch between where Martin should have been picking up souls and where he actually was."

Luke pulled out a pencil and began pointing out discrepancies across the documents. No one could match his ability to drill down through piles of data and then build what he found into a beautiful cathedral of cause and effect. Luke knew his stuff, and the evidence was incriminating. Martin had played it fast and loose with his assignments and charges. For every visit to an exotic locale, there was a corresponding missed pickup and the creation of a mulligan. There were hundreds. Luke's graph put to shame the one discussed at Hamelin's performance review. Damning in every sense of the word.

Half an hour later, Luke stood up from his crouched position, stretched, put his pointer down, and said, "Enough?"

"More than enough," Hamelin said. He leaned back in his chair and breathed a sigh of relief. He had some control again, and there was no doubt he could take on Martin. He began shuffling the papers together into a pile. "You do have copies, right?"

Luke shook his head. "I'm not about to get caught with the likes of this. Just show him the summary sheet." Luke reached down and pulled the paper from the bottom of the stack. "Oh, and I haven't had any conversations with you since the contest began. *Hai capito?*"

"Yes. Is there anyone else I shouldn't be thanking?"

"Charlotte, and don't. She'll deny any involvement, too."

"No, I understand." Hamelin patted Luke on the back. "Just wish me luck. I'll check in with you later." He tucked the evidence under his arm, and they climbed the spiral stairs back up from the depths. Luke pointed him toward the hallway that would put him outside Martin's private office. Martin's turf wasn't Hamelin's first choice. Neutral ground was preferable, but a row in a public area would announce his return and surely prevent him from returning to earth. Advantage Martin.

As he walked the corridor connecting the generic office space of the working elite with the lusher digs of upper management, expansive windows let in bright natural light. He wondered what Martin would do when he found out Hamelin had the power to take away this and all the other perks of his newfound success. In the end, it didn't much matter. Even if he never got to witness Martin's reaction, booting him from the realm would be gratification enough.

He found Martin's office and barged in. Martin seemed rattled—an uncontrolled emotion rolling across his face before he pulled together a stonier visage. He put down his pen. "Hamelin! You're back."

"Momentarily."

"Sit?" Martin asked, gesturing to a collection of comfortable chairs spaced around a rectangular glass table.

Hamelin put Luke's summary sheet on the table and sat down with his back to the door. He took in the room. As a rule, managers' offices were spartan. Not this one. An assortment of playthings and personal pursuits were on display: an enormous silver and black telescope in one corner, multiple sets of rich-looking leather-bound books in a case running beneath the length of a large window that overlooked some pastoral area of the universe, and a tower of deluxe sound equipment within easy reach of Martin's desk chair. The sound of soft jazz—Coleman Hawkins, Hamelin thought—created a rather different ambient mood from that of the religious intonations piped in like Muzak throughout the common areas of the complex. He wondered how Martin had any time to serve others when he was so immersed in material luxuries.

"Are you here for a meeting?" Martin asked, settling down into the chair across from him.

"Business. It's interfering with the retreat." He caught Martin glancing toward the door. Who was he afraid would join them? "Am I interrupting something?"

"I *do* have an appointment, but he's late," Martin said, dismissing the consideration with a wave that seemed more practiced than spontaneous. "So what can I do for you? You should be out enjoying yourself, Hamelin."

"It's more what *I* can do for *you*." Hamelin turned the summary spreadsheet around and slid it over the coffee table so Martin could read it. He brushed his hand across the data points plotted on the paper. "A bit like the Milky Way, don't you think? Looks pretty, but actually, it's a great swath of ineptitude and indifference spiraling through the cosmos."

Martin slid to the edge of his seat and pulled it closer. "What are you talking about?" As his finger traced over the labels on the graph axes—*souls to be conveyed* on the horizontal, *vacation* on the vertical—a deep groove formed between his eyes. "There's a point to this, I'm sure."

Hamelin pointed to a key in the bottom right corner. "Look. It's even color coded. And have you noticed how often you seem to be on vacation on the opposite side of the globe from where your assigned pickups are?" He put his hand to his chin. "How is it that you manage to get your work done in Calcutta while climbing peaks in ..." He looked more closely at the graph. "*California?* That must have been a new time record for scaling El Capitan. Roped or free solo?"

Martin crumpled up the paper and threw it at Hamelin, nailing him on the chin. "Someday, you might make it out of the rank and file, but you'll have to lose that streak of jealousy to do it. You're wasting your time taking potshots at me.

"Not that it's any of your business," Martin continued, "but my performance review was last week, and as always, the feedback was glowing. Not so much with yours, huh? You're a disgrace, Hamelin, and I've not held my tongue over the years about what a hopeless case you are. Now others have taken up the call to drum your sorry bum out of here. It won't be long. Now, get out," he said, pointing toward the door. "Come back after your meeting today. Then we'll talk about reality." He leaned back into his seat with an air of untouchable smugness.

Hamelin took his time smoothing the wrinkles out of the summary. "Others? Pshaw!" he said at last. "Sniveling Curtis, whom you sent to spy on me and screw with the Tippy? That'd be these *others* you're waiting on? If he's not here now—and there's no reason he should be running to you to report anything out of the ordinary—he's not coming. He's the meticulous, punctual sort."

When Martin's gaze flitted to the door again, Hamelin knew he had him. Martin *had* nothing. If he and Curtis had spoken, Curtis had kept his information close to the vest.

Hamelin put the paper back down and placed a newspaper front page alongside it. "Seen the latest from Brazil?" he asked, pointing down at the front page of Rio de Janeiro's *O Globo,* the English-language version: "HEALTH OFFICIALS PUZZLED BY SPIKING DEATH RATE."

"I hear Abraham's team in Receiving is overwhelmed with a sudden influx of deliveries. It seems the reaping season has suddenly gotten very busy, it's like watching a dam breach. So many souls yearning to come home."

Martin flipped the newspaper over to view the other side. His eyes now looked beady and snakelike. "Where did you get this?"

Gloating inside, Hamelin pressed forward. "There's quiet talk of an epidemic of mulligans. Amazing how much furor this sort of thing stirs up." He replaced the newspaper with a third document, another chart. "They're just streaming in from Ipanema, Búzios, Paraty," he said, pointing. "Oh, and look. You were there in July two years ago. Fact-finding trip? Otherwise, it's an extraordinary coincidence, if I do say so myself."

"Just you." Martin walked back to his desk and sat on the edge like a hawk hunting out his next meal. "I'd be the first to admit I've missed a few over the millennia. *Everyone* does."

Hamelin chuckled. It was human nature to attack or intimidate when out of better options. Imperfect immortals were no different. "Admit it, Martin. The rising mortality rate is all your doing—one gigantic cover-your-backside move. You're running scared, so you've begun collecting all the souls you left dangling out there."

Hamelin folded the newspaper in half and tossed it back on the table. "I am puzzled by your lack of planning. Why didn't you trickle the mulligans back in a few at a time? No one would have noticed. Why the hurry?"

Martin studied the ceiling, and a long, disgusted sigh escaped his lips. He pointed to Hamelin's stack of papers. "Show and tell over? Because I do have things to do."

Hamelin rifled through and nodded his head. "I think we've hit the high points. I could go on, but why bother? You thought you would nail me with this new crackdown on mulligans, but it's backfired on you. You didn't anticipate what a bit player you'd be and how little control you'd have. The task force has thrown a wide net, and they're moving quickly. It won't be long before they've snagged you in it. In fact, right here is enough to, I don't know, finally get you out of here and off to a permanent home—though I don't think it's the one you were shooting for, *Mulligan* Martin."

They sat for a moment, locked in a staring match. Hamelin had him dead to rights, but the man was a tough nut to crack. His eyes stayed focused on Martin while his thoughts wandered to the door behind him. How long could he afford to sit here without someone catching him and forcing him to stay for the inquiry into his suspension.

Martin blinked first. "What do you want?" he asked.

"Quit hounding me, or I'm going to complain. *Loudly.*"

"Puh-*lease!* As if your list of mulligans wouldn't rival mine."

Hamelin shook his head. "Not even close, and don't think for a moment that I'm going to plot it out for you." He looked back down at the first chart's spatter design. "The difference between what you and I have done? I took into consideration the needs and desires of the dying when I gave them extra time. Your decisions were purely self-serving. Want to take in a thundering migration on the Serengeti?" he asked, setting his fingertip down on one of the points on the graph. "Or maybe a splashy aurora on Zebulon Thirty-Eight?" His finger slid to the right. "Screw that needy soul." He looked back up with a gleam in his eye. "You should have been smarter, *my friend.*"

Martin walked back over to the seating area. "You are more on the ball than I gave you credit for, Mr. Russell," he said, fingering the graph.

"There are other copies."

Martin laughed. "I'm sure there are. Who did this? Luke?"

"You, all by yourself."

Martin studied the first graph a moment. "Maybe it's accurate, maybe not. But I agree that it doesn't look good. I can still control the flow to Abraham, however. And it stops here. No more mulligans. Problem solved. Satisfied?"

Hamelin snorted and shook his head. "Not in the least, you hypocritical bastard. Running a task force to identify and curb mulligans, what were you going to do, Martin? Scrub your own personal data as it came in? A few IT people in your pocket raring to cover up your indifference and ineptitude? I can't even begin to imagine what you offered them in exchange for their help."

"You're letting your imagination get the best of you, Hamelin. My indiscretions are no greater than yours. I might take a step back just to keep the peace, but if you think you're going to blackmail me into something for your benefit, you're delusional. You know you can't stand against me." He slid the report across the table toward Hamelin. "Your move."

Hamelin slid the documents protectively under his arm. "Nope. Still all yours. You can't report me without opening the door to your own activities. Your mistakes are already a matter of record in the databases."

"What do you *really* want, Hamelin?"

"As I said, to be left alone. Recall Curtis, and get him out of my hair. Then stay away from me. Don't talk to me, look at me, or even pass my way. As long as you respect those boundaries, I think we can serve out our time here without further conflict. Otherwise, I'll take my lumps with the committee. And they will be few because I'm in the process of terminating all my mulligans." He took a slow, exaggerated look around the room at the trinkets: the elegantly bound books, the Takahashi telescope, and those sound components that could make jazz sound almost as great as the blues. "You have a lot to lose here, Martin, and a lot further to fall than I do. Let's both be smart about it."

There was a light tapping on the door. The men exchanged a brief glance, and Martin tipped his chin toward the corner near the door. Hamelin stepped into it just as the door swung open.

"Private meeting," Martin said.

The advance of the door halted, and whoever stood on the other side remained there. "Are you still meeting with us?" asked a timid voice that Hamelin did not recognize.

"Sorry, Martha. Be down shortly. Can you get started without me?"

The voice agreed, and the door closed.

Martin looked back at Hamelin. "Very well. I'll recall Curtis and put him on something else challenging. That should soothe his disappointment at leaving the contest early. But if I get one inkling of you—"

"You just worry about your little clone-in-the-making. I'm not sure he's as pliable as you think."

And with that, Hamelin left—out of the detached progressions of jazz and into the rise and fall of faint a cappella prayer wafting from hallway speakers. The chanting filled the space with a sudden holiness. Hamelin quickly pulled the door tight to keep the moment uncorrupted.

He fled in the direction of the nearest earthly portal—not so much to exit as to maintain an avenue of escape while he considered his next move. As he had hoped, the corridor was empty. He leaned up against the door, ready to propel himself through it at the first sign of company. If necessary, he could leave and circle back around for reentry at another portal.

At the moment, he trusted Martin more than he trusted Curtis, and that was troubling. Martin appeared to be expecting his little gunslinger, and he should have arrived first. Where was AWAB? Had he decided to gain glory for himself? Gone rogue to inform on Hamelin to a higher-level authority than Martin? Hamelin quickly dismissed the thought. Curtis might be sharp, but no newbie knew the ropes well enough—or had the chutzpah—to play the upper-management structure to his advantage.

A door clicking shut resonated down the hall and snapped his head up. And right after that came the drone of deep, soft voices from the same direction. Hamelin closed his eyes and slowed down the space-time continuum, pushing the bubble surrounding him until it gently bumped up against and compressed the bubble of the approaching people. He could hold it briefly, but that would be enough.

The voices disappeared immediately, and he returned to his reverie. His instinct told him that Curtis wasn't as noble as he came across, either. Odds were good that Curtis was still on earth—

Two men in flowing robes rounded the corner, and Hamelin's time construct shattered like a thin pane of glass. He stepped through the portal.

Chapter Twenty-Six
Gains and Losses

As Ryan approached the secret entrance to Delaney's, he wondered whether the brute manning the door would recognize him. But if the man knew he owned the competition down the street, he didn't show it, or maybe didn't care. He seemed more preoccupied with his cell phone than with the patrons' identities. Upon hearing the correct password, the doorman nodded and worked his magic on the hidden door in the bookcase.

Ryan walked inside and took stock of his dimly lit surroundings. It was indeed a speakeasy as he and Bennie had suspected. The walls were awash in posters of flappers and fedora-wearing Al Capone types from the 1920s. "Delaney here?" he asked an approaching waiter.

A waiter led him across the room to the far back corner and tapped lightly on the closed door marked "Office." When Delaney bade them enter, the waiter left and Ryan went in.

Delaney was at his desk. A filing cabinet stood to his right, and two empty ladderback chairs took up space near the door. The only tchotchke was a small metal replica of a model T Ford sitting on top of the cabinet. The austerity of the room stood in stark contrast to the glitz of the bar area. Just as Delaney had left no personal imprint during his tenure at the Phoenix, he didn't seem inclined to add any touches to his new office, either. Ryan's eyes quickly settled on the small black notebook spread open on the desk.

Delaney flipped the book shut. "Ryan," he said, rising. "This is a surprise."

Ryan smiled sheepishly. "I didn't like the way we parted so I thought I'd come down and congratulate you on your opening. The place looks terrific, by the way."

Delaney nodded. Ryan watched him spread a hand protectively over his reading material.

"And I wanted you to know that if you need anything, please give a holler. If we work together, we can build a strong social scene here. A win-win for everyone." Ryan thrust out a hand. "Bygones be bygones?"

Delaney glanced down at the book and then back up at Ryan. "Sure. Winning always feels good." He reached out and shook his hand.

With Delaney's hand in his, the notebook—whoever's it might be—now lay unprotected on the desk. Grab and go? Delaney was a big guy …

***

Curtis moved from the kitchen into the dining area. "Delaney around?" he asked. A ponytailed young woman with a gray tub of dirty dishes on her hip pointed with her chin toward an open door across the room. He moved quickly, his heart pounding out a counterrhythm to the bluesy strains playing softly above the chatter of nearby patrons. He didn't bother rapping on the doorjamb. Delaney would be thrilled to see him.

"And how are things …" Curtis's eyes moved from Delaney to the pub owner, to their hands clasped in a hearty handshake. Then he saw a notebook between them on the desk. Which one? And what deal was this involving the fruits of *his* labor? "I, er, uh …"

The two men dropped their hands, and Thomas locked eyes on Curtis. He said nothing, but Curtis could feel the ill will. There was no mistaking it. Hamelin had looped him in.

Delaney, on the other hand, broke out into a brilliant smile and rushed him. "I don't know how to th—"

Curtis threw his hands up. "Stop! Didn't know you were indisposed. I'll wait out here until you're finished." He backed out of the office but didn't go far. If they didn't bid their adieus soon, he'd have to push it along.

***

Ryan glanced at Delaney, who now stood between him and the door. The book was still on the desk. All he needed was five seconds alone and a chance to get out of the office before Delaney came after him. He could sprint two blocks. Possibly. "It sounds important," he said to Delaney, and tipped his head toward the door.

As Delaney moved for the door, Ryan swept up the notebook and slid it down his underwear. Then he pushed out right behind Delaney. "Catch you later," he said, and glided out of the office and past the other two men. He took a sharp right turn toward the kitchen. As he did so, he collided with a waitress carrying a tray of beers and a nacho salad. Beer went up; she went down. He skidded through the cheese like a novice skater, to the rear service entrance. And when he hit the fresh air, he ran like his ten-year-old self did when little Bucky Thurmont threatened to beat him senseless with a thirty-one-inch Louisville Slugger bat. He wasn't sure which book was chafing his buttocks, but someone owed him profuse thanks.

***

Delaney muttered an oath as he watched alcohol and cheesy lettuce rain down on a table of customers. He moved forward to minimize the damage and smooth any ruffled feathers. Then he reconsidered and made an about-face back into his office, to retrieve the Tippy book. His eyes swept the empty desk, and his mind replayed Thomas's hasty retreat.

"*Shit,*" he said aloud, not caring who heard him. "Two-faced son of—he took my book!"

"Which book?" Curtis asked coming in behind him. When he didn't get an answer, he clutched Delaney by the forearm. "I said, *which book*?"

Delaney yanked his arm free and turned on him, his eyes raging with a ferocity that would have cowered any mortal man. "The *bar* book you sent down. Thomas took it." He tried to sweep Curtis aside, but the immortal cast him off easily and fixed him with a steely gaze that rooted Delaney where he stood.

"And the other one?" Curtis asked.

"The joke book that didn't open?" Delaney pointed out the door. "Trashed it. Not funny. Now, get outta my way. I'd hate to have to move you." For the first time in his life, the threat sounded hollow.

Curtis poked a finger into his broad chest. "You did wh … No, you're right. Not funny at all. Show me where. *Now.* Only then will I consider helping you out of the mess you've created."

Delaney stood towering over Curtis. He blinked rapidly but seemed unable to move. He pointed toward the door again.

"Dear God in heaven, I really don't have time for this," Curtis said. And grabbing Delaney by the arm, he dragged him out of the office and past annoyed patrons pulling rabbit food and cheese out of their hair.

"I'll pay for your clothes," Delaney said as he passed. He led Curtis to the end of the bar, where he had been bookkeeping. "Artie," he bellowed. "Where's the trash?"

A curly-haired man in a full-length white apron stepped back from a long stainless-steel prep table. He glanced at Delaney and pointed a thumb at the rear service door. "Pickup anytime now." He resumed chopping his tomatoes.

The dumpster was empty, and the ground was littered with refuse. No book. Curtis glimpsed the flashing hazard lights of a dark-green trash compactor receding into the distance and disappearing over a gentle rise in the road. Curtis checked the other way. A homeless man slept leaning against the foundation of the next building, with his shopping cart pulled close by, and no Ryan Thomas in sight.

Curtis wanted to kick himself. He had no excuse for letting Thomas beat him to Delaney. If he had been but a moment sooner … He shook it off. When had self-pity helped anything?

"It's no big deal," Delaney said. "I'm telling you, it was garbage. You couldn't read it. But that other one …" He turned toward the Phoenix.

Curtis started walking, haltingly at first, and then with determined speed that had Delaney hurrying to keep pace. He stooped next to the derelict and picked up a book lying on his lap. It was a soul runner's manual, but strangely light. When he opened it, he found no pages, just a folded piece of white cardstock keeping place for absolutely nothing. It fluttered out and onto the sleeping man's chest. He picked it up. It was another fisherman's card.

The man's face was taut and darkly tanned, like the skin of an oven-baked chicken. The narrative was all too clear. As a creature of the street, the man had no home, decent food, or medical care. He scavenged for what he needed to survive. His was a precarious life, and he lived constantly with one boot in the hereafter. The power of the manual had simply overwhelmed him. Curtis's heart filled with pity.

But then alarm replaced the pity. With the transportation moratorium, there were to be no deaths. How had this happened? Where, pray tell, had the man's soul gone? A mulligan? Unlikely. There would need to be a second death and an available body. The thought of two deaths occurring here during the moratorium would be most unusual. He took in the scene around him. It was just him, Delaney, and the corpse. If there was a new mulligan, he hoped the man's new life would be easier than the one he had left behind.

Curtis's mind raced. He wasn't trained for this. His job was to transport as instructed, nothing more. Should he walk away and make the irregular death someone else's problem? He fingered the bookmark. Yeah, walking away would be the smartest. Then he ran his fingertips across the empty cover. No, that was crazy thinking—heretical, in fact. Mulligan or not, a soul was out there *somewhere.* Still, he decided, not really his problem. He stood up and backed away, sliding the card into the manual's cover.

"Is he ... *gone*?" Delaney asked, standing his ground a few feet away.

"Afraid so. Curtis studied Delaney's ashen face and wide-eyed stare. It brought back forgotten memories of the fear of death. "But he was an elderly man."

Delaney's gaze shifted to the book. "How did you get that open?" he asked, reaching for it.

Curtis slid the empty cover into an inside jacket pocket. Delaney's deepening involvement in otherworldly affairs was troubling. The bartender wasn't quick enough to understand unfolding events, but he could easily blab it all to an immortal over a cold glass of suds. Curtis needed to find a way to dispense with his services.

First things first, though. He wanted to reap the benefits of rescuing Hamelin's manual. What would Hamelin give to get it back—or what was left of it? He would give Hamelin first crack at being grateful. If he wasn't, Martin would be.

Curtis took off for the Phoenix, motioning Delaney to follow. "Come on. This isn't finished yet."

Chapter Twenty-Seven
Devil's in the Details

Ryan locked his office door, tossed Delaney's book on the floor, and doubled over with his hands on his knees. He had expected Delaney to give a more strenuous pursuit. Considering how Delaney had obtained the book, Ryan didn't see him bursting in now to demand its return. He tried to tell that to his quivering leg muscles. For the moment, the door would remain secured.

"Why is it you seem unable to accomplish any task I set out for you?"

Ryan started and then sagged back against the door as Hamelin reached down and picked the book up from the floor. "Right one?" he asked, panting heavily.

Hamelin tossed Bennie's book on the desk, where it landed with a smack. "Of course not."

"Best I can do, Hamelin. I only saw the one book." Ryan slid down the length of the door into a sitting position on the floor. "*You* go get 'em. I'm tapped out."

"Curtis?"

"He had just come in to see Delaney when I grabbed the book and ran for it. If Delaney has the second book, it wasn't out."

"If Curtis is there, so is the book," Hamelin said. "Now, get out of the way so I can take care of this."

Ryan did a half roll away from the door. Hamelin opened the door and slid him farther aside until he could squeeze through.

"Damn you, Hamelin Russell!" Ryan called after him. "Please don't come back with more drama." He looked at the Tippy book across the room. Poor Bennie would just have to wait until he got his second wind.

***

Hamelin flung open the service door, catching Delaney full in the face. Delaney stumbled backward into Curtis, and they both went down in a heap. Hamelin advanced on the two, yanking Curtis out of the tangle and to his feet. Then he swung him around and slammed him against the brick wall of the building.

"Hamelin. Praise be," Curtis said, gasping for breath. He tried to pry Hamelin's fingers loose from the front of his shirt, but he couldn't divert any of the rage Hamelin was channeling. "A terrible mistake, I assure you."

Hamelin slammed him into the rear wall of the Phoenix a second time. "A *most* terrible mistake, I'm afraid."

"If you don't remove your hands at once, I will be forced to report you. Section One: Respect. '… the heart noble, thy hands and …"

Hamelin tightened his grip to quiet him. "Oh, I'm going to do much worse than report you, Mr. Merriweather." He saw a notebook sticking out of Curtis's pocket and jerked it out. It wasn't his. "Where's my book? I know you have it." He frisked Curtis's other pockets and pulled out what was left of his manual, the card still peeking out of its top.

"I s-s-swear, Hamelin, I found it just like this. I was bringing it back to you."

Hamelin gave him one more slam against the bricks. Curtis was a lousy liar.

"Care to rethink that?"

"As God is my witness, I found it just like that with the card in it."

Hamelin let him go and pulled the card free. He read it through slowly, and then once again. "*Beelzebub's* card? You traded my book to the *devil*?" he asked, his voice rising to anear shout. "Are you insane?" Hamelin crumpled up the card and tossed it into the air, where it burst into a cold white flame and disappeared with a flash. Hamelin crossed himself.

"I, er ... It's *what*?" Curtis's eyes were wide with fear.

"Where are the pages? And be quick about it. Otherwise, I'll dragging you straight to hell and let others be the judge of whether you should stay there."

"Delaney trashed it, the bum found it, and now he's lying dead down there outside *Delaney's*." It all came tumbling out with Curtis pointing frantically in various directions to convey what happened.

Hamelin turned and looked toward Delaney's. There was still something dark piled against the foundation of the building. The deceased, he assumed. "You reported it and transported the soul?"

Curtis gave him a wide-eyed look. "The moratorium ..."

"So you've just left a soul alone and unprotected, and our operating guidelines to boot? Oh, Curtis, Curtis, Curtis, why is it that extremely bright people have so little common sense? You have failed utterly to live up to your heavenly obligations. Your ineptitude is the devil's gain."

Curtis's face fell. "Dear Lord, save us. I didn't realize. But we can get them back, can't we?"

Hamelin turned away from him. "Possibly."

Curtis tugged his jacket back on straight. "Oh, thank you, Jesus. I knew you could take care of this. Let's get this done, then."

"Easier said than done," said Hamelin. "The devil loves to barter. I'm afraid the recently departed was merely a stepping-stone along the way to something much more desirable. And if I'm not mistaken ..." Hamelin let his eyes wander over their surroundings. "He's somewhere close by, waiting to offer and seal the deal for something much grander than a down-and-out homeless man's soul."

"But what would he want a soul runner manual for?"

Hamelin turned hard eyes on him. "He doesn't. And he knows he can't keep the soul. He'll just torment it a bit. It's part of his game, not an ultimate objective. He's pushing all our buttons, waiting for one of us to make a mistake. Beelzebub is trolling for the soul of an immortal."

Curtis blanched. "Im ... immortal? Management would never allow—"

A sudden breeze buffeted them and rustled the leaves of the hickory grove at the far end of the Phoenix parking lot. A leaf blew end over end across the empty parking spaces before coming to rest at the feet of a man standing alone under a tree at the far edge of the lot. He took a step forward and ground the leaf under his foot as if it were a discarded cigarette butt.

Hamelin's skin flushed with goose bumps. It was the fisherman he had met earlier on the beach. He was city blocks from the water, but he was, without a doubt, still fishing. He didn't call out or make any move toward discourse, but Hamelin felt the unspoken offer hanging in the air. Unlike the last time they met, it would be up to Hamelin to close the distance between them and initiate the encounter.

Hamelin hesitated. He really didn't want to entertain that invitation. He just wanted something back that was rightfully his, without any hellish deals. He glanced at Curtis, who had apparently also sensed the man and was now staring intently across the way.

"Hamelin, is that who I think … Because if it is, we're in over our heads, aren't we?"

"In the flesh, and yes, we are."

Curtis took hold of Hamelin's arm and began edging him back, as if any sudden move might bring hellfire raining down on them. "We should go. Let someone else locate the soul."

"Not until I have my book back."

"Are you willing to pay the price he'll be asking?"

Truth be told, Hamelin wasn't sure. Crossing that gravel parking lot, he would be moving into the grayest area he had ever traversed. How culpable would he be for even entertaining some sort of deal with the dark side? With each second he wasted waffling and considering, the pull to find out grew stronger, until he felt unable to walk away.

He ran his thumb along the sealed gilt pages of Curtis's manual. Unexpectedly, the book fell open, and before him was a consolidated list of pending soul runner transportees—not only Curtis's, but those of everyone else in his group, including his own. "Where did you get this?" he asked, trying to keep his voice even as he frantically searched the list.

"Martin. And you're not authorized," Curtis said, tugging on the book.

Hamelin elbowed him away as his finger went down the column. His list included all his remaining mulligans, starting with the oldest and continuing through his last: Livia Williams, aka Marie McGallagher. All the safeguards he had created to hide them had been stripped away. And Ryan Thomas was still showing up as a mulligan. After the drowning incident, Hamelin had been unsure about him.

"Dear God, what have you done, Martin." He ripped the page from the book and shoved it in his pocket."

Curtis flushed, looking as if he were about to burst a blood vessel. "You can't … That's my …"

Hamelin pointed a finger at him, and he shut his mouth. "*Can't?* You seem to forget yourself, Mr. Merriweather. It's time you remembered who's in charge here, sir. You are the bearer of an unauthorized document, or my name isn't Russell. Since we currently have more pressing issues, I will deal with it later. Now, stop your blubbering."

He slid Curtis's book into the jacket pocket where he usually kept his own. Then he checked on their friend across the parking lot. He hadn't moved an inch and was no doubt enjoying the little celestial dust-up going on before him. "I'm going to get the other one back. *He* certainly can't use it, and I'm certainly not going to give him what he wants."

"Which one of us does he want? Maybe we should just get out of here."

"Either will do. But that does raise the question: Why are you even still here? You have no manual and limited skills. I can't babysit you right now. Do everyone a favor and go home, Curtis." He glanced at Delaney, still sprawled on his back and hearing bells. Hamelin was battling on too many fronts, and this nonsense had gone on long enough. He accelerated the time-space continuum and started across the lot. "Don't be here when I get back."

He was halfway across the parking lot before the sound of crunching gravel brought him back around. He turned and saw Curtis coming at him, low and fast. The newbie hit him hard, driving him backward as he grappled for the backs of his legs.

"Aww, Curtis." Hamelin down-blocked him with his right arm and countered by wrapping him in a headlock. They both tumbled sideways and began barrel rolling. Hamelin was considerably taller, but the nerdy little fellow was wiry. They rolled several times before fetching up against the tumbledown brick retaining wall edging the Phoenix lot—Hamelin on top, Curtis underneath him and wedged against the wall. They lay like that a moment, the sound of ragged breathing filling Hamelin's ears.

"I'm going to get up now, Curtis. And if you so much as breathe on me again, you won't make it home to Martin. Am I communicating?"

Curtis turned his face away, squirmed another moment, then nodded. When Hamelin felt him go limp in submission, he got up and walked away.

The sharp blow to the right side of Hamelin's head came out of nowhere. He staggered and then swung around, catching Curtis full in the chest and heaving him away with all the strength he could muster. As he went down in pain, he heard a crack and thud.

All went black.

***

The tapping was like the dripping of a faucet: continual, predictable, and annoying. Hamelin's eyes popped opened, and he pulled his head up out of loose gravel. Inches from his face sat the fisherman, his black sandal bouncing to some unheard rhythm against the green lichened wall.

Hamelin scrambled up. He lunged for the black notebook, which lay open on the wall, but the Beelzebub surrogate was quicker. He wrapped a long-fingered hand around it and shook his head once.

Hamelin reconsidered his options. The manual was a divine

document. This devil's minion couldn't possibly believe he could retain control of it. But did Hamelin really want to brawl with this one? To take on an emissary of darkness was to sail in uncharted territory. "Where's Curtis?" he finally asked, changing tack.

The Beelzebubette motioned behind him. "In the soul-running vernacular? Free fall, I believe."

Curtis was lying motionless along the low wall, his head resting at an odd angle. Hamelin crouched down next to him and put his hand on his back. He didn't react. He wasn't hot or cold. There was no spilled blood or gore. Soul runners were of the spirit, not the flesh. Hamelin rose to his feet, exuding righteous fury. "There is no death for an immortal. What did you do to him?"

"Me? Nothing." The Bubette came off the wall with a graceful slither. "Didn't your mother ever tell you that horseplay can be dangerous? And no, *duh,* we both know you can't kill the dead. But surely you also know that there is a more *final* designation for all you soul runners."

"Yeah, but you don't determine where or when he goes. You can't just walk off with him. Now, get lost before I call the might of heaven down upon you and you are cast into the fiery cesspool you call home. You can't have him!"

"Yet."

"Not *ever.*"

Bub twitched an eyebrow and approached Curtis. Hamelin reached out to stop him, then reconsidered. What was Bub's power? One did not touch an immortal, be it a servant of light or of darkness, without consequence. He withdrew his hand as an odor like rotting fish wafted over him.

Bub crouched down beside the fallen immortal. "Hmm. A physical altercation between two of God's children. Isn't that a violation of Section One? Most unbecoming. Like a modern-day Caine and Abel, wouldn't you say?"

"There was no ill intent here. Only two hotheads who let their tempers get the better of them."

Bub plucked the second calling card from Curtis's hip pocket and secreted it into a fold in his dark shirt. His face showed no pity or concern, nor any malicious intent. Rather, he had the detached air of someone considering the best way to move a piece of furniture and be done with it. "Soul runners are a different breed, aren't they? It's interesting that you have no authority to transport one of your own. I do believe your hands are tied, are they not? Feel free to run along, Hamelin Russell. Don't you have some sort of bacchanalian contest to attend to?"

The hell-bent soul runner spoke the truth: Hamelin had no official standing here. Yet he wasn't positive Bub did, either. This smacked more of opportunity than obligation—a mistaken transport that would take a while to tease out, and a hellish experience for Curtis.

Hamelin's mind raced. So far, he was at fault for losing his book. Yes, he had violated Section One by putting his hands on Curtis, but given the circumstances, that might be forgiven. It was Curtis who had escalated the Caine-Abel clause. So should Hamelin play it by the book—even though he didn't have an operational one at the moment? Back off and report the unfortunate series of events and hope for mercy from his superiors? Or should he do what his heart was telling him to do? Something that he had done so often that, with the grace of God and good intent, he just might be able to pull it off without the use of his manual?

"You're right," he said. "I can't transport him, but I *can* do this."

Hamelin dropped to his knees and placed a hand over Curtis's. The simple gesture released Curtis' soul. As the temporal body remained prostrate, the ethereal rose like a gossamer wisp that dissipated into fine particles that glittered as they caught the sun. The mass gathered itself into a tight cluster. And then, with a swoosh, it shot forward and hit Hamelin full in the chest—and vanished.

Hamelin grabbed his chest and shuddered. For a split second, he felt dazed and disoriented. The feeling passed, and he looked at Bub and laughed. "I may not be able to transport him, but I sure as hell can create a mulligan. Check and mate."

Bub studied the point of entry on Hamelin's chest and seemed to contemplate his own course. Then, with a shrill, hair-raising keen, he was gone.

Hamelin sank down against the wall. It was all going wrong. And this was bad, really bad. He could already hear the Jake-braking of the massive soul-running machine as it ground to a halt. A missing soul runner would not stay so for long. And exactly how long could he lug Curtis around like this? Casting him back out would be a complicated task and would leave both of them vulnerable during the process.

He looked toward the Phoenix and one of the only true friends he had ever had. Ryan Thomas and his symbiotic co-soul had spent years entwined within the same corporal vessel. Could the same be said for two immortals?

Hamelin ran his hand across his chest, but it was his gut that was yelling at him. He hated to admit it, but he had run out of options. So he snatched up his book, dematerialized, and entered the nearest portal into the afterlife.

Chapter Twenty-Eight
Fission

Luke was all over him before he cleared the portal threshold. His eyes went straight to Hamelin's midsection.

"I'm not nine months pregnant," Hamelin said. "Where—"

"Sh-h-h!" Luke grabbed his arm and hustled him down the corridor, past door after door of residential rooms arranged like a Holiday Inn. This was the newbie wing of Building 25, but it was currently deserted, with all its residents out participating in the Tippy. Luke grimaced at the only sound in the silent corridor: the squeak of his rubber-soled shoes on the polished floor.

As they passed the great picture window opposite the elevator bay, Hamelin glanced outside. To his chagrin, the scene had changed. The peaceful tropical waterfall that splashed gently into clear pools as it tumbled down a lush mountainside was gone, replaced by a raging torrent of muddy floodwater that submerged everything in its path. He averted his eyes and pushed on.

When they had gone halfway, Luke unlocked the door marked "21." They entered, and he locked it behind them. The room was tidy and spare: a twin bed, a desk, and a dark wooden armoire of simple style.

"The *darkness* stalking you? What did you …? How can you …?" Luke threw his hands up in frustration. "Now what?"

Hamelin's eyes darted about. "Curtis's room? Yeah, this is good. Come back in ten minutes, Luke."

"Hamelin, I doubt you have five minutes before they figure out you've sneaked back home. I can't come back. This is the last favor I can do for you. Gotta figure it out yourself."

"I know. And I appreciate all your help. I'll never forget." Hamelin gave him a quick embrace. "You'll need to come back and do a wellness check on him, so don't go far. I can't afford to send you a shout-out. That would be tantamount to sending out an all-points bulletin on myself." He pushed Luke out the door and locked it.

Hamelin sat down at the desk and put his head in his hands. He and Curtis were safe without risk of anyone swooping in and laying claim to either of their souls. But Luke was right. The elders would soon find them. He closed his eyes and prayed for discernment as he tried to drift into a place of quiet contemplation and, he hoped, insight.

Creating a mulligan was a relatively uncomplicated procedure. One simply allowed a soul released from one mortal body to drift into another. And ending a mulligan was equally simple. One merely terminated the flesh and transported the spirit. He had done it many times over the years. But Curtis wasn't technically a mulligan. While soul runners could assume human form, they were never of the flesh. Curtis had been a spirit of the law before Hamelin mulliganed him, and he would remain so after. Hamelin had never drawn a soul into himself as he had done with Curtis. So, how, exactly, to extricate Curtis's being from his own?

He didn't think he could hurt Curtis. Sending the newbie's soul on to heaven or hell would be above his pay grade. Maybe it was wishful thinking, but Hamelin hoped he had been granted some sort of spur-of-the-moment authority to do what he had just done. It was probably the most selfless act he had ever performed, but that didn't mean he wouldn't pay for it in the end.

He reined in his galloping thoughts and tried to visualize Curtis prostrate on his bed. He cast aside the distracting baubles, paper wads, and bits that pulled his pockets tight across his pants, and tried to blot out the black cat on the pillow, rumpled bedclothes, and half-dozen unhelpful visual images that popped into his head as his control failed him.

This was not working. He shook out his hands, shook each foot, and resumed his pose. Picturing blackness, he reached within, softly calling Curtis's name as he sank deeper and deeper within himself. He embraced the nothingness. Slowly, almost imperceptibly at first, he felt a growing pull, the draw of power like a mild electrical current flowing out in all directions from his core. He let go and traveled with it, floating on an uncontrollable surge of emotion that built into a raging river as it coursed through him. His body shook, and just as he felt he could bear it no longer, the force surged into his fingertips and exploded out into the room in a flash of white, burning heat.

Hamelin fell forward and cracked his forehead on the table. When he raised his head, Curtis lay on his bed, eyes closed, breathing deeply as if in sleep. Outwardly, there was no mark on him. And inwardly, he seemed at peace.

Hamelin fled the room. There was no time to learn more. He couldn't imagine the blip this would create on the radar search for Curtis, only that there would be one. A big one. He broke into a jog and headed for the conservatory in Building 1. One final stop and far too little time.

When he reached Building 1, it seemed a ghost town. But this was merely an illusion. The greatest concentration of offices in the complex was here, and many souls were toiling quietly away behind closed doors.

By the time he hit the Hall of Masters, he was sprinting. He skidded to a halt in front of the Berlinghiero Madonna. She starred back at him with pleading, soulful eyes. "*Perdonami,*" he whispered as he reverently touched his forehead, heart, and shoulders in the sign of the cross. He reached up and tried to lift the painting from its wall hooks. The left side came free with ease; the other refused to yield. He lowered it, shifted the frame slightly, and tried again, this time lifting the stubborn side first. It remained stuck fast. He turned it loose and peeked behind the edge of the painting. One of the metal hooks was crimped down tight on the hanging wire.

He rattled the picture in frustration and eyed the portal two doors down. There was no more time. In desperation, he took the right side of the painting in both hands, braced his foot against the wall, and yanked. Both anchors broke loose from the plaster and sent him and the Madonna reeling backward. He landed on his backside in the middle of the corridor, the picture still firmly in his hands.

He examined it. The frame was split across the top from one hook to the other, but the painting appeared undamaged. "*Tutto andrà bene,*" he said reassuringly to Christ's mother as she continued to plead with him. He tucked her under his arm and bolted.

***

Martin hurried toward the White Corridor. The impromptu meeting would play havoc with his already packed schedule. But that was okay. He was a firm believer that gossip came in two forms. There was accurate scuttlebutt, which had contained kernels of truth, and there was idle, empty chitchat. Martin knew how to cultivate the former and ignore the latter. And what he had cultivated this morning made him ecstatic. There were big problems with the Tippy—no names yet, but he could guess. Hamelin had somehow screwed himself over. Marin had hoped Curtis would enlighten him, but the greenhorn had failed to keep him informed. What a disappointment he had proved to be. He would let him know that as soon as he reported in.

Martin turned into the Hall of Masters and froze, his eyes immediately drawn to a man exiting through the portal door with something under his arm. He zeroed in on the blank space where a picture should be, the gouges on the wall, and plaster on the floor directly beneath it. Someone had the audacity to steal the Madonna? A flash of fear rolled over him. A person capable of stealing a religious painting was capable of .... He backed out of the hallway.

What to do? There was no way he would confront the culprit. He didn't want a hero's role—just a nice job title, a corner office, and a slavishly obedient staff. He wouldn't get involved. He took off on a quickly rerouted course to the meeting.

He took two steps and hesitated. Had the man seen him? Because if he had, there would be no place Martin could hide if the thief came after him. No, the thief had never turned looked his way. Martin had seen him only from the back, and maybe a split second in profile. A few neurons pinged his memory bank, like a little hammer dinging a brass bell. He knew that face. Hated that face. Wouldn't rest until he nailed the whole sorry hide to the tanyard wall. Only Hamelin Russell was despicable enough to steal Berlinghiero's masterpiece. Martin set off to report the crime. This would be the most excellent of days.

***

Curtis awoke from a dark and troubling dream whose specifics he couldn't remember. He bolted up into a sitting position. No Hamelin, no agent of the devil, and no parking lot. Just a king-size headache and almost debilitating confusion.

He swung off the bed and put fingertips to his ears. “Martin? Martin, are you there?”

Martin’s voice immediately flooded his brain. It was loud and clipped, irritated. “Curtis! Where are you?”

Curtis turned about the room, wide-eyed and thunderstruck. “My *room*? Although I’m not quite sure how I got … Actually, sir, I might be in a bit of trouble …”

“Don’t. Go. Anywhere. I’ll be right there.”

“Yes sir. I think it might be for the best, sir.”

He tuned Martin out and began pacing back and forth between his bed and the door. Whatever he did, he would not put himself in the position of falling back to sleep again. At the moment, there seemed something very unholy about that.

Chapter Twenty-Nine
The Weigh Station

Hamelin found Ryan Thomas sitting atop a wooden crate by the Phoenix's service door. Maybe he wasn't waiting there for him, but it was a comforting thought. He seemed small and lost, a look of powerlessness and resignation on his face.

"Book?" Ryan asked, his eyes searching.

Hamelin patted his pocket.

"A part of me was hoping you wouldn't come back. But the rest of me still needs you." He tipped his head toward the public room. "There's a big crowd out there, but I'm afraid to go out into my own pub. Contest still on?"

Hamelin glanced that way. "Most have moved on, but you were wise to stay here." His gaze returned to Ryan. "I am sorry, Ryan Thomas. I have blundered spectacularly. I must leave. If you like, you can come with me, or if you prefer, take your chances here. I can offer little protection, but it's more than you would have at the Phoenix. Whatever I have is yours, but you must choose immediately."

Ryan hopped up and headed for the bar area. "Just let me—"

Hamelin slid in front of him. "No! I've already wasted enough time. *Now.* Or this is goodbye." He watched Ryan take stock of his surroundings. He had seen that look too many times to count—an unwillingness to let go of what one had, to grasp at an uncertain future. Free choice could sometimes be painful to watch, and even Hamelin couldn't tell him the right one to make.

Ryan clapped his hand on Hamelin's shoulder and closed his eyes. "Wherever. I'm with you."

Hamelin gently shook him until he opened his eyes again. "Your house, but we're going the old-fashioned way. Collect your car keys and get us out of here. There is no hiding, so skip the scenic and circuitous. It's only a matter of time before we face consequences."

***

The only sound in the Carrera was that of the air whipping through Ryan's open window. Hamelin rode shotgun, slouching down in the seat as low as he could manage. There was little he could do for either of them. He had never been good at planning, but at least he could keep things calm and dignified to the end. How had he gotten himself into such a mess? Sure, he was known to dog it occasionally, but his basic intentions were generally good. Stubborn pride was to blame. Why couldn't he accept authority? If only he had returned home as soon as they locked his book! His dear friend Luke was right. He should have toed the line and ignored Martin.

Ryan's quiet voice interrupted his ruminations. "Hamelin. Am I going to die today? Because if I am, there are people—"

Hamelin pointed down the road. "You have always talked too much. Keep driving. I need to think."

Ryan tapped his thumbs on the steering wheel. "And sometimes *you* don't talk *enough*."

Hamelin rolled his eyes toward Ryan. Unless he smote the man, he would just keep blabbing. He put his feet on the floormat and pushed up in the seat. "Perhaps."

Ryan pulled up to the front steps of his house and killed the engine. "Perhaps you don't talk enough, or perhaps I *am* going to die?"

Hamelin gave him a scorching look. The last thing he needed was a Q & A from a despairing mortal. He took his painting from the car and went inside.

Ryan scrambled up the steps after him. "No! Come back here. You don't have the right to walk away from me. I have a stake in this. At least let me die knowing what's going on!"

Hamelin ignored him. He walked through the galley kitchen and turned down a short hallway of bedrooms. When he reached the room at the end, he entered. It was the smallest bedroom—twin bed, easy chair, and a built-in nook with drawers and a computer desk. He stood the Madonna upright against the computer monitor and motioned Ryan toward the chair. "I can think of many other things that we could choose to do."

Ryan took the chair. "No. Knowledge is power. Tell me."

Hamelin stretched out on the bed as he considered the request. There would be no power plays from here on out, but Ryan Thomas had been more game than he had ever expected him to be. He deserved to know. And it would keep him distracted. Hamelin closed his eyes and began to recite as if it were yesterday.

"It started long ago. I was charged with escorting a soul to heaven—someone Martin knew during life and felt wronged by. He wanted me to, er, take the soul the *other* way."

"I though you said that God was the … What's the word you used? *Distributor.* So how is Martin getting off deciding fate?"

"Precisely. I refused his despicable, unauthorized request."

"But if you had, would the soul have remained in hell?"

"Of course not. One can't game the system. Martin knew that. He just wanted to inflict as much terror and suffering as he could before the assignment was reversed and the soul was sent to its proper place. Of course, everything would have been my fault. I knew there would be repercussions no matter what I did. The proverbial rock and a hard place? Scylla and Charybdis? Devil and the deep blue sea?" He paused a moment as he watched it play out again in vivid detail through his memories. "In retaliation," he continued, "he wrote me up on a series of bogus charges, and I was removed from my plum assignments to heaven and busted back to making deliveries to hell."

Ryan shuddered. "I thought angels were supposed to be honest."

"They are, but we're not angels. The career paths are different."

Hamelin placed his hands behind his head and studied the ceiling. "Every time he's in charge, it's something—a subtle chipping away of me and others. Particularly me."

Ryan got up and walked over to the Madonna. "Hamelin?" he said as he ran his hand along the crack in the frame. "You *are* dead, aren't you?"

"You shouldn't have to ask that."

Ryan turned and looked at him. "No mortal should be having *any* of the conversations I seem to have with you. But hey," he said spreading his arms out wide. "Here we are."

Hamelin looked around the room with its blank walls and insipid decor utterly lacking in character. "Yes, here we are." His gaze settled on his beloved Madonna. He nodded once at her.

Ryan's eyes shifted back to the painting. "Berlinghiero's Madonna? This isn't real, right?" He turned the frame over as if he would find a yard-sale tag.

"You couldn't tell the difference between the real thing and a velvet

Elvis. Of course it's real."

Ryan put the painting back and took a respectful step back. "Oh. And you took it … why?"

"Borrowed."

"You have a very strange way of defining reality," Ryan said. "Then why did you borrow it?"

"Because it was mine to begin with. I poured my heart and soul into that work, and now, in this trying time, I need a little of that back."

Ryan raised an eyebrow. "Is this another of your Robert Johnson I-wanna-play-blues-like-the-master stories? You're going to lie there and tell me you gave Berlinghiero a little extra time on earth in exchange for learning how to paint?"

"No." Hamelin joined him in front of the Madonna. "Quite the contrary. It was *I* who bartered for time. This was my last painting before I passed on …"

"No shit, Sherlo—"

Hamelin cut him off with a glare.

"Sorry, Hamelin. I didn't mean that as an insult. It's just I don't often get to hobnob with medieval painters." He admired the painting again. "One more question. Well, many, but for now …" He shot Hamelin a tentative look and waited.

"I'm listening."

"You're quite rebellious and can be very annoying at times. That leads me to believe you couldn't possibly have made it past Saint Peter and through the gates. Do you normally reside in heaven, or hell?"

Hamelin drew back in horror. First, Beelzebub thinking he was compromised enough to approach, and now this? "How hurtful. I thought we were friends."

Ryan shrugged. "I don't know what we are, but I'd hate to think I was complicit with one of the devil's own."

Hamelin tipped his head back and roared with laughter. "This from the *honest* man who was begging me to take his soul instead of Livia's? The one who begged me to go away and come back in sixty years? 'A single tick of the clock for an immortal' was how, I think, you once put it. You mortals do have your moments, don't you?"

"For heaven's sake, Hamelin! Heaven or hell?"

Hamelin wiped the moisture from his eyes and walked to the window. The river was calm and smooth as glass. "Neither. It's a temporary state of being some of us find ourselves in after death. For some, it is but a blip in the journey to eternal bliss or damnation, but for others, a longer period."

"So you're in purgatory?"

"Not exactly. Think of it as a weigh station of sorts."

Ryan nodded. "A *way* station. I suppose that makes sense. There's no need to hurry; eternity's a long time, isn't it? I must say, though, I never expected heaven to be so … so haphazardly run."

A quiet, wistful sigh escaped Hamelin's lips. "From what I have heard, Ryan James, I don't think we would be disappointed at all. Lemon meringue pie and the delta blues played all day long," he whispered. He was quiet a moment before turning back to Ryan. "But we aren't addressing heaven here. These people may be immortal, but they aren't heavenly. At least, not yet."

He noticed a work boat push off from the dredger, leaving him with an unobstructed view of the operation. He watched with fascination as a conveyor belt moved silt and debris up from the river bottom and ran a discharge out the other side. "Until then, we have the Weigh Station. The more mundane governances of transporting souls are determined there. In theory, it all should run smoothly, but in truth, it's an imperfect business run by immortals full of pettiness, visions of grandeur, and stupidity."

"Not really the company man, are you, Hamelin? So that raises the question: If you understand all this, why can't you just follow instructions and get yourself out? Why stick around and fight it?"

Hamelin threw himself down in the chair and put his head in his hands. "I fight it because I feel. Okay? I *feel.* Is that so wrong?"

"I, uh, suppose not."

"I've given many lovely people a second chance."

"Sometimes, you might have gotten it right, but the man you mulliganed me with, Ryan Llewellyn Thomas, was a despicable human being."

Hamelin raised his hand. "I didn't choose that vessel. It was a same time, same place issue. Mistakes do happen, but for the most part, I don't believe what I've done is wrong. If creating mulligans were wrong, the might of Saint Peter would have come thundering down and crushed me like a dung beetle. Don't you see? I'm exercising free will in a compassionate way for the benefit of others, and *I'm getting away with it.* Doesn't that tell you something?"

Ryan sat down on the edge of the bed. "Yeah. Saint Peter's apparently not paying enough attention, or he would muster you out. Meanwhile, *they* are coming to get us. I wish I had never jumped in that water and gotten you suspended. You're screwed. I'm screwed. Marie McGallagher is ..." He began to wring his hands.

Hamelin tipped his chair back and propped his feet up on the bed. "Forget it. I made the choice to put aside the book and save you."

"I can't do that. You told me there would be a price to pay, and I stupidly thought I would be the one paying it. At worst, my life would end early. Marie's, too, but it would be okay because she and I would be together. I didn't stop to think that you would also have to pay."

Hamelin shrugged. "I understood all the consequences."

"Because you always know what you need to know." Ryan gave him a long, thoughtful look. When he spoke again, his voice was soft but deliberate. "You have your book back now. Go ahead and take my soul." He reached up and wiped one eye. "But I, uh … one final request. Then you can get at it." He choked up and had to wait a moment as he struggled for the words. "First opportunity? Go get Marie. Maybe we can't be together in this life, but if there is any happiness in heaven, I'll see her there."

Hamelin watched him brush away tears now flowing freely down both cheeks. He felt a tug inside. Pity, or a loving memory? A little of both, maybe.

"I'll be there at the gate."

"I'm afraid it's now out of my hands, Ryan James. After I left you, I had a little run-in with Curtis. I believe he's okay, but I've attracted some bad sorts. When Curtis repeats everything to Martin …" Hamelin shook his head.

Ryan exhaled slowly and seemed to pull himself together. "How soon?"

Hamelin could feel the fear creeping into Ryan's heart like a lengthening evening shadow slowly eating up the light. "Best say a prayer, Ryan James. Our time is nigh."

Chapter Thirty
The Black Zone

Martin stood before Curtis, hands clasped behind his back. He had never seen an immortal in such sad shape. When he could finally get the newbie to look him in the eye, he saw trauma and fear swirling there.

"And you're sure it was a demonic soul runner?" he asked, trying to be as gentle as possible.

Curtis lifted his eyes from the bedroom floor. "Yes sir. He gave me his card. God forgive me, I was so intent on getting even, I thought it was a joke. And then he started leading me, filling me with doubt, cankering my soul. I could feel myself sliding …" He shuddered, and his eyes reverted to the floor.

"Yes, yes, that's all right." Martin patted his shoulder and sat down beside him. "Don't think this is anything personal. We've seen it before—the underworld trolling for unsuspecting souls. Not frequently, but enough. A rogue soul runner can do much damage, but once we've identified them, we make short shrift of them and put things back to right."

And at present, he needed to make quick work of all this before others muddied the waters. Team lead and perpetual screw-up Hamelin Russell was the problem. Ineptitude, failure to follow manual guidelines and restrictions, and theft were severe charges, but he needed something more. If he had all the pieces, he could present an airtight case for judgment and damnation.

He got up and moved to the desk to give Curtis a little breathing room. "Who struck the first blow?" he asked, absently moving a round glass paperweight in line with Curtis's matching pen-and-pencil set.

"I'm afraid I did, sir."

Martin shook his head. Curtis was the last person he would ever expect to inflict violence on another. He picked up a discarded wad of paper and began smoothing it out. "Why?"

"Because he was going to make a deal with the devil to get his manual back." Curtis launched into a play-by-play of the drama leading up to his attack on Hamelin—including his taking of both their notebooks, and Hamelin's apparent friendship with the owner of the Phoenix bar.

Martin didn't respond. Much more riveting was the list of transportee names he was holding—transportees under Hamelin Russell's care. Some of them had pending dates going back years. "Curtis, what happened to the universal transportee list I gave you? Did you access it?"

"Uh …"

Martin turned around and waved the crumpled paper at him. "Curtis?"

"Hamelin was here?" He looked around wildly. "It was Hamelin, sir. I tried to stop him. He tore his list of names right out of my manual. I suppose that's his, sir."

"Relax. If he was here, he's long gone now. And the bar owner Hamelin is so chummy with—you said that's a man named Ryan Thomas?"

"That's right," Curtis said. He got up and moved toward Martin, a spark of life returning to his expression. "He's on the list?"

Martin tapped the paper with his forefinger. "Yes. And his pickup date is way overdue. He's a mulligan. Number three, from what I see here."

"Sweet Jesus," Curtis said, making the sign of the cross. "I swear I never read this. If I had known, I would have told you immediately." Curtis leaned in to read the list. "How much trouble am I in?"

Martin pulled it away. Here was his smoking gun. "Clearly, you've been duped. If we act quickly, we can clean up what Hamelin's done. Save management a lot of time and headache. A good turn here would go a long way toward proving you've been an innocent bystander. Might even move us both on to better things. Would you like to help, Curtis?"

Curtis nodded.

Martin clapped him on the back. "I thought so. We'll start with tracking Hamelin down. My guess is, he's still in Nevis. If we catch him in the company of the mulligan, even better. I have the authority to take him into custody and bring him back here."

"And if he resists?"

"If he's smart, he won't. But even if he does, you needn't worry. By the power of two, he will be no match for us."

"Violence?" Curtis backed away. "Maybe we should—"

"Shh, Curtis. You've been through a difficult time. I need your full trust on this. The devil has many tricks and disguises. Let clearer, less troubled heads prevail in this time of peril. That's what management is for. Hamelin Russell has been creating mulligans in direct violation of Section Three-Eight-Three and courting the dark side."

Curtis studied him a moment and then nodded. "Right, sir. This is all making my head spin and pound. Just tell me what I have to do."

"Count on it," Martin said, rising. "I'll tell you exactly what I need you to do. Now, hurry. We've wasted enough time here."

***

"Hamelin!

Hamelin snapped out of his meditation and responded immediately to the telepathic voice. "Luke! Problem?"

"Several," Luke replied. "But they are not all on the home front. I've been parked outside Curtis's room, waiting to see what shakes out. Martin hightailed it down here right after you left. From the conversation I heard through the door, he has complete buy-in from Curtis. They're headed your way and they're going to do a mulligan cleanup. If you get in the way, Martin has the authority to take you out, and by the excitement in his voice, it sounded like he's itching to do just that. Take care of the problem yourself, and avoid all the heartache."

Hamelin's gaze flicked to Ryan, who was watching him closely. He turned away.

"Hamelin, your lack of enthusiasm scares me. Better idea?"

"Hardly, but there is something else. I want you gather up all the graphs you prepared and take them to Stephen. If you can't get in to see him, start working your way down the hallway until you find someone available who has the authority to get involved."

"You might want to rethink that. Martin's got some sort of list with your mullig—"

"I know the list. It's an illicit concoction no one should be privy to, and I'm not sure it's even accurate at this point. It'll probably update when the moratorium lifts. I've whittled my numbers down and I'm prepared to answer for those few."

Hamelin felt Ryan still watching him. He walked over to the closet door, which stood half open, and swung it wide. Inside were three wire coat hangers, a pair of black rubber boots, and a battered acoustic guitar. For a moment, he considered stepping in and closing the door behind him. Reconsidering, he reached in and pulled out the instrument. "Just do what I asked, and I'll take my chances with the rest."

"I'm already halfway to Stephen's."

Luke's steadfast tone bolstered Hamelin's courage. "Thanks. Talk to you later."

"Hamelin! If you need me, I can be there."

Hamelin stifled a smile. "You might want to weigh that offer carefully."

"Not necessary. You might be the most screwed-up soul runner …"

Hamelin frowned and leaned forward. "Didn't catch that. What again?"

"We just need to stop that son of a bitch."

Hamelin laughed. He doubted Luke had ever cussed in the living world, let alone tried it in the afterlife. "I appreciate that, but no, concentrate on your end. I owe you."

"And you shall pay, my friend. You shall pay."

As Hamelin felt the connection between them break, he reconnected with his immediate surroundings. Ryan sat riveted in his seat, eyes glued to him.

"You're telepathic," Ryan said, still staring.

"What did you expect, an unlimited Verizon plan? I'm also multilingual, left-handed, and famished."

Ryan got up and moved closer. "Who's coming?"

"Martin and Curtis," Hamelin said, softly strumming the guitar. He sweep picked across the strings. Surprisingly, it was in tune. "Relax," he said, looking at Ryan. "Luke is a good friend. And contrary to what you may think, I do have a few. He's never failed me." Hamelin stopped strumming and cradled the guitar in the chair. "Sandwich?" he asked, and walked out.

"My last meal is going to be bologna?" Ryan followed him into the kitchen galley. "No thanks. I'll skip eating. If I'm going to have to fight for my life, I'll take something sharp in high-carbon steel. You eat."

***

With a wash of relief, Luke noted Stephen's open door. Then panic set in as he saw that the antechamber was packed with twelve high-level managers. He stutter-stepped and glanced over at Stephen's receptionist, Anita. Her amiable smile gave him a spark of hope. With renewed determination, he excused his way through the crowd.

"Hi, Anita," he whispered, leaning in as closely as decorum allowed. "I have an emergency." He placed his blue folder in the middle of her desk. "I need to get this to Stephen immediately."

Her eyes moved from the folder to the crowd, then back to Luke again. She picked it up. "As soon as the crisis ebbs."

"This *is* the crisis," Luke said, tugging on the folder.

"Luke!"

It was Gabe, a low-level supervisor in Martin's new group, coming his way. "You've saved me steps. Do you know where Hamelin is? Seems he and another runner have fallen off the radar. Last known location, Nevis."

Luke was fairly sure Hamelin had jumped rather than fallen, but he listened and nodded solicitously. "No idea." He turned back to Anita.

"He should have been back by now," Gabe continued. "The retreats have all but wrapped up." In a hushed voice, he added, "Moratorium is about to be lifted, too. Stephen needs us to find him. If there's a problem, we need to provide aid or do … Well, at any rate, he's needed back here."

Luke stood rooted, horrified. *Or do what?*

Gabe tipped his head toward the door. "High priority, so let's go. We'll split up once we get to Nevis."

With no way out that he could see, Luke followed him through the crowd. As they reached the door, he managed one last desperate look toward Anita. "He's expecting that." He hated lying, but desperation sometimes compromised good people.

A moment later, he stepped through a portal and hurtled toward Nevis.

Chapter Thirty-One
Playing Our Song

From the moment he began to play the guitar, Hamelin's talent held Ryan spellbound. He was a sight, hunched over the instrument and rocking gently, a soft shimmer of light encircling him—Hamelin's happy contented glow. He and the guitar were one, or maybe it was more than that. Ryan knew his Delta blues, and sometimes the riffs were so complex, he would have sworn Hamelin had summoned the souls of all the great Mississippi Delta bluesmen to accompany him. Gradually, the music shifted to the short but magical catalog of Robert Johnson, perhaps the greatest of them all. Ryan wasn't surprised. Hamelin had told him Johnson had taught him how to play before the immortal escorted his soul into the afterlife. If he played long enough, maybe other familiar styles would emerge—evidence of secret deals between the dying and a soul runner whose greatest joys were music and baseball. Ryan smiled as he pictured Hamelin smashing his guitar à la Jimi Hendrix.

"So, to recap, you're musical; you paint. What other abilities? Gourmet cooking? Talking to animals?"

"The last comes with the territory, so I wouldn't exactly call it an ability."

Ryan's gaze drifted to Hoffa, curled up against Hamelin's back. The sting of being rejected by his own dog lessened a bit. He closed his eyes and floated effortlessly to a place of safety and calm. At some point, and he wasn't sure when, the melody slowly shifted to something sweet and gentle, something so quiet it almost seemed as if someone had put music to his thoughts. Ryan stopped fighting the urge to sleep. "This is good. What's it called?"

When Hamelin didn't answer, Ryan looked his way. Hamelin had set aside the guitar and was gazing out the window at the waning light, yet the enticing strains continued. He scrambled off the bed and took a center position in the middle of the room. Mrs. Mattingly never played music, and he had no other close neighbors. "Hamelin? What is that?"

"There's always music. No two quite the same, but all lovely and soothing." Hamelin's head moved ever so slightly to the beat.

"There's nothing soothing about that. They're coming for me?"

Hamelin seemed lost in the melody. "Yes. The moratorium is lifting. It appears you will be the first problem solved."

"Is it Martin?"

"I'm not yet privy to that, but I'll let you know soon enough."

"I don't remember any music when I died the first time."

"There is always music, but not for the living. No need for you to remember it. Your wife's music was exquisite. I can hum it, if you like."

Ryan shuddered. "Certainly not! I don't need an earworm to go along with the horror of what happened that day. God, you're emotionally empty!"

"If I were, you'd be facing this alone." Hamelin took up a position in the chair. "Sit here next to me," he commanded. "We wait."

Ryan sat back down on the bed, his eyes darting from the window to the door and back to Hamelin again. "Help me appeal this, Hamelin."

"Relax. Dying is all part of the process. Be grateful for what you've had, and look forward to what awaits."

Ryan's hands stopped. "So I *am* going to heaven?"

"Oh, I have no idea. But you seem like a good enough sort. I've certainly encountered worse. Much, much worse. My guess would be that you will at least make the Weigh Station. At any rate, transporting for a while won't hurt you. Look at me."

Ryan put his head between his knees. "Oh, dear God. And what's going to happen to you when they find out how you've obstructed?"

"Well, it's not like they can execute me," Hamelin said, and laughed. It sounded forced. "They'll convene a hearing, which will involve issues of failure to protect my manual. That will pale in comparison to the issues of interference when I rescued you, willful violation of my sacred trust to transport the souls of those assigned to me, and inflicting violence on a fellow immortal. I, too, will soon be facing the final judgment."

There was a sudden shift in the air as a cool breeze blew through the open window. Hamelin rose. "I need to take care of something. Stay here."

Ryan ignored the order. He followed Hamelin to the kitchen and watched as the immortal held his manual over the sink.

"Don't come any closer," Hamelin said over his shoulder. "No need for senseless collateral damage."

Ryan stopped at the doorway.

Hamelin grasped the manual firmly in both hands. "I am ready to be taken out of this dreary existence, Lord. Thy will be done. As given, so shall it be returned." A flash of brilliant light immolated the text. Hamelin staggered forward, grasping at the faucet to steady himself and crumpled to the floor.

Ryan blew out of the doorway and came to some fifteen feet away on the living room floor. His eyes immediately settled on two figures silhouetted in the light from the French doors onto the deck. The soft, beautiful music he had been hearing was now sweeping and loud. He scrambled to his feet.

A quick look to the left showed him Hamelin in a heap on the kitchen floor. He began crawling that way. "Hamelin! Friends here to see you."

No response.

He focused on his visitors. "Curtis, isn't it? And I assume you must be Martin," he said, looking from one to the other. "but at a time like this, assuming probably isn't the way to go. So at the risk of sounding rude, may I ask who's calling?"

Curtis stepped forward. "Yes. Curtis, a friend of Hamelin's. It was a little crazy at the Phoenix. I don't think we were formally introduced." He thrust out his hand and began walking forward. "Curtis Merriweather, Mr. Thomas."

Ryan felt an undercurrent of throbbing power—indefinable but terribly wrong. "Phobic," he said, nodding at the offered hand. "Only under extreme duress for business purposes."

"This is business," Martin said, propelling Curtis forward. "Just think of us as another Hamelin."

There was movement in the kitchen. Ryan bolted that way. As he reached Hamelin, some unseen force sent him tumbling. When he came to rest, he lay against the dishwasher. The air crackled and grew hot as brilliant yellow light and thunder exploded around him, rendering him momentarily blind and deaf. As his senses returned, he saw someone standing in between himself and Curtis, but it wasn't Hamelin.

"Step aside, Luke," Martin said. "He's a mulligan. The moratorium has lifted."

The man called Luke remained steadfast. "Designated by whom? What list?"

And the strangest of dialogues began between the three as the air pressure in the room rose unbearably, forcing Ryan to clear his ears. He cowered against the cabinets as light pulsed off the walls and ceilings as if in some otherworldly stadium rock show.

Martin pointed at him. "He's on the list, Curtis. Do your duty while I deal with this."

Luke raised a hand, and golden flame licked angrily across the floor. It danced and roared before the immortals' feet, barring their advance. "Stop, Curtis," Luke demanded. "I've been sent to intervene in this travesty of justice. That list is unsanctioned and unlawful. Stand down or be damned."

Curtis hesitated and looked at Martin.

"Then we'll *all* be damned," Martin said, stepping over the line of flame.

In an instant, the room filled with a blaze of white light so intense that Ryan was forced to hide his face. And then, just as quickly, the room darkened and all was quiet. Ryan's ears popped, and he opened his eyes. All four immortals were gone, and he was alone in the kitchen.

Chapter Thirty-Two
All God's Mulligans

Once again Hamelin sat reflecting on white furniture, bleached curtains, and upper management. Stephen sat before him, Barnaby and Patrick flanking him at each shoulder. It was Stephen's show. This meeting would be quick—a swift judgment on a life well lived. Or not so well. If Hamelin's destination was hell, he had brought this all on himself. Somehow, the immortal, soul runner thing didn't wear well on him.

There were no papers on the conference table—just hands folded in cathedral poses. He watched the gentle tapping of Stephen's forefingers. Reluctance to damn him?

They locked eyes. Stephen said, "Hamelin Russell."

"Sir?"

"I was hoping we would not be meeting again for a while, but what's a week in the grand scheme of eternity, eh? Why do you think you're here, Hamelin?"

Hamelin raised an eyebrow. If Stephen didn't know, he would deny, deny, deny.

"At this Weigh Station," Stephen said, gesturing at their surroundings.

"Oh. Healing and purification—a chance at transition to something purer."

"You and your peers have been blessed with a second chance to get it right."

"A mulligan."

Stephen paused a moment to consider and then nodded. "Close enough. And just as on earth, the decisions you make here—ones that we hope are guided by love, compassion, and obedience to the law—determine your final judgment and destination." He leaned across the table as each hand closed into a tight fist. "Mr. Russell, have you ever met a regulation you liked? Why is it you must insist on pursuing the *spirit* of the law?"

Before Hamelin could formulate a response, Stephen regained his saintly bearing and continued. "The one mitigating factor in your rather lengthy stay with us has been your compassion. Of particular note is your recent rescue of a fellow soul runner. At great personal risk, I might add. It was selfless and heroic."

This was a good direction, Hamelin thought. "Well, anyone in my place—"

"But!" Stephen said, raising an index finger.

God, there was going to be a "but."

"You're making no real progress here. Isn't that an accurate assessment, Hamelin?"

Hamelin ran a finger along the edge of the table as he considered his options. A no answer might have catastrophic consequences. "I'm still having, uh, some difficulties. I'm getting better. It's not time to throw in the towel yet."

Stephen appeared unmoved. "Yes, um, the *attention deficit.* Your stay here started out so promisingly. But you can't seem to keep on task. And after all this time, you still haven't managed to transform yourself to a higher plane of existence. Picking up souls is a sacred trust."

Hamelin felt flushed. "Slow and steady—"

"Doesn't win this race, I'm afraid. Mr. Russell. Do you know why Section Three-Eight-Three prohibits the creation of mulligans?" He didn't wait for an answer. "Because nobody gave you the authority to play God. But you decided to, and quite frankly, you ran with it. And that's nothing to be proud of. There is no spirit of the law here, Hamelin Russell!"

"No sir." Hamelin didn't know which way to go with that one. Stephen's view of him was bouncing around like a Ping-Pong ball.

Stephen's steely eyes studied him a moment before the elder filled the awkward silence between them. "We have interviewed all parties involved in this dreadful Tippy debacle. You've been accused of failing to follow instructions, losing your manual, creating mulligans …" He stopped and sighed. "On and on it goes. However, without the records in your manual, which you report—and I quote—'*spontaneously combusted,*' we are left with an incomplete record of exactly what you've been doing these past few eons. What we have been able to determine is that a thread of compassion runs through your indiscretions."

Stephen's eyes softened. Their expression hurt Hamelin worse than if they were flashing anger or abject disappointment.

"The last time we met," Stephen continued, "you were put on thirty days' probation, with the understanding that you would maintain a certain level of performance. And you were told in no uncertain terms that failure to do so would trigger a final judgment. Considering what has occurred since that meeting, it has been deemed that you have violated your probation. Therefore, by the authority invested in me, Hamelin Russell, I am pronouncing judgment upon you."

Hamelin's mind blanked, and the statement bounced around in his head. "So it's hell, then?" he finally whispered.

"I don't think so."

"Angel?" Hamelin asked, brightening considerably.

Stephen uttered a sound somewhere between a sigh and a chuckle. "Let's not get carried away, now. The creation of mulligans alone should damn you. But there is this redeeming quality in you that *seems* to want to make considered heartfelt choices even when you should be following the letter of the law. The little Mississippi boy, Tyler Parson, for example."

"How do you know about Tyler?"

"A feathered friend," snapped Barnaby.

"Barnaby!" Stephen said, giving him a sharp look. He cleared his throat. "We have many avenues of information. And after thorough review of all, a judgment has been rendered. Domenica Rossellini di Hamelin," he said, locking eyes with Hamelin, "you are hereby mandated back to earth, where you will live out your days until such time as your purifying journey is deemed complete. Then you will receive final judgment."

"As a mortal?"

"No, but not as an average immortal, either. I want you to use that compassion and your knowledge and sense of the divine for the good of others."

Hamelin clutched at his chest. It was as if someone had plucked out his beating heart. "God have mercy!" he murmured. "You're kicking me out of the afterlife?"

"Always. And no, not forever. Just until …"

Hamelin looked down and realized his fingers had somehow entwined themselves into a tight prayerful clasp. He loosened them. "No more soul running?"

"I'm afraid not."

"Appeals?"

Stephen shook his head.

Hamelin bowed his head. "Then thy will be done. I have but one request. If I may make one last pickup ... There's a personal connection."

"Granted," Stephen said. "But under strict supervision. He exchanged glances with the other two elders. Each nodded but added nothing further. "Very well, Hamelin. Lucky are those who receive two chances, let alone three. See what you can do with it."

"I shall do my very best."

And that was it—quick and not at all as Hamelin had expected. He watched the three elders file out: Barnaby, then Patrick, and finally, Stephen. As he reached the door, Stephen suddenly turned.

"Oh," he said. "I almost forgot. Return the painting." And then he, too, was gone.

Hamelin put his head in his hands. So it was done, or nearly so. He briefly considered returning to his room for his guitar but rejected the notion. They could either forward it to him or give it to someone else. He would find another and start a new history.

He walked halfway down the hall. *Never return.* As much as he hated this place, it was a sobering thought. He took one last thoughtful look around and stepped through the nearest portal.

Chapter Thirty-Three

A Date to Remember

Bennie looked around the pub. They had been going gangbusters all week, and now this: quieter than four-thirty confession at Saint Peter's. "Too much to ask," he said to himself. He took another swipe at the counter he had just cleaned.

Vanessa looked up from the *Washington Post* she had spread out across the bar top. "The contest? You think it's over?"

"Yeah. You don't feel it, Van? The energy is gone." His gaze wandered above the bar, to the shelf that held his shot-glass collection, and he sighed. "Coulda' put it right there."

"Bennie." It was Jean, on the stool next to Vanessa, thoughtfully swirling a celery stick around in her bloody Mary. "I'm sorry. I gave you such a hard time about coming back, but watching your passion, how hard you've worked, how hard *everybody* worked …" Her voice trailed off, and she took a long, thoughtful drink.

"Yeah, so don't give up yet," Vanessa said, bypassing sports for the food section. "Maybe they're tallying votes, or something. Or visiting other places. Right?"

He shook his head. "No, from what I know, it's all pretty quick. I guess we didn't have what it takes."

He frowned.

"What is that?" he asked, and marched over to his collection. He pulled down a glass, and his frown deepened. "Monkey's uncle," he breathed. "Who did this?" he asked, turning around. This is great!"

Jean took the shot glass from him and ran her finger across the red embossed sketch of the Phoenix on one side, and the three lines of black inscription on the other.

Tippy Winner 2020
Bennie Bertollini
Nevis, Maryland

"Aww. Wish I had," she said, eyes shining as she looked up at Bennie. She handed it to Vanessa, who likewise admired it but disavowed any involvement.

And then it traveled down the row of regulars warming their bar stools, and through the gathering crowd of servers and kitchen help drawn by all the excited chatter. No one fessed up or could even offer a report of suspicious people or activity behind the bar. But they all agreed on one thing: Bennie guarded that shelf as jealously as a mother duck.

Vanessa handed the little glass back to him. "Congratulations, Bennie! The Tippy judges got it right. This place is the best, and I can't think of a better trophy for you."

Bennie held it up to the light, turning it to and fro as his eyes widened with awe. "All these years … You really think so?"

"Know so," Jean said, wrapping an arm around him.

He kissed her on the forehead. "Gives me goose bumps just thinking about it." He glanced around the room. "Anyone seen Ryan? This is gonna be a day he'll never forget."

***

Hamelin picked up a flat rock and flicked it sidearm out across the water. It skipped several times along the surface before disappearing into the Patuxent River. He saw a few more good candidates at his feet, but he would much prefer to get on with business. Where was the supervisor Stephen had insisted on? He picked up a fragment of oyster shell.

"Living to fight another day?"

It was Luke, standing quietly behind him, hands clasped behind his back as he looked out across the river. There was a radiance in the way his curls caught the sunlight. He looked like a redeeming angel. "And what, pray tell, is *that*?" Luke asked, pointing at the blue dredger in the channel.

Hamelin broke out into a wide smile. *"You?"*

"And I even volunteered," Luke said. "I thought you would be more comfortable with someone … well, you know. And I'm truly sorry anyone has to be here, Hamelin, but I guess that's how it is." He shrugged.

"No, I'm glad it's you. And it's me who should be apologizing. And thanking you. You averted much evil by showing up when you did. If it weren't for you—"

"Don't," Luke said, raising his hands in protest. "It's done, and I'll be all right. Probation for the foreseeable future, but it's nothing I can't handle. When I revealed all of Martin's machinations, the focus shifted."

"What happened to him?"

"I haven't seen him since I transported the three of you back. No one's seen him. I think judgment's already been passed."

"Burning, no doubt. And Curtis?"

"Probation, and Barnaby-of-few-words as mentor."

Hamelin snorted. "I'd give anything to see that."

Luke gave him a pained look. "I'll share it with you someday—in the blessed realm."

Hamelin felt a catch in his throat. "To the blessed realm," he said, flicking the shell fragment out into the water, where it immediately sank with a soft *plunk*. "I would shake your hand, but that may not be wise."

Luke shook his head. "And they will soon be wondering where I am." He gestured toward the house. "Shall we take care of business one last time?"

Hamelin led him to the back door. It was two minutes till noon. It was time. "You'll like this one, Luke. Mrs. Mattingly has a fierce exterior but a very tender heart. It'll be the Weigh Station's loss and heaven's gain."

***

Ryan wasn't sure what pulled him away from his reading. There was no shift in the air, exotic new smell, or sudden flight of the osprey from its perch high atop the light pole at the end of his pier. But there was something. He put down his book and looked past the yellow rose hedge dividing his yard from Mrs. Mattingly's. There was Hamelin, standing on the little stoop that looked out over her vegetable garden. He had been staring out across the river but almost immediately turned his attention toward Ryan. He offered a half salute and came down off the porch.

Still in the business. Ryan felt misty-eyed as he thought of sweet Mrs. Mattingly's soul winging its way to her new beginning in the afterlife. *Godspeed, Irene.* Certainly, she would be pausing only briefly, or most likely skipping entirely, the Way Station.

He watched as the immortal made his way through the tomato

plants that Mrs. Mattingly so lovingly attended, and on a little farther past a rainbow of flowers in what she called her cutting garden. He walked with a calm grace to the retaining wall at the water's edge and sat down—in a strange, beautiful harmony with his surroundings.

He was back on the job, and apparently, whatever problems he had with mulligans, Martin, and his superiors had been resolved. It was great news. Now Hamelin could push on and leave him alone. While that might sound self-serving, Ryan didn't see it that way. It was for Hamelin's sake, too. Somehow, hell didn't suit him. Not that Ryan would ever fully understand what made the immortal tick, but he knew him well enough. He was a walking contradiction—endearing and childlike one moment, and terrifyingly calculating the next. However, there was nothing malevolent about him. Had immortal life made him that way, or merely heightened what was already there? Ryan could only guess. He got up and went out to say goodbye.

Hamelin—praying, perhaps, or conducting some sort of morbid postaudit of his activities—said nothing as Ryan sat down beside him. They sat on the wall for a while, each in his own thoughts, and watched the quiet ways of the waterfowl and the river as it flowed past in a journey it had begun long before their time began.

It was Ryan who broke the silence. "The good place?"

"The best. She will love it."

Ryan nodded. "I don't want to know what happened about any of this. I'm just glad to see that everything has worked out for you." He looked at Hamelin and stuck out his hand. "I'll miss you."

Hamelin looked at the proffered hand and smiled. "Ryan James Thomas, we have come a long way if you trust me enough to shake my hand. How do you know that Mrs. Mattingly is my last acquisition here?"

Ryan dropped his hand. "Good point."

Hamelin chuckled. "Relax. When my book was destroyed, all record of my mulligans went with it. You are home free, as they say."

"And Marie?"

"*All* of you. We will have to get you back on the death schedule, but I don't think we need to stress about that anytime soon."

Ryan gave a silent prayer of thanks. Manual or no manual, God was omnipotent and omniscient. If the Almighty was willing to let him stay earthbound for a while, he'd take it. The Big Guy must have other plans.

"But don't ask me to help you find her," Hamelin said as if reading his mind. "At least, not yet. When that time comes, I will certainly consider it. Until then, you have to wait, and you have to put up with me."

"Put up with you? As in remaining in Nevis?" Ryan stood up. "No, no, no. You said I'm home free, so it's time we parted. Nice knowing you, pal." He gave Hamelin a half-wave and started off the wall.

"It seems I failed miserably in the role of soul runner," Hamelin called after him. "Rather than a judgment of heaven or hell, I have been sent back to earth for another go at it. I'm to be of service to others, and when I have redeemed myself sufficiently, I will be on my way again. It could be a long time," he added.

Ryan made an about-face. Hamelin's eyes were filled with determination, but his voice was flat and emotionless. "No more soul running?"

"The touch is gone," Hamelin said, shaking his head. "But if you dislike me that much, I can find somewhere else to be." He slid off the wall and extended his hand. "No hard feelings?"

Hamelin might have lost *the touch,* but Ryan was fairly certain that shaking hands would invite all sorts of new problems. But how could he just send his favorite immortal out into the world friendless, penniless, and brokenhearted? Friends didn't do that. Yeah, there was no use denying it. They were friends.

Ryan grasped his hand and smiled. "As long as you don't put a bid down on the Mattingly house, I think we can work things out." He swept his arm toward his own home. "Pancakes? Learned from the best. And I'll have to make a call for Mrs. Mattingly."

Hamelin returned the smile with a sly grin. "The same one who taught you how to make a *virgin* daiquiri?"

"Don't worry, there's no alcohol in a short stack."

"No. I was thinking more along the lines of Italian. How about the new place downtown?"

"Nonni's? Yeah, sure, but don't get into the habit of thinking I'm going to wine and dine you all around town. I have my financial limits. We could go see how Delaney is surviving."

Hamelin brushed past him and headed toward the house. "He's recuperating at a friend's house. I doubt we'll see him again. We'll enjoy Nonni's, and no need to worry—I have considerable means at my disposal. Car still out front?"

"Yeah, but you still can't drive," Ryan said, pulling out his keys as he hurried to catch up. "They give you a golden parachute before they kicked you out?"

"Something like that. But just because I am here doesn't mean you should underestimate me, Ryan James. I am beholden to no mortal, and my knowledge and abilities are many. Best remember that."

"Oka-ay," Ryan said, unlocking the car doors. "Can you tell me what the status of the Tippy was before you got kicked—er, relocated? Bennie still in the running? He's so good at what he does."

"The Tippy is all about spirit, judgment, and intuition—like Byron Berline when he plays the fiddle. He's in the moment, the zone, the flow, if you will. Free to enter a higher creative plane, and it elevates the work. He's tapped into something magical within himself that is unlimited. For Bennie, bartending is like that. It's intuitive. He just had to let go and trust his instincts."

"Just answer my question."

"In the end, it was a tie between your place and an earthy little dive in Istanbul. As the ranking member of the group, I cast the deciding vote. *Voila!* And well deserved. My last official act—well, outside of Mrs. Mattingly, that is."

"Does he know yet? He'll be out-of-his-mind happy. Let's hit the Phoenix so I can congratulate him."

"He knows. Lasagna first. Then you're free to follow your little heart's desire." With that, Hamelin pulled his feet up onto the seat and zoned out of any further discussion.

***

Nonni's sat in the middle of the downtown block and directly across from the town green's spectacular carousel from the early 1900s. One of just three buildings approved for renovation by the newly created Nevis Architectural Commission, its long history included use as a general store, printer's shop, and, most recently, a flophouse. Hamelin thought it the perfect place for new beginnings.

He and Ryan stopped at the broad front window and watched as a white-toqued chef tossed a pizza skin into the air. Nearby, an attractive dark-haired woman scattered shredded mutz onto an unfinished pie. Several completed ones sat to her right, awaiting their turn in the nearby brick oven.

"Looks like they're getting some business," Ryan said. "The Phoenix doesn't serve pizza, so bully for them." He leaned closer to the glass and squinted. "Wonder who owns the place." His forehead hit the glass. Twice. "Marie? Marie *McGallagher*?" He turned to Hamelin, a shocked look on his face.

"It pays to have friends in high places," Hamelin said, glancing skyward. He pointed to the U-Haul being loaded up at the curb. "The boyfriend—funny how things don't work out."

Ryan put his hand to the glass and rested his forehead against it. "Whose place?"

"Hers. No rush, I suppose, but what are you waiting for? This is what you've been badgering me about."

To Hamelin's amazement, Ryan hesitated.

"What if she rejects me?" Ryan whispered.

"Ryan *Doubting* Thomas. By now you should have come to realize that love transcends time and space. Souls are all about love. Now, go in there and get this destiny thing rolling. I've got things to move along elsewhere."

"I owe you," Ryan said, pushing past him to the door.

"And I'll remember."

Hamelin stood for a moment, watching Ryan approach the counter, and the way Marie's face lit up when she looked up at him. It was out of his hands now. He left them to work it out—and he was pretty sure they would—and proceeded uptown with a sense of deep contentment he hadn't expected. Maybe this earthly sentence wasn't going to be as bad as he had anticipated.

His eyes wandered down the long row of Italianate storefronts, searching for a delicatessen. Surely, good kielbasa could be had somewhere local. And after a good meal, inquiries were needed about putting a roof over his head. He wanted to line that up right away. Settlement of the Mattingly estate would be quick, and the house wouldn't be on the market long. It had such a lovely view, and a neighbor who owed him big-time.

Thank you for reading *Spirit of the Law*. I hope you enjoyed the story. If you have a moment, please consider leaving a quick review on the book's Amazon page.

The sequel, *Edgar and the Flyboys* should be available soon on Amazon. In the meantime, if you would like to read more about the first meeting between Hamelin Russell and Ryan Thomas, check out *Bayside Blues*.

Would you like to know when I release new books?
Here are three ways:

Join my mailing list at:
https://www.louisegordaybooks.com/contact

Like me on Facebook:
https://www.facebook.com/louisegordayauthor

Follow me on Twitter
https://twitter.com/LouiseGorday

Made in the USA
Columbia, SC
14 November 2020